Sounds Like a Happy Train Today

By

Kenneth Lee McGee

For Denise

Who years ago gave me
credit for having the courage,
if not the skill,
to tackle a rather
controversial subject.

I would like to thank everyone
who has taken time to visit my website
or my Amazon author page.
I appreciate the support
and kind words.

Thank you Cory Woodward
for the cover photo.

Prologue

"I'll be right back, guys. I'm going to run Caralyn up to her room," Tucker McKay said.

Derren Stanfield and Richard Laderman got out of the car. "Take your time, Tuck. Richard and I are going to walk home. He needs the exercise."

"Good night, Cara. I hope you had a good birthday." Richard stared at her until Derren nudged him in the side.

Tucker and Caralyn rode the elevator in silence and avoided making eye contact. Tucker followed to her room and stood behind her as she unlocked the door.

"Can I come in for a second, Cara?"

"Of course you can." *I'm not going to call Jeremiah now. I haven't been thinking about him all night if you're wondering.* "Thank you for dinner tonight, Tuck. It was thoughtful of you guys to remember."

"You're welcome. You look so pretty tonight. Like you did the first time you wore that dress."

"I hope you don't mind that I wore it again. I didn't know if you would remember, and if you did, afraid you would be upset."

"I'll never forget that dress. Did you realize Derren called you Carrie tonight?"

"Yes, and I hope you didn't mind."

"Not a bit." He reached in his pocket and pulled out a small box wrapped in gift paper. "I got you something. It's not much. I hope you will like it." He handed it to her and she smiled at him.

She nervously opened the gift. Inside was a small charm for her bracelet—a small teddy bear.

"Oh, Tuck! This is perfect. I love it!"

"I found it a month ago."

He watched as she attached the charm to her bracelet. She hugged him and began to sob.

"It's all right, Carrie. I can take it back if you don't like it." Tucker fought to keep from crying.

"You better not," she whispered.

They held each other tightly. She thought about how much he had meant to her over the years as she looked at the teddy bear nestled against the pillows on her bed. She remembered when they would play with it even though Tucker would rather be outside playing ball.

He looked at the teddy bear on her bed and remembered how they used to pretend the bear was their baby. Without saying a single word they both remembered the same moment in time.

Finally, Caralyn said, "You were so quiet tonight, Tuck. I was afraid you were mad at me."

"I wasn't mad at you, Carrie. I didn't know if you would like my present."

"You always get me the perfect gift. How could I not love it?" She looked into his eyes and smiled.

He leaned down and kissed her on the cheek. "Happy birthday, Tarry."

Tears again filled her eyes. He hadn't called her Tarry since they were little kids. He turned to leave, and she followed him to the door and leaned against it after he left. He hurried to the elevator because he didn't want anyone to see him crying.

"Shoot! Why didn't I tell him to stay?" She threw open the door and sprinted after him, but it was too late. The elevator door closed.

"Open! Come on open!" She stabbed the button repeatedly.

When it didn't, she ran back to her room and fell on the bed. She wept for several minutes and then got off the bed. "Oh, crap. I hope I didn't ruin this dress." She took it off and smoothed out the wrinkles before hanging it back in the closet. She had just closed the closet door when the phone rang. She bounded to her desk, yanked her cell phone from her purse and answered before the second ring. "Oh, Bubby, I'm sorry," she cried.

"Who's Bubby?" Jeremiah asked.

"Someone special," she answered.

Chapter One

With the end of the fall semester only a few days away, Caralyn Dawson worked on a way to get to Meyersdale, Wisconsin, without Mom and Dad McKay knowing the reason. She checked the ride board in the student union daily for anyone heading to the Meyersdale area.

"Yes! Finally, someone's going my direction. All I have to do is pay my share of the gas."

"Who are you calling?" Tucker asked. He watched her punch a number into her cell phone then looked at the notice. He wrote the number on his wrist.

"None of your business, Tucker."

The girl she knew only as Betsy kept her on the phone for twenty minutes. Tucker called the number when he got back to his apartment. He arranged to be the fourth person in the car, but didn't tell Caralyn.

"Dad, I'm going to be a few days late coming home. I really need to take care of a friend."

"That's all right. You do what you need. Does it have anything to do with basketball?"

"No, Coach gave us two weeks off. I could use the break."

"See you when you get home."

Caralyn called home and told Mom, "I'm catching a ride to Meyersdale with Betsy and Tim. They are going home for the holidays."

"Where are you going to stay, honey?"

"With Betsy. She's kinda quirky, but we get along."

"Am I correct in assuming you will see Jeremiah?"

"Yes, and he will bring me home so you can meet him."

"We are looking forward to meeting him, Cara. Have a good time with Betsy. Call us if you need anything."

"Thanks, Mom. I will be fine." She felt guilty for lying.

Mom stared at the phone. *Caralyn, you've never lied to me before. I hope you will be safe.*

"Thank God! Finals are done. I have ten minutes to pack and meet Betsy outside Matteson Hall." Caralyn brushed her palms together and bounced on her toes. "I will be in Meyersdale by tonight." She quickly packed, threw on her winter coat, grabbed her organizer, locked her room and hurried to the elevator.

She dragged her suitcase and saw a couple waiting by an old Ford Escort station wagon. She looked at the car. At one time it had been blue, but now was a combination of bondo, rust and a white passenger door from another vehicle.

"At least it's a ride," Caralyn said with a sigh. "It only has to make it in one piece."

"Are you Caralyn Dawson by any chance?" the girl asked in the annoying high-pitched voice Caralyn recognized from her phone conversation.

"Yes, I am."

"I'm Betsy Cooper, and this is my boyfriend Tim Walters. It's so good to actually meet you. I feel like we are best friends already. We are waiting for one more person. Tim can put your suitcase in the back."

Tim smiled and adjusted his red bow tie. "My pleasure."

Caralyn checked out Betsy's beehive hairdo as Tim loaded her suitcase. She rolled her eyes and muttered, "They must be dressed for a costume party." She got in back and started to read.

"Here comes the other rider now, I think." Betsy waved her arms. "Over here! Here we are!"

"Egads. How will I put up with that voice?" Caralyn kept her nose in her book. Betsy got in the front passenger seat, and Tim casually tossed the other rider's backpack in the car. Caralyn didn't pay any attention to the other person until he got in the backseat. She glanced at him and her mouth dropped.

"Tucker McKay! What are you doing here? Where do you think you're going?"

"Oh, didn't I mention? I'm going to Meyersdale to see an old friend."

"No way! You're going there so you can ruin my time with Jeremiah. Get out of the car this instant. You are not going."

"Yes, I am, and you can't stop me. This isn't your car, and I made arrangements to ride exactly like you did." He leaned forward and held out his hand. "I'm Tucker. Thank you so much for the ride. I love your costumes, by the way."

"What costumes?" Tim asked.

"Never mind," Tucker said and sat back in his seat.

"Get out, Tucker," Caralyn ordered.

"Not a chance." He crossed his arms over his chest.

Tim and Betsy watched them argue from the front seat.

"You've met before, right?" Betsy asked.

"Yes."

"No!" Caralyn hollered.

"It doesn't matter," Tucker said. "We are grateful for the ride."

Tim started the car after a couple tries and they took off. "I hope you don't mind, but I don't like to drive on the Interstate. We're going to take the old highways and see some sights."

Caralyn didn't say anything. Tucker grunted a reply.

Betsy added, "I have been planning this trip and there are several interesting sights we should see. In Mt. Olive there is a red and white six-sided barn. We have to see it, and in Jamison Grove is the largest working five-sail wooden windmill in the state."

"Sounds like fun. I don't mind if we don't get to Meyersdale until Christmas," Tucker told Betsy with a fake smile.

Betsy turned around in her seat to face the front—puzzled over whether he was making fun of her or not.

Tucker grinned at Caralyn because he knew she wanted to get to Meyersdale as soon as possible.

"Don't even look at me, Tucker McKay. You are not going to ruin my plans."

"I'm not trying to ruin your plans with Jerry."

"His name is Jeremiah. Jeremiah! Can you remember that? Don't talk to me."

Caralyn tried to ignore Tucker, but he kept trying to engage her in conversation. Tim and Betsy tried to tune them out by turning up the radio, without success.

They actually stopped outside of Mt. Olive to look at the odd barn to Caralyn's annoyance. She stayed in the car while Tucker followed Betsy and Tim. He feigned great interest in the unique barn. When they got back in the car, it wouldn't start.

"Don't worry. This happens once in a while," Tim said. "I know how to fix it."

"Take your time, Tim," Tucker said with a grin. "We aren't in any hurry. Betsy, thank you so much for telling me about the barn. I've never seen one so interesting before," Tucker smirked as he looked at Caralyn.

"I am ignoring you, Tucker James McKay," Caralyn said turning away.

"Not if you're talking to me."

"I'm only talking to... oh, never mind."

Tim worked for an eternity to get it running again. They stopped in Grayling Falls to get gas and in Jamison Grove to see the windmill. Tucker and Caralyn quarreled the entire time.

As they left the windmill site, Tim pounded the steering wheel, turned around and yelled, "If you don't stop this endless bickering, I will leave you stranded in the middle of Converse County."

"Actually, dear, we are in Weston County now," Betsy said.

"Thank you, Betsy," he said sweetly then turned back to Tucker and Caralyn and shouted, "And I totally mean it."

Tucker and Caralyn looked at each other without speaking.

Tim took a deep breath, exhaled slowly then looked at Betsy. "What's the next exciting place to see?"

"There is the car on stilts outside of Chippewa River Falls."

Caralyn read her book. Tucker rolled his eyes.

"That's where we are heading then, dear," Tim said. As he pulled onto the blacktop, they heard the air horn from a Freightliner truck.

"Look out!" Betsy squealed.

Tim slammed on the brakes.

Caralyn cringed. "God help me."

"I see it," Tim replied. "How can I drive with them arguing all the time?"

Betsy glanced over her shoulder. "They are quiet now," she whispered. "Do you need another pill?"

"No! I am fine." He looked in both direction four times before slowly pulling out.

"I can't wait to see Jerry," Tucker said.

"His name is Jeremiah! Jeremiah! Jeremiah! How many times do I have to tell you before you get it through your thick skull?"

"I was talking about my friend Jerry Monroe. He goes to school in Meyersdale. That's who I'm going to see."

Caralyn looked at him and punched his arm.

"Ow! What was that for?"

"For being a jerk and spoiling my plans."

"I am not spoiling your plans, little Missy."

"Yes you are, and I hate you!" Caralyn screamed as she punched him again.

Tim slammed on the brakes. The car swerved from one side of the blacktop to the other, through an intersection then skidded to a stop on the gravel shoulder amid a cloud of dust.

"Tim! Try to remain calm," Betsy shouted. "You didn't take your blood pressure pill yet."

"I am fine, Betsy dear."

He got out of the car, tilted his head back and forth and whistled as he walked to the rear of the car. He opened the back of the station wagon, grabbed Tucker's backpack and tossed it out as Tucker and Caralyn watched.

"Serves you right, Tucker. Now get out so I can ride in peace."

Tucker watched as Tim grabbed Caralyn's large suitcase and heaved it out of the car also. He poked her ribs and said gleefully, "Looks like you're out of luck, too, Carrie."

"What?" She turned around and didn't see her suitcase. "No! Tim, wait, please. Don't do this to me. I have to get to Meyersdale tonight. It's a matter of life and death."

Tim screamed, "Get out! Both of you. Get out now. I don't ever want to see either of you again." He opened the doors and waited for them to get out of the car.

"This isn't my fault," Caralyn pleaded.

As soon as Caralyn was out, he jumped in and he and Betsy took off with gravel flying and tires squealing on the pavement. The passenger doors banged against the car without closing.

"Tim, we didn't get their gas money," Betsy said. She looked out the rear window and waved.

Tucker waved back then turned to Caralyn. "Now what are we going to do?"

Caralyn looked at Tucker with the most hateful expression. "I don't know what you are going to do, but I am going to get to Meyersdale today if I have to walk." She pulled her coat tighter and stood in the middle of the intersection. "Which way, Tuck? Never mind. I'm going this way."

He waited a few seconds then shouted, "Caralyn Ann!"

"What?" She stopped and turned around.

He pointed in the opposite direction. "Meyersdale." He clicked his tongue. "North."

She looked in both directions. "Are you sure?"

"Yes."

"Thank you, Tucker. I appreciate it."

"You're welcome, Carrie."

Caralyn turned around and as she passed Tucker, slugged his arm. "Don't walk with me. You can walk behind me but not with me. I am still mad at you."

They walked for what seemed like an hour, but only fifteen minutes passed before a man in a pickup truck stopped and offered them a ride to the next town.

"Thanks, but we're fine," Tucker said closing the pickup door. The driver drove away weaving from side to side.

"We're not fine," Caralyn said. "We need a ride."

Tucker shrugged and said, "I hate riding in green trucks."

"Why?"

"He reeked of booze and pot," Tucker answered.

Caralyn tried to call Jeremiah but realized her cell phone battery had discharged.

"I'm hungry, Cara. Are you?"

"I'm starving, Tucker. Truce?"

"Yeah, I guess so."

They trudged into the next town, stopped at a local convenience store to grab some food and sat on the sidewalk to eat.

"What are we going to do? Jeremiah will be worried about me." She looked at her phone again. "I need to charge it."

"I'm not sure, " he said then looked at her. "Why do you like this guy?"

She answered with an elbow to his ribs.

"No, tell me. He acts weird. What normal twenty-five year old wants his young girlfriend to dress and act like a thirty year old?"

"He isn't weird, Tuck. Granted, he can be a bit controlling at times."

"He tries to dress you like an old lady." Tucker waved his hand while holding a chicken salad sandwich. "That's more than controlling. He a weird dude, Cara. He's a freak."

"He wants me to be taken as a mature young woman."

"Whatever." Tucker pointed to the sky. "I don't like the looks of those clouds."

Right then it started to pour. Within a minute they were soaked to the skin. Tucker saw a motel sign a block away. He pointed it out to Caralyn, and they hurried to get out of the rain.

"This storm is supposed to last all day. At least it's not snow," the desk clerk said. "Do you kids need anything?" He winked at Tucker.

Tucker asked, "Do you have any rooms available?"

"Only got one left for tonight. You can have it if you want, but you gotta pay up front. Fifty bucks cash." He leaned close and whispered, "I don't care if you spend the night or stay an hour."

What should have been an easy six hour trip to Meyersdale had turned into a nightmare. Tucker didn't see any other option but to take the room.

Chapter Two

Caralyn took off her coat, looked disdainfully at the one small bed and then frowned at Tucker.

He saw the problem. "I'll sleep on the floor, Cara. I don't want to upset you any more than you already are."

She looked at him, but didn't say anything.

Tucker plopped onto the bed. "You can use the bathroom first. I'll wait out here while you change clothes."

"Thanks, Tuck. I won't take long. Will you plug in my phone so it can charge?"

"Sure thing," Tucker answered in a disgusted way.

Later, she stepped out of the shower. "Shoot. I need clean clothes." She wrapped the towel around her and walked into the room. "Don't make fun, but I forgot my clothes."

Tucker watched as she got a sweatshirt and pajama pants out of the suitcase. She tried not to let him see her underwear but he noticed and smiled.

"Pink polka dots, huh? Weird dude, Cara."

Caralyn blushed. "Shut up, Tuck."

He smiled again, and she started to grin. "Jeremiah told me he likes polka dots. Silly, huh?"

Finally, you don't seem to be upset with me anymore. "I don't think it's raining as hard now. Do you want me to get us something to snack on?"

"That would be nice. Are you going back to that little store? If you are, could you see if they have those fudge cookies I like."

"Sure. What do you want to drink? Dr Pepper, okay?"

"That would be fine. How about something for breakfast?"

"I'll check. Make sure the door is locked."

She dressed, sat on the bed and called Jeremiah.

"Where are you, Caralyn? I thought you'd be here by now."

"You would not believe the day I've had," she said with a sigh as she inspected her toenails. She told him everything. He listened without interest.

Tucker returned, and Caralyn let him in and motioned for him to be quiet. He set the bags on the table and listened.

"Was there someone at the door, Caralyn? I thought I heard someone knocking."

"I ordered a pizza and had it delivered. I'll be all right tonight, Jeremiah. I will get to Meyersdale tomorrow, and we'll be together."

"I can't wait to see you. We are going to have so much fun. Did you bring what I asked?"

Tucker stood close enough to hear Jeremiah, and he grinned at Caralyn.

"You will have to wait and see, Jeremiah. I have to go. The battery is low. I'll see you tomorrow. Bye."

Tucker sat on the edge of the bed, grinned and teased, "Oh, Jeremiah. I am wearing the panties you like so much. Do you want to see them?"

"You're going to get it, Tuck."

She pushed him back on the bed and sat on top of him. He didn't try to get away. He lay on his back in the middle of the bed as she straddled him. She laughed as he kept teasing her about Jeremiah. Suddenly, he grabbed her and switched positions.

"Tucker," she whispered.

He smiled and she smiled back. She raised her hands above her head. Tucker looked at her exposed belly button. He reached under her sweatshirt and touched her. They stared at each other for several seconds without speaking.

"Don't, Tuck. Please not now," she said softly.

"I'm sorry, Carrie. I got carried away." He got off the bed, but she stayed there. "I found the cookies you like and the Dr Pepper. They had some donuts. I'll be back."

"Where are you going?" She sat up quickly.

"For a walk. I need some fresh air. I won't be gone long."

"I'm sorry if I made you mad."

"It's okay. I shouldn't have touched you like that." He stepped out. "Make sure you hook the chain."

She lay on the bed and stared at the ceiling.

16

An hour passed and she heard someone banging on the door.

"It's me, Cara. Can you open the door, please?"

She jumped off the bed and opened the door for him. "Oh, Tuck. You're not mad at me. I was afraid you would leave me here to die."

"Carrie, I would never leave you in a place like this no matter what. Were you asleep?"

"I couldn't get to sleep. I was worried about you. Where did you go? You are soaking wet."

"Nowhere really. I walked around town. There's not much here. It stopped raining, but now it's snowing and getting colder." He wrapped his arms around his chest. "I guess we're lucky we got this room."

"You need to get out of those clothes before you freeze to death."

He grinned at her.

She smacked his arm. "I didn't mean it like that. Now I don't care if you freeze or not."

"Sorry. I'll use the bathroom to change."

He came back and stood by the bed.

"Are you hungry? I didn't eat the cookies yet."

"Yes, please."

They sat on the bed and shared the cookies and the room temperature Dr Pepper. He noticed her yawning.

"Are you ready to sleep now, Carrie? It's still kinda early."

"Yes."

"Okay, let me have a pillow, and I'll sleep next to the bed on the floor. I will survive one night on the hard floor."

Caralyn looked at the dirty carpet then looked at Tucker. "Fine! You can stop looking like you just lost your favorite dog. I will share the bed. You better behave though and don't you dare tell anyone."

"I will, Cara. I won't try anything."

You better not," she warned. "I need to use the bathroom. I won't take long."

"Everything okay?" he asked when she came out thirty minutes later.

"Yes. Jeremiah told me I should use a moisturizer before bed."

"Really? Do you think it would work for me? I think I'm getting a zit on my chin."

"Buy your own. Mine is for women." She climbed into bed and watched as he pulled off his sweatshirt then dropped his jeans.

She giggled.

"What?" he asked with a shrug.

She pointed and said, "I remember those boxers with the smiley face."

"Maybe I have more than one pair."

"Take your socks off, Tuck. They probably smell."

He climbed in bed next to her. He slipped under the thin blanket and looked at her. She lay on her back with her arms over her breasts as if shielding them. They could feel their hips touching in the small bed.

Tucker turned onto his side and looked at her. "Are you absolutely sure you want to head to Meyersdale in the morning?"

She looked at him with sad eyes and nodded. "I have to see Jerry."

"Do you mean Jeremiah?"

"That's what I said, wasn't it?"

"You said Jerry."

"I meant Jeremiah."

"Right! How could I forget?"

"He's coming home with me, and I think he is looking forward to meeting Mom and Dad. You should give him a chance. You might learn to like him. He's so intelligent."

"Whatever you say. Good night, Carrie. Sleep well."

"Good night, Bubby," she answered softly and childlike.

Tucker turned away and turned out the light.

18

Chapter Three

Caralyn opened her eyes as the sun warmed her face. She felt Tucker's arm around her and smiled then fell back to sleep. When she woke an hour later, Tucker still had his arm in the same place, and she could feel something poking against her.

"Tuck," she whispered. "Tuck, you need to wake up."

He opened his eyes, yawned, rolled his shoulder then smiled at her. "What time is it?"

"I don't know, but it's light out."

She moved her hips to the edge of the bed and he suddenly realized his position. He threw back the sheet and jumped out of bed. He noticed she had the blanket to herself.

"I didn't do anything, Cara. I swear." He covered his boxers with both hands.

"You kept me warm, that's all."

"I wasn't trying anything. Don't be mad at me."

"I'm not upset."

He stayed up and got ready to leave while Caralyn slipped back to sleep.

"Cara, you need to wake up. We need to get going if we were going to make it to Meyersdale by one."

"Crap, Tuck. I need to call Jeremiah."

"Go ahead." He pointed to her phone.

Jeremiah answered on the fourth ring. "I am working until six, but I can meet you at one to give you a key. I'll be on my break, so I only have a few minutes."

"I will make it there if I have to take a cab."

They shared the donuts and the last of the flat Dr Pepper then caught a ride into Meyersdale with a middle-age couple who had stayed at the motel.

"She really needs to meet her boyfriend by noon. She's pregnant and needs to tell him," Tucker said.

"I am not," Caralyn whispered.

Tucker shrugged then added, "That's what popped into my mind, and they don't know the difference."

19

The couple drove them into Meyersdale with time to spare.

"Thank you for the ride," Tucker said. "She's in time to get the abortion."

Caralyn slugged him. "I hate you, Tucker. Why did you say that awful thing?"

He shrugged and said, "Because I'm a blockhead. Do you know how to get to Jeremiah's apartment from here?"

"I have the address in my organizer. I'm pretty sure I can find it. Do you know where Jerry Monroe lives?"

"Not a clue. He told me to call him when I got here, and he would pick me up."

"Do you want to use my phone, Tuck?"

"I can find a pay phone somewhere, Cara."

"Don't be silly. Pay phones are obsolete. You'll never find one. Use my cell and call him."

Tucker called Jerry and arranged to be picked up. "How will I find you when it's time to head home, Caralyn?"

"I'm going home with Jeremiah. Remember? He is coming with me to meet Mom and Dad."

"Oh, yeah. I forgot."

"Let me write down his address in case you need to find me." She gave Tucker the address then checked the time. "I better run."

"Yeah, I guess so. Bye, Carrie. I'll see you sometime."

"Bye, Tuck." They looked into each other's eyes for a moment before she turned to leave.

"There you are, Caralyn. I was afraid you weren't going to make it." Jeremiah pulled his hands out of his coat pockets and squeezed her shoulders. "I have to get back to work but here is a key. It's number four on the second floor. Make yourself at home, and I'll see you around six. I'm so glad you're here."

"I am thrilled to be here at last."

She smiled and Jeremiah kissed her cheek.

"I need to get back. I am meeting a potential client this afternoon."

He left her with the heavy suitcase to lug up the stairs. She dragged it up one flight and down the hall to his apartment then opened the door. She hung up her coat and checked it out. "It's ten times cleaner and neater than the guys' place. I should take a picture to show Tucker and Derry."

She looked in the fridge for something and picked up a half-empty carton of milk. "Not much to choose from, Jeremiah. We better shop for necessities." She drank a can of pop and found some cheese. "Why did I rush to get here if he has to work, and why am I talking to myself? It must be nerves." She sat on the couch and watched TV for an hour. "This sucks. I should check out the campus while I'm here. At least it stopped snowing."

She put on her coat, made sure she had the key and left. She spent the afternoon outside and let the sunshine, and crisp fresh air, invigorate her. Around four o'clock she spotted a sandwich shop and entered.

"Crap! Why are you here, Tucker?" She saw him sitting at a table with two college-age girls and who she supposed was Jerry Monroe. She was about to leave when Tucker spotted her and rushed over.

"Carrie, what are you doing here? Where is Jeremiah?"

"He's still at work. I was walking around the campus when I spotted this place. I thought I would get something to drink and maybe something to eat. I'm starving."

"Why don't you join us. That's Jerry and his friends."

"No, I don't want to intrude. It looks like you are having fun. I don't want to spoil your party."

"Come on, Carrie. You can be social for a few minutes."

"Fine, but I can't stay long." She sat at the table and noticed the beer. She glared at Tucker and asked, "Were you drinking?"

"No." He held up his Coke. "You know me better."

"Hi, I'm Jerry, and this is Mary Sue. That's Kim hanging all over Tucker."

Caralyn smiled then pulled out her cell phone.

"Would you like a beer?" Jerry asked. "Tucker refuses, but you look like you could use a beer."

21

"No, thanks," she said waving dismissively.

"More for us. Right, girls?"

Caralyn caught Tucker's eyes and he shrugged.

"I should leave. Jeremiah will be getting home soon," Caralyn said.

Tucker pushed Kim away and stood up. "I'll walk you out." He glanced over his shoulder at Kim. "To his apartment if you want."

"No need. Looks like you will be busy with Kim," she told Tucker sarcastically.

"It's not what you think, Cara."

"Yeah sure, Tuck. Have fun with your new friend."

Jerry ran over and handed Caralyn a piece of paper. "We're having a party at this address tonight. If you and your boyfriend aren't too busy, you are welcome to come and have fun. There will be lots of beer and music and probably some food and lots of pretty girls." He slapped Tucker on the back and laughed. "Lots of girls. Oh, you probably don't care about the girls. Anyway, hope to see you there. My phone number is there, too. Call me." He held his hand to his ear. "It will be the bomb."

"Thanks, but I think I will pass."

Caralyn walked back to Jeremiah's apartment and waited.

"I'm home, Caralyn. How are you doing?" He tossed his keys on the table, took off his black wool trench coat and hugged her. "Are you hungry? I thought maybe we could order your favorite. There is a Chinese place two blocks away. They make a wicked orange chicken."

"Jeremiah, I don't really like... Oh never mind. Order what you think best. I'm hungry enough to eat anything."

Jeremiah called in the order and picked it up.

"I asked for an extra egg roll. I hope you don't mind sharing the orange chicken."

After they finished dinner, Jeremiah rubbed his stomach and said, "I will be hungry again in an hour, and we have just enough chicken chop suey left."

"I've had enough, thank you," she said with a wry grin.

"Caralyn, I need to read. Would you like to read or maybe watch TV? *Family Entertainment Hour* is on channel eight. I think you would like the dry humor in the dialogue."

She watched the show as he read, but her mind wandered. *I wonder if Tucker is still with Kim. She's such a bimbo.*

He looked up from his book. "Cara, are you paying attention?"

"No, this show sucks. Can we go out tonight? I know where they are having a party. I want to have some fun."

He plucked at his shirt cuffs. "Are you sure that's what you want to do, Caralyn? Wouldn't you rather spend a quiet evening here?"

"No. I want to party and dance. It's the holidays." She looked at the address Jerry had given her and handed it to Jeremiah. "Do you know where this is?"

He inspected the nearly illegible handwriting. "It's only a few blocks away. Do you seriously want to spend time at a frat party? I thought you would be above that nonsense."

"Yes. I want to get drunk and dance with you."

Jeremiah's eyebrows shot up. *That is unexpected. Could I be wrong about you? I might need to rethink my strategy.* He rubbed his jaw and pressed his glasses higher up his nose. "Okay, but let's not stay too long."

Jeremiah and Caralyn walked to the party. They could hear loud music blaring from outside the house. As soon as they entered, Caralyn removed her coat, tossed it in a pile with other coats and said, "I want a glass of beer, Jeremiah. Would you be a dear?"

At that moment someone walked by carrying a tray of plastic cups filled with beer. Jeremiah grabbed one and handed it to her. She drank it and asked for another.

"Don't drink too fast, Caralyn. I don't want you to pass out," Jeremiah cautioned.

She wandered through the house looking for Tucker as Jeremiah followed.

"Are you looking for someone, Caralyn?" Jeremiah asked. He saw several guys tossing ping pong balls into red plastic cups on a table and rolled his eyes.

Finally, she spotted Tucker and Kim dancing in a corner of the basement. Kim's low-cut dress barely covered anything, and she was obviously braless.

Caralyn walked straight to Tucker, put her hand on her hips and shouted, "Are you having fun, Mr. McKay?"

He put his hand to his ear and shrugged.

"I said are you having fun," she shouted to be heard over the music.

The song ended but people kept dancing.

"Caralyn. What are you doing here, and is that beer in your cup?"

"Yes, it is. I'm here with Jeremiah. I told him I want to get drunk. What do you think of that, Tucker McKay?"

"If that's what you want to do, Carrie, then go right ahead."

Caralyn looked at Kim and shook her head. "Really?" Caralyn said staring at Tucker.

"She's not... never mind. Where is Jeremiah? Is it past his bedtime?"

"Very funny, Tuck. Hah. Hah. He had to make a call if you must know." She was bumped by a guy trying to dance with a drunk coed and spilled part of her beer. "Watch out, bucko."

The music resumed but at a less ear-shattering level.

"I think I will head upstairs and see if he wants to dance."

Tucker followed Caralyn upstairs and Kim followed Tucker like an obedient puppy.

Caralyn saw Jeremiah and took his hand. "Let's dance, Jeremiah, and then I want to go back to your place."

He put his cell phone in his sports jacket pocket and adjusted his tie. "This isn't proper music for dancing."

"I don't care. You are dancing with me," she ordered.

Tucker watched as Caralyn danced with Jeremiah and pressed close to him.

"Let's dance too, Kim," Tucker yelled.

"Do you want me to take my dress off now or later?"

Tucker, Caralyn and Jeremiah stared at Kim.

"Do you attend college here, Kim?" Caralyn asked.

"Oh, no. I work at a dance club near here."

"Really? What a surprise."

"Caralyn, do you have to be so mean?" Tucker frowned.

"Oh, sorry. Am I being mean to your new friend?"

"Knock it off. Why don't you and Justin leave."

"Maybe we will, and you know his name. You are trying to irritate me."

Jeremiah listened and asked, "Why are you arguing?"

"It's not important. Let's go. I've seen enough here. I want to return to your place so we can make love."

Kim asked Tucker, "Are you ready to go upstairs so we can have sex? Jerry told me he would pay this time."

Tucker stared at her then said, "Just a minute."

Caralyn scowled at Kim and told Tucker, "Have fun with your new girlfriend."

"I didn't know about this, and I'm going to kill Jerry."

"Don't lie to me, Tucker," she shouted.

"I'm not. I only came here to make sure you were okay."

"I don't need you to take care of me."

"Caralyn, why are you arguing with him?" Jeremiah asked. "Are you her cousin from the bar in Cornell Lakes?"

"Shut up!" Tucker and Caralyn told him simultaneously.

Caralyn glared at Tucker then turned to Jeremiah and said, "Come on, Jeremiah. We're leaving. I'm ready for bed."

"Carrie, don't do it," Tucker pleaded.

"It's none of your business, Tucker McKay. I can do what I please."

Jeremiah shrugged and followed behind. "I have no clue what just happened, but I think it's working to my advantage. She's ready for about anything." He looked over his shoulder at Tucker and nearly tripped on someone passed out on the floor. "This is why I hate college parties."

Chapter Four

"I put clean sheets on the bed, Caralyn." He put an arm around her waist, pulled her close and kissed the top of her head as they stood in the bedroom doorway.

"What did you say, Jeremiah? My mind is elsewhere."

"There are fresh sheets on the bed. If you are ready, you can change in the bathroom." He opened a dresser drawer and pulled something red and shiny out. He held it up and smiled. "I would like you to wear this. It's silk and will feel so smooth on your bare skin."

"Thanks. I'll be right back." Caralyn undressed, put on the nightie while Jeremiah stripped to his boxers and waited in bed.

She came out and adjusted the thin straps. "It's a little loose. I usually wear a smaller size." She stood by the bed.

He pulled back the covers and she slid next to him. "Are you nervous, Caralyn?"

She moved onto her back and pulled the sheet up higher. "Not really. I am still a little upset."

"Is it because of the argument with that guy earlier?"

"He doesn't matter to me anymore."

Jeremiah turned on his side. "How well do you know him?"

"I don't want to talk about him. Can we go to sleep."

"All right. I'll turn out the light." He put his glasses on the nightstand and turned off the light. "I have envisaged this moment with great anticipation. I am sure you been looking forward to it, too?"

"Yes, Jeremiah, but I don't think I'm ready now."

"Why not? You look so sexy in... that nightie." He moved the sheet lower and moved a finger from her neck to her chest.

"I know what I said earlier, but now I'm too upset."

He moved his hand to her breast. "We can wait until morning if you want, honey, but I think you will relax after a few kisses." He leaned close to kiss her, but she turned her head.

"Would you mind? You have been awfully patient, but I am too upset right now."

He clenched his jaw and muttered, "I won't force you to do anything tonight if you're not ready."

She looked at him and tried to smile. "Thank you. I'm sure I will feel better tomorrow."

He kissed her cheek. "I could give you something to help you sleep. It will settle your nerves, and I promise you will feel better in the morning."

She chewed her lip for a second. "I could use some help falling asleep tonight."

He got out of bed. "I'll be right back."

He returned a moment later. "Take this. I broke it in half. It will settle your nerves." He ran his hand through her hair.

"Thank you, Jeremiah." She put the pill in her mouth and drank the water. "I'm sorry for disappointing you. I promise I will make love to you in the morning, or maybe sooner."

"You haven't disappointed me, Caralyn. Try to sleep. Have you ever thought about dyeing your hair brown?"

They fell asleep, but in the middle of the night Jeremiah woke up and checked on her. "Caralyn, are you asleep?"

She moaned but didn't open her eyes.

"Cara," he nudged her but she still didn't open her eyes. He put a hand on her stomach. When she didn't stir, he moved it to her breasts. "You may want to wait, but I don't," he whispered. He pulled up her nightie, pushed his boxers down and moved into position.

"Ow! That hurts," she mumbled. "What are you doing, Tuck? Slow down. I will let you make love, but..."

"I am not Tucker," Jeremiah hissed.

She opened her eyes and in the dim light could tell it wasn't Tucker. "Jeremiah, what is happening?" She tried to push him away.

He grabbed her shoulders and pressed deeper into her.

She realized who was on top of her. "Stop, Jeremiah. I don't want to do this." She tried again to push him off. "Stop! You're hurting me."

"Come on, Caralyn. You know this feels good. I can tell because you put your arms around me when we started."

"No! It doesn't feel good. Stop! Stop it, Jeremiah!" She hit him hard with both fists. "Get off me." She continued to hit him as the tears cascaded down her face.

He pushed into her one final time and collapsed.

She shoved him to the side and scrambled out from underneath. She stood by the side of the bed and hit him repeatedly. "I hate you! How could you do this? I told you I wanted to wait until the morning."

"It is morning," he said.

She hit him once more, then ran to the bathroom, slammed the door and locked it. She collapsed onto the floor between the toilet and the tub. She wrapped her arms around her chest and sobbed. "Tucker, where are you? I need you, Bubby."

"Caralyn. Caralyn. Are you all right?" Jeremiah pounded on the door later.

She opened her eyes and could see the sun shining through the window. She realized she was on the cold tile floor.

"Caralyn, open the door. I need to make sure you are all right." He knocked on the door again. "Talk to me, honey. If this is about last night, I am truly sorry. I don't know what came over me. Please let me in."

"No," she whispered. She reached up for the bath towel above her and covered her legs.

"You can't stay in there all day, sweetie."

"Don't you dare call me sweetie. I hate you."

"You are just upset..."

"You better believe I'm upset." She used the tub for leverage and stood up. She looked in the mirror and saw her red eyes and tangled hair. She turned on the water and cupped her hands to get a drink.

"Cara," he whispered while tapping softly on the door. "I'm sorry for what happened, but it wasn't all my fault. Please let me in. I need to take a leak."

She turned her head to look at the door. "Not all your fault? You raped me! You..." She let loose with a string of expletives normally used by longshoremen and seedy politicians. She held onto the vanity for balance and unlocked the door.

He opened it cautiously. "Can I come in?"

"The door's open," she said.

He took one step into the room. When she didn't hit him, he moved in front of the toilet and began to urinate. "How can you say I raped you?"

"What else would you call it?"

"You were in my bed of your own free will," he said without looking at her.

"You miserable bastard." She pushed him with all the force she could muster.

"Cara!" he shouted losing his balance. He fell into the tub with a sickening thud as his head hit the wall.

"Are you okay?" she asked staring at him with hands on her hips.

He rubbed his head and moved his arms. "I don't think I broke any bones."

"Too bad." She kicked his leg, then shouted, "I wish you were dead!"

"You don't mean that," he said struggling to get up.

"Yes I do." She slugged him again, but only succeeded in hurting her hand. "I want you to leave and never come back."

He managed to sit on the edge of the tub. "This is my apartment."

"I don't care. Go away."

"I can tell you're a little upset..."

"A little upset!" she screamed. "You raped me."

"No I didn't. You said you wanted to do it in the morning, and it's morning."

She thought about the glass of water he gave her last night. "What did you give me? Was it some kind of date rape drug?" She pointed to his pajamas. "Put that thing away before I... before.... Just fix your pajamas."

"It was Ambien," he said fixing his pajamas. "I use it occasionally because of my insomnia. It's not a rape drug. It helped you fall asleep."

"Then why did you have to do what you did? I was sleeping and the next thing I knew you were screwing me," she took a deep breath and realized her heart was racing. "You didn't use a condom. I will kill you if you got me pregnant." She put a hand to her mouth. "I'm gonna puke..."

He couldn't get out of the way in time.

"Aw. This is gross." He grabbed the hand towel, turned on the tub and tired to clean up. "Are you going to claim I raped you?" He felt bile rise in his throat. "It was consensual."

"That's not how I see it." She rinsed out her mouth. "You didn't use protection. Why would you do that?"

"I thought you were on the pill."

"I never told you that. You should have... never mind."

"Do you really want to face the humiliation and emotional trauma you would experience? You told me you wanted to wait until morning, and it was the morning. You can't change your mind in the middle of doing it."

"I told you to stop."

"And I did," he said. "I'm sorry if you feel taken advantage of, but..."

"Go to hell!" She kicked him where it would count the most.

He doubled over and fell to the floor. "You just assaulted me. I should call the police on you."

"Since you won't leave, I will. Stay in here while I change and pack, and don't try to stop me."

"Good riddance to you." He waved with one hand while massaging his groin. "Leave and I won't press charges."

She looked at him with contempt and debated her options. "Maybe I can't prove it was rape, but that's how I feel."

"It wasn't rape. I woke you up and you said yes."

"I don't remember that. When I woke up enough to realize you weren't Tucker, I tried to get you to stop."

"And I did."

"You're trying to confuse me, Jeremiah."

"No I'm not, Cara. We both know we were going to make love. That's why you came up here. It was just bad timing."

"I'm still leaving," she said gathering her clothes. "Don't try to stop me."

"If you feel you need to, I won't stop you." He sat against the tub. "I can't get up."

"Good!" She turned around and walked away.

He leaned his head back and exhaled while holding his genitals.

She was dressed with her coat on and totally packed when he walked out of the bathroom.

"Do you want me to take you home?"

She looked at him blankly. "Seriously? You think I ever want to be that close to you again? I called Tucker's friend and talked to Tucker. He will be here soon."

"Did you tell him what happened?"

She shook her head and tried to close her suitcase. "I told him we had a fight."

"I could take you to the bus station if you want."

"No, thank you. I can manage on my own without any assistance from you." She threw a photo at him. "Who is Anna?"

"My sister," he said.

She shook her head. "Not according to the writing on the back. It says she loves you and the ring is perfect."

"I can explain."

She waved a hand. "Save it. I don't want to hear."

"I will pay for the abortion if you need one."

She threw a book at him. "You'll never know."

Tucker knocked on the door and Caralyn opened it after looking through the peephole.

"Are you okay, Carrie?"

"I'm ready to leave." She turned to Jeremiah and started to say something, but couldn't.

"I can take your suitcase."

"Thank you, Tucker. Let's go."

They left the building and stood in the brisk air.

"Caralyn, I'm sorry you guys had a fight, and I won't ask you to talk about it until you're ready."

"Thanks, Bubby. I found out he has a girlfriend named Anna. He tried to tell me she was his sister, but they're engaged."

"I'm sorry."

She chewed on her lip and asked softly, "Did you spend the night with Kim?"

"Are you kidding me? I would never sleep with anyone like her. She drove me nuts. Can you believe how dumb...?"

"She was as bright as a burned out light bulb."

"I think that would be giving her too much credit."

"Tuck, I want to go home. I feel like such an idiot. Can you take me home?"

"I've got bus fare for us to get home, Carrie. We can leave whenever you're ready."

"We have to leave now."

"Okay, it's not far. We can walk."

"I feel so dirty. I never want to see him again. You were right about everything. God. What a fool I have been. Do you still love me, even after what I've done?"

"You know I still love you, Carrie. You're my best friend, and I'm sorry you had to find out about him like this."

They walked to the bus station; purchased tickets and waited for the bus for home. She fell asleep against his shoulder on the ride to Butler.

Tucker gazed at her as she slept. *Carrie, I know you've been hurt. I'm not stupid. I won't ask what really happened, but please know I still love you very much.*

They were nearly to Butler where Dad McKay would pick them up when Caralyn looked at Tucker and he saw the sadness in her eyes.

"Are you okay, Carrie?" Tucker asked tenderly.

She nodded as her lip started to quiver, and the tears started flowing.

He put an arm around her and said, "Everything will be all right." He let her sob softly for several minutes.

"Tuck, will you promise not to say anything about Jeremiah to Mom and Dad? Please? I don't want them to know I spent the night with him."

"I won't tell them, Carrie. I hope I don't have to lie to them, but I certainly won't volunteer any information."

"Thank you, Bubby. There's one more thing."

"You don't have to tell me if you don't want to."

"He didn't use a condom," she whispered.

He thought about what that meant.

"I won't have his baby, Tuck."

"We will deal with that if we need to," he said. He wiped her brow then gripped her hand. "It's all right. You will get over Jeremiah and move on. Someday you will find the right guy for you."

She looked out the window and whispered, "Not a chance. I'm never getting serious about a man ever again."

"You don't mean it. You're upset. It will pass."

"No it won't." She dried her eyes and wiped her nose "I had the right guy, and I tossed him aside. Now you are going out with Laurie."

"Laurie and I are friends for the most part."

"Have you slept with her, Tuck? I saw you kissing her before."

"We haven't slept together, Carrie."

"Are you hoping to? I know you think she's pretty and all."

"Carrie!"

"What? I can't talk to you about sex now."

"It's not the right time," he said.

"You're right. I can't talk about it now."

"You know we always share things with each other. Are you going to keep secrets from me now?" he asked.

"I have to."

He didn't press her for details.

"Okay. I have thought about how it would be to make love to Laurie, but I'm not sure she's interested in me that way."

"Oh. She's interested all right. I can tell."

"How can you tell? You haven't talked to her lately."

"I don't need to talk to her to know she finds you attractive and sexy."

The bus pulled into the Butler station, and Dad waved as soon as he spotted them. Caralyn ran to hug him and started crying.

"Did you miss me that much, honey?" Dad held Caralyn and looked at Tucker. "Did something happen? We thought Jeremiah was bringing her home?"

Tucker shook his head, and Dad understood something had gone wrong. They got in the car to head home. Caralyn sat quietly in the back. Dad and Tucker talked about school and the weather merely to make conversation. When they got home, Tucker carried in the luggage for Caralyn. She saw Mom and burst into tears.

"It's all right, baby. You can let it loose."

After sobbing for a few minutes, Caralyn regained her composure.

"Jeremiah and I broke up. He was not the man I thought. He was already engaged to another woman. He led me to believe I was his only girl, but he lied. We had a fight, and I never want to see, or talk to, or ever hear his name again. Promise me you won't ever use his name out loud."

"We won't mention him ever," Mom said. 'You have my word."

"You were both right about me being too young to think about getting married. I am sorry I didn't take your advice."

Chapter Five

Cara, I haven't heard you mention... his name... since we got home after... you know. You need to talk about it."

"Tucker, I know you never liked Jeremiah from the start, and as it turned out, you were right," she said as they walked back to her dorm after lunch. "I'm sorry I don't want to talk about that night. I'm fine now, but it will take time before... never mind."

"I'm not going to gloat or say 'I told you so,' Carrie. I'm really sorry about whatever happened. If I ever see him again, I will punch his lights out for lying about his girlfriend."

"You will have to wait until after I kick him in the balls, Tuck."

They laughed as Tucker thought of her punching Jeremiah.

"What about... you know... the condom thing? You haven't said anything. I could tell how upset you were but you never talked about it."

"I started my period before New Year's Day. You can never tell anyone, Tuck. You have to swear it."

"I won't tell a soul, Carrie. You have my word. That's a relief. I've been worried about it."

"I'm sorry. I should have told you right away," she whispered.

"It's okay. I'm glad you got your... you know."

"Are you and Laurie getting serious about each other? Can we still be friends if you're with her?"

"Not really, Cara."

"But I want to be friends."

He laughed and waved a hand. "I was talking about getting serious with Laurie. You and I will always be friends."

"Do you love her?"

"I like her, but we are more friends than anything. Are you seeing anyone?"

"Trent from across the hall, but it's not serious. We hang out, but he hasn't even tried to kiss me lately."

"A-ha, so you've kissed him before."

Caralyn looked at Tucker and grinned, "Yes, he has kissed me, and I've kissed him back. So what?"

"Is there any chance for us, Cara? I know we still love each other, but everything is different now."

"Do you want to get back together, Tuck? Do you want to try again and see what happens?"

"I'm not sure, Caralyn. We'll see how it goes."

"Carrie, are you going to talk about it sometime?" Tucker asked the next morning. "Meyersdale, I mean."

"Not in the dining hall, and not at breakfast. How was practice last night?"

He shook his head. "Nice segue. Coach ran us ragged. Since you switched subjects, I will to. I heard you and Richard were all over each other the other day. Is it true?"

"We kissed and... I wanted some affection. It didn't go too far." She picked cold cereal and a fruit cup to eat.

"Why are you and Richard suddenly after each other? You do know he is quite a player, right?" Tucker loaded his tray with eggs, bacon and potatoes O'Brien.

"I don't care. We want to see where it will lead."

"You know where it will lead—right to bed. Do you want to became another of his girls? Do you think you can still be friends after having sex with him?"

"You're the one to talk." she said then pointed. "There's an empty table."

He followed and sat across from her. "Come on. You know it's different between us. You know I love you, and I always have. Do you know how much it hurt when you were with Jeremiah?" He heard his name and waved to a teammate.

"Don't mention his name. You know how sorry I am about the whole thing. I fell into his web like a spider into a flytrap. And what about Laurie? Are you still sleeping with her?"

He jerked his head toward her. "Carrie, we have never slept together. You are still the only one I have ever made love with. I'm only going out with Laurie because you were with... him."

"Do you think Derren or Richard know we did it?" she asked stabbing a piece of cantaloupe. "Richard said something last night that made me think he might know."

"I never told either of them anything about those nights. Have you?"

"No, of course not." She poured milk on her corn flakes.

"Are you sure?" he asked.

"Why would I tell them you were my first? They both think Jeremiah was my first, if you want to call what he did... I won't talk about it. I'm so glad we did it the way we did, Tuck."

"Carrie, I did it because I love you. I wanted your first time to be memorable."

"You accomplished that, Tuck. I'll never forget our night. First it was awkward because we couldn't get it right, but then it was the most romantic night of my life."

"Well, I hope so. I mean you were only seventeen. How many romantic nights have you had?"

"Just the nights with you."

He added more ketchup to his eggs and asked, "Do you think it would be romantic if you and Richard sleep together?"

"No, it would just be sex. You know that." She swiped a slice of bacon. "He may be a charmer, but it's just sex to him."

"I still wish you wouldn't be so, what's the word..."

"Easy? You think I'm being easy and promiscuous, don't you? Because I made a mistake with Jeremiah means I've lost my sense of morality. You think I would jump into bed with anyone who shows an interest, huh?" Her breathing quickened and her heart raced.

"That's not it at all. I know that jerk hurt you more than simply lying about his fiancee..."

She crossed her arms over her chest. "Do not go there, Tucker McKay."

He took deep breaths to calm down. "I won't."

"Do you think we will ever tell anyone about our nights together?"

"I don't know, Carrie," he answered sharply.

"Do you think it would change the way they view us or change our friendship?"

"I really don't know. What's with all the questions? Do you think we should tell them?"

"Yeah, I think we should. I don't want to keep it a secret anymore. They will understand. I know Richard thought I was your little sister for so long, and, sometimes, I think he still does."

"Do you ever think of me as your brother anymore?"

"No! I haven't thought of you as my brother for a long time. You're my protector and my knight in shining armor, but not my brother."

"We better get going. I've got to get to class. Are you coming over for dinner tonight?"

"I don't think so. I'm gonna grab something quick after my last class and then head to the library."

"Is Richard still coming to your room?"

"Maybe."

"Carrie, please don't let him... you know."

"I can't promise anything. I love you."

"Love you, too, Carrie, see you later."

Later that evening Caralyn heard a knock on her door. She closed her textbook and said, "Hi, Richard, come on in."

"Hey, Cara, how was your day?" He sat on the edge of her bed and smiled at her bear.

She pivoted in her desk chair. "All right, yours?"

"Typical day. Classes, girls chasing me everywhere."

"I hope you were able to get away from them and still save some energy for chasing me." She stood up and walked closer.

"Are you going to make me chase you, Cara?" He touched the tip of her nose.

"I think I will, but I probably won't run too fast."

"I brought something with me tonight. Do you want to see?"

"If it's what I think it is, no. I don't want to see. How many did you bring anyway?"

"Caralyn, are you telling me I need more than one?" Richard grinned wickedly as Caralyn turned red. "I brought two. One for me and one for you."

"What on earth will I do with one?"

"Eat it, of course."

"What are you talking about?" She grabbed for his hand. "Let me see, Richard."

He held out his hands palms up. "Mounds bars, of course." He closed his hands before she could see what he held. "What did you think I meant? Did you think I... you thought I brought condoms, huh? You did, didn't you?" He drew a sharp breath. "I'm shocked. Shocked, I tell you." He laughed and added, "That's from a Bogart movie in case you weren't aware."

"I've seen *Casablanca*, and we will always have Paris, Rickey."

"Good comeback."

"Richard, let me see what you've got, right now!"

"Here. Mounds, like I said. This one is for you and this one's mine." He raised his hands straight up.

"Let me have mine." She tried to grab it but only succeeded in pressing close to him.

"Say please."

She poked him in the stomach instead.

"Ow! That wasn't nice."

Caralyn looked surprised and confused. "You didn't come here to finish what we started?"

"Caralyn, believe me you'll never know how much I would like to. I'm sorry, but I can't bring myself to do it."

"Why? The other night you were ready to do me on the couch with Tuck and Derren home."

"I know, but we let our emotions and physical needs cloud our judgment. I don't think we would have gone all the way. I think we would have stopped."

She reached for the Mounds again. "I wasn't going to stop. I was ready to do it even if Tuck and Derren were in the room. Haven't you heard I'm a slut?"

"You know that's not true, Caralyn. I know something's changed since you were..."

"Since I let that jerk do me? Is that what you want to say?" She shoved her hands into her jean pockets. "I deserve it."

He put his hands on her shoulders and said softly, "I think it would change our friendship, and I don't want to lose that. I'm sorry, but that means more to me than ten minutes of sex."

"All right. I wouldn't have done it with them watching of course, but ten minutes? Is that all the time you were going to take to do me?"

"You said that's all the time Jeremiah took."

She shoved him away with both hands. "Screw you to hell and back, Richard! Don't ever talk about him."

He stumbled back but regained his balance. "Caralyn, you know I would never be that way with you, and I'm sorry Jeremiah was such an ass. You deserved better."

"Can we head back to the apartment? I want Tuck and Derren to know we aren't going to do it."

"Sure, if you want. Let's go." He held out the Mounds and she grabbed it.

They walked into the apartment and surprised Tuck and Derren. She took off her coat, threw it at the new wooden rack by the closet and kicked off her shoes.

"Hey, Carrie, I'm glad to see you. Didn't expect you so early. Everything all right?" Derren asked.

"Yes, everything's fine and so you guys know, we didn't do it." She shifted her eyes from Derren to Tucker. "Richard decided he didn't want to waste ten minutes on me."

"That's not what I said, Caralyn." He picked up her coat and hung it up properly.

Tucker walked up behind her and hugged her. "I'm glad you didn't do it," he whispered.

"Tuck, we need to tell them about us tonight."

"Are you sure?"

"Yes, let's tell them right now."

"Okay." Tucker faced his flatmates. He rubbed his jaw, stared at the ceiling then said, "Derren, Richard, we have something to tell you, and it's important." He took a deep breath. "There is this thing we have been keeping secret since last year." Tucker paused.

"Just tell them, Tuck." She poked him in the ribs. "Don't turn it into a mini-series."

"All right. Carrie and I made love last year one night when you guys were gone. In fact we spent two, no three, different nights together and made love all night long. We went out for dinner. She surprised me by wearing a dress You saw it on her birthday. I had candles in the bedroom and..."

"You don't need to tell them all the details." She looked at Tucker and bumped his hip.

"I thought you were going to tell us a secret." Derren grinned and said, "We've known about that all along."

"What?" Tucker and Caralyn shouted.

"How could you have known?" she asked. "We never told anyone."

"We aren't blind or stupid," Derren said with a grin. "We could tell you guys were crazy about each other, so we arranged to be gone that weekend to let you have the place to yourselves."

Caralyn looked at Derren and said, "I can't believe you have known all along. You never said a word. You knew when we went camping in Wisconsin. Is that why you would disappear at night? You were giving us a chance to be alone in case we wanted to make love while I was trying to set him up with Nancy."

"Yeah, I guess so. I knew you had made love, and I wanted to make sure you have some privacy in case you wanted to do it again. We thought as long as you guys were keeping it a secret, we would too. I'm glad it's finally out in the open."

"How could you tell we followed through with it?" Caralyn asked as she fiddled with her new stud earrings.

"Caralyn, you were glowing for a week afterward. We could tell by the look on your face. Plus we saw you guys kissing and holding hands like two newlyweds."

"I can't believe you've known all this time. Richard, you knew about me and Tuck, and you still almost made love to me on the couch that night. If you hadn't finally run out of condoms, we would have had sex right here with these two home."

"What do you mean? Richard is never out of condoms. He still has a whole drawer full in his room," Derren said.

"What?" Caralyn looked at Tucker then turned to Richard and grabbed his arm. "You told me you were all out, and that's why we stopped."

"I'm sorry, Cara. I lied to you. I wasn't out, but I couldn't go through with it."

"You had your hand on my pants and I had my hand on you. In another couple minutes you would have had my pants off and been inside of me. Was it all a joke or something?" Caralyn balled her fists. "Is that the way it is with all men? I hate every last one of you!"

"No, Cara. Not at all. I really was turned on by you, but I guess my conscience wouldn't let me continue. I'm really sorry. I would never want to hurt you. Will you forgive me?"

"I guess I will, but now I feel ashamed because of how much I wanted you."

"I can understand. I am the school's and maybe the world's greatest lover."

Everybody groaned at once.

"Listen to Casanova here. Caralyn, do you want us to hold him while you take your revenge on him?"

"No, Derren. It's enough to know he could have had the best night of his life, but he passed it up. He will have to be content with what could have been."

"Caralyn! How can you say that?" Tucker frowned at her.

"Tuck, I'm sorry I got carried away with Richard."

Richard told everyone, "Well, I, for one, am glad it's out in the open now. We don't have to pretend you guys didn't have an affair any more."

"Let's order a pizza and garlic bread. I'm hungry," Tucker said.

"After we eat, do you want to jump into bed, Tuck? She asked. "Since everyone knows, we can keep our 'affair' going."

"Caralyn!" the guys yelled at the same time.

She lifted her shoulder in a half shrug then inspected her fingernails. "Just kidding. I'm never letting another man touch me."

"Really?" Richard asked.

She looked at Derren and Richard. "You guys are dead meat if you touch me." She moved behind Tucker and thought about Jeremiah.

"What do you think, Derren? Should we?" Richard asked. "She deserves it for being a tease."

Derren looked at Caralyn, saw she was trembling and shook his head. "Cara, we aren't going to touch you. No one will ever hurt you like that again."

Chapter Six

A few days later, Caralyn and Tucker studied at the dining table—all alone in the apartment. She kept bumping Tucker's foot.

"Cara, I'm busy. I need to finish this."

"Sorry, Tuck. I thought I was touching the table."

After she did it a few more times, Tucker looked at her and asked, "Cara, are you trying to tell me something? I may not be a rocket scientist, but I'm not a dumb jock."

"Well, since Derren and Richard know we have been lovers, and we have the apartment to ourselves..." Caralyn smiled at Tucker and put a finger to her mouth in a sexy way.

Tucker closed his book and stared at her. "I don't want to do this unless you tell me you aren't doing it to get back at Jeremiah."

"What about Laurie? I don't want you to cheat on her."

"That's over. She dumped me."

"Why? Is she crazy?"

"She found an older man she liked better. She said she couldn't compete with basketball."

"You can have me again." She moved to the couch.

"That doesn't sound very romantic."

"It's just sex," she said.

Caralyn lay on her back and Tucker moved next to her.

"Kiss me, Tuck."

He leaned closer and let his lips touch hers just as Derren and Richard walked in. Tucker froze.

Derren told Richard, "I guess we got here too late."

"Maybe we got here too early," Richard replied with a grin.

"We weren't doing anything," Tucker said.

Caralyn punched his arm and tried to sit up. "Stand up, and they aren't stupid."

Richard pointed to his bedroom and said, "You can use it if you want to finish."

Tucker got up and Caralyn fixed her jeans which were unsnapped and unzipped.

"When did you do that?" He looked at Richard and Derren. "I didn't do that."

The guys laughed. Caralyn stuck out her tongue.

She took Tucker's hand and pulled him into Richard's bedroom. "You guys have the worst timing possible." She stuck her tongue out at Derren and Richard again and closed the door.

"The condoms are in the drawer," Richard hollered. "Feel free to borrow one... or two."

Caralyn looked at Tucker. "Did you tell him what you told me? About condoms?"

"Of course not. I may be a jock, but I'm not a blockhead. I swore I'd never tell anyone, and I haven't."

She joined Tucker on the bed and the bed squeaked. They kissed and the bed squeaked. She touched his jeans and the bed squeaked again. They tried to remain completely still... and the bed didn't squeak. She kissed him... and the bed squeaked louder than ever.

"I can't do this now, Carrie. The bed is so noisy and the thought of them knowing what we are doing in here is too much."

"I know. Maybe we should bounce around on the bed and make them think we are doing it. Maybe they will leave."

"I don't think it would matter, Cara. Let's forget about it and finish studying."

The bed squeaked as they got off. The door squeaked as Caralyn opened it. They walked back to the table and sat down. Her chair squeaked. Derren was in the kitchen, but didn't say anything. Richard sat in the living room watching them. Finally, he couldn't stand it.

"Either that was the fastest quickie in history, or you didn't do anything. Which is it?"

Caralyn gave Richard a dirty look and a quick gesture using one finger.

"I'll take that as you didn't do anything."

Caralyn blushed as she said, "That lousy bed makes so much noise. You can't move a muscle without it squeaking. Why do you tolerate it?"

"I only use the bed to sleep in, Caralyn. I don't use it like you were trying to," Richard joked.

Caralyn was embarrassed and mad, too. "Richard, you have used that bed for sex so many times you would need a supercomputer to keep track of how many girls have been in there."

"Not true. I know exactly how many girls have shared that bed with me." Richard grinned at her. "And the bed only started squeaking a couple days ago. I guess I wore it out."

She tossed a pen at him, but missed.

The next afternoon Tucker and Caralyn were alone in the apartment once more. They bumped into each other in the kitchen.

"Sorry, Tuck. I didn't see you." She looked at him and her lip began to quiver."

"Carrie, what's wrong? Did something happen?"

She shook her head, raised her arms and whispered, "Hold me, Tuck."

He held her tenderly. "Carrie, is this because of... him?"

"I'm afraid to... do anything. I tried yesterday, but I couldn't go through with it. I can't concentrate on classes and I can't sleep."

He took her hands and gently kissed the top of her head. "You can talk to me, and I promise not to say anything."

"I want you to hold me, Tuck. I need to cuddle."

They moved to the bedroom and lay beside each other.

"Please hold me. No kissing, okay?"

"Are you shaking, Carrie?"

"I don't want to get hurt again, Bubby."

"I would never hurt you." He wiped a tear away, moved her hair out of her eyes and rubbed her forehead with a finger.

He had been holding her for several minutes when the door opened and Derren walked in.

Tucker saw him and put a finger to his mouth. "She's trying to sleep."

"Sorry." Derren nodded and walked away closing the door slowly.

Tucker walked out to the living room where Derren was studying. "She needed to be held."

"You don't have to explain. Is she feeling better?"

"I think so."

"She won't talk about that night, but is it possible it was more than she let on?"

"Like what?" Tucker sat down.

He closed his book. "Maybe she wasn't willing."

"Are you saying what I think you are?" He drummed his fingers on the table.

Derren nodded.

Tucker swore under his breath. "If I thought that for a minute, I would drive up there right now and..."

"No, you wouldn't."

"Should we ask her? She won't talk about it voluntarily."

Derren shrugged. "I have no clue. Maybe she should talk to a counselor."

"She would kill me if I suggested it."

"What are you going to do?"

"Nothing. If what you think happened. The last thing she needs is someone taking advantage of her."

Caralyn came out a few minutes later looking half asleep. She stood behind Tucker, ran a finger through his hair and asked, "Why did you leave?"

"You fell asleep, so I came out here to study. Do you feel better now?"

Caralyn looked at Derren. "Did he tell you what happened, Derry? Wait, don't tell me."

"If you guys are going to use the bedroom during the day, we need to have a signal like Richard," Derren said trying to be funny.

"Richard has a signal?" Caralyn asked as she crossed her arms over her chest. "Why does he need a signal? That bed is so noisy. I bet the whole building can hear it."

"Yeah, it wasn't always so noisy. Anyway, he puts his tennis racquet by the door if he is busy."

47

"Doesn't it embarrass you guys if he has a girl with him?"

Derren shrugged and leaned back in his chair. The chair squeaked. "It did at first, but we are used to it now." He leaned forward.

"Do you ever see the girls?"

Derren and Tucker looked at each other.

"You do, don't you? I bet you have seem them naked."

"Not all of them, Cara, but we have seen a couple," Tucker admitted.

"Naked, you mean? You've seen a couple of them naked, right?" She thwacked the back of his head.

He rubbed his head, turned in the chair and tried to grab her hand. "Not intentionally, Caralyn. A few times they walked out of the bedroom to use the bathroom."

The kitchen timer dinged. "That's my pizza," Derren said. He stood up and scooted to the kitchen.

Tucker tried to stand, but she put her hands on his shoulders and forced him down.

"Stay right here, dweeb brain." Caralyn looked at them and shook her head. "I suppose I should walk around naked if I have sex, huh? I will let you and Richard and Derren and whoever else might be hanging around see me naked."

"You know you aren't going to do that, Carrie."

"No, I won't, but Richard's girlfriends shouldn't either." She walked to the stove and looked at the pizza. "I want a slice."

Derren and Tucker felt embarrassed as they looked at each other.

Caralyn noticed. "What? You're hiding something. Spill it."

Tucker looked at Derren and rolled his shoulders.

Caralyn shifted her eyes back and forth. Then she smacked Derren's arm. "Don't tell me. Natalie did it, too. Tuck, have you and Richard seen Natalie naked?"

"Richard, did one time, but I never have."

"Partly naked?" Caralyn frowned at Tucker with her hands on her hips.

"Carrie, does it really matter? Are you going to be upset?"

"What part of Natalie did you see? Tell me."

"All right. I saw her topless for a few seconds one time. That's all, I swear it."

"Did you know about it, Derren?"

"Yes, I was here, but it wasn't a big deal."

"What? How could it not be a big deal?"

He leaned against the counter and rubbed his chin.

"Did she let Richard see her totally naked?"

"She didn't know he was here, and she walked into the kitchen to get some water from the fridge. She was as surprised to see him as he was to see her."

"I can't believe you guys." Caralyn hollered. She pressed her hands to her temples. "You are all pigs."

Richard walked in and heard part of the conversation. "What's going on? What happened?"

Derren and Tucker were too embarrassed to tell him so Caralyn did. "I hear it's normal for girls to walk around here naked, so I figure the next time after I make love with whoever, I will stay naked so everyone can see me."

"Ooops! I guess someone is upset." Richard hung his coat on the rack and held out his hands with palms up. "What can I say?"

"Oh, you guys are such imbeciles." Caralyn yelled as she marched into the bathroom.

Richard looked at Tucker and Derren. "I haven't had a girl here in weeks."

Two days later, as Richard and Caralyn ate lunch, Richard asked, "What did Derren see when he walked in on you guys?"

"Richard. Are you trying to embarrass me again?"

"Not really. I'm merely curious." He added salt and pepper to his burger. "And don't call me a cat."

She tossed her hair, looked around to see if anyone could hear them and whispered, "I was on top of Tucker. I think the sheet covered my butt, but I'm not positive."

"Get real!"

"I didn't hear him so I didn't cover up. I know he has seen me naked before but certainly not while Tuck and I were in bed."

Richard smirked.

"Are you wishing it had been you to walk in on us?"

"Yeah, sorta. I know we are friends and I had my chance with you and couldn't follow through with it, but I still wish I could see you naked sometime."

"You're a creep." She pounded her fist on the table spilling his water. "He didn't see anything. Tucker was holding me because I was upset and tired."

"So you weren't making love, huh?"

"No! I was upset."

He took another bite of his burger, and added more ketchup to his tater tots. "Want to try a tot?"

"No, thanks. Do you remember how many girls you have slept with? Have you ever had one change their mind? Never mind. Forget that."

"Do you think I'm a jerk for sleeping with so many girls?"

"I think you are afraid to get serious about a girl, so you use casual sex to prevent getting in a serious relationship. One of these days you will find the right girl, and I hope you aren't afraid to make a real commitment."

"What about you and Tucker? Are you going to get serious about each other?"

She added the rest of her French dressing to her salad and shook her head. "I'm never getting serious about anyone ever again."

He leaned closer, grabbed her hand and whispered, "Was Jeremiah serious? I think you tried to convince yourself it was, but deep down I think you knew it wouldn't last. I think you pretended it was meaningful in case you slept with him. You could use 'being in love' as an excuse."

She jerked her hand away. "You don't know what happened."

"Nobody does because you won't talk about it."

She crossed her arms over her chest and stared at him.

50

"The truth hurts, huh?"

She took a sip of Dr Pepper and said, "Maybe you are right, Richard. Maybe I was fooling myself. I will regret that night for the rest of my life. Do you have any regrets about not having sex with me? I mean, what if that was our only chance to ever sleep together, and what if it was great—like the best sex either one of us is ever going to have and we missed out."

Richard picked up a tater tot with his fork and waved it halfway between his mouth and hers. "Are you offering me a second chance? If I ever have another chance, I will not stop."

She stole his tot and asked, "Where would we go? I wouldn't want to use the apartment because we would get caught."

"What about your dorm room?"

"Tucker has a key, but he rarely uses it."

Richard looked at her with a wicked smile.

"We're not going to do it now. I have class in a half hour."

"What about later tonight?"

"You are serious about trying again, aren't you?"

"Yes, I guess I am. I might regret it later if we let sex ruin our friendship, but I don't think it would. Think about it, Cara, and let me know. I am getting aroused talking about it."

She rolled her eyes. "You guys are so horny. All you ever think about is sex."

"Yeah, so."

"If we do, you have to promise never to tell anyone." She stole his last tot. "Not a soul unless you want to die a slow and agonizing death."

He raised a hand. "I swear it will be our secret forever."

"Call me at seven, and I will let you know."

"Seriously?" he asked with a smirk.

She sneered and shouted, "No! I'm never sleeping with another man." She saw several people staring at her.

"That's what I thought." He tugged at his shirt collar. "Maybe we aren't mean to be lovers, Cara, but we can still be close friends."

51

"Caralyn, where have you been all weekend?" Tucker asked Sunday evening as Caralyn walked into the apartment. "Mom called. She said your cell phone went straight to voicemail so she called here. I didn't know what to tell her."

"I'm sorry I didn't tell you, Tuck. I took the train to Carrier Grove."

"Why? Who do you know there?"

"Duh! Sandy Young. Nancy was going with me, but she had to work an extra shift. I should have called you, but I got busy and forgot."

"It's okay as long as you're all right. You are all right?"

"I'm fine, just tired." She plopped onto the couch. "The train was crowded for some reason and I couldn't take a nap."

Tucker stared at her for a moment then asked, "Was it really a guy you went to see?"

"Tuck. I stayed with Sandy. Call and check."

"I don't want to make you mad. I was simply wondering."

"Well, I didn't have sex with anyone while I was gone if that eases your mind."

"Hey!" He raised his hands with palms out. "Don't be mad at me for caring about you."

She pointed to herself. "I'm sorry. I'm mad at myself."

"How's Sandy doing? I heard she's engaged."

"She is engaged, but he was gone. I realized Sandy and I are not as close as I had thought. She has moved on with her life and probably won't ever live in Stockton Woods again."

She decided to tell Tucker the truth. "I didn't originally plan to see a guy, Tuck. That was not my intention at all, but on the train I scrolled through my phone contacts and saw a number I got while in high school. I called it on a whim and to make a long story short, I met him for lunch. Sandy was busy studying in the evening and without Nancy there, I got bored. I slipped out for a walk and stopped at a place and ran into him and a couple friends..." She told Tucker the entire story.

"Were you going to have sex with him like you did with Jeremiah?" Tucker asked as he snapped back in anger.

"Maybe. It's not your business if I want to sleep with someone. I'm not your property."

"I didn't mean you were. Why are we shouting at each other?"

"Because I hate all men." Caralyn left in tears.

"What time are Mom and Dad supposed to get here?" Tucker asked. "Is all your stuff packed."

"Mom said around noon, and I wish I could put everything in your apartment. Richard is living there all summer, so you can leave stuff there. Why can't I leave some things?"

"What? All you have are clothes and teddy bears," he teased.

"And books and my little fridge though I should toss it. It stopped working a few days ago."

"Let's put in in the dumpster," Tucker suggested.

"I suppose you're right. Why isn't Richard going home?"

Tucker looked around Caralyn's dorm room. "He's taking classes and interning for a local lawyer."

"Why do you have to leave right away?" She tried lifting a suitcase but struggled. "What's so important about some basketball camp in North Carolina?"

"Let me get that, Cara." He set the suitcase on the mattress with ease. "It's run by Coach McNealy, and only a few players are invited."

"Are you leaving tomorrow afternoon?"

"If I want to be there on time, I have to. Why?"

"Could we stop at The Curve for a shake or something. It would give us a chance to say goodbye."

"Maybe. If Stanley's working, will you flirt with him, so I can have free food, too."

"No way. You have to pay like everyone else." She made a face. "I do not flirt to get free food... all the time."

"Caralyn, would you be interested in a job? Natalie and I had a fight, and now she's not going to help at camp this summer. Are you interested?" Derren asked Friday evening. "I'm rather desperate."

"Maybe. What would I have to do?" She put the last of the clean plates in the cupboard.

"You would be assisting with the athletic program. I would help you get everything set up. Then you would be responsible for some activities."

"Would I get paid?"

"Two hundred and fifty dollars a week plus room and board. Same pay as Natalie."

"That's more than I would make working at The Curve. Would I have to share the same cabin as you?"

"No way. There's a cabin for the single ladies."

"I'll call you back after I talk to Mom. She said I need to do something other than mope around the house all day."

"Let me know as quick as you can, please."

Mom and Dad were reluctant to consent. After much discussion, they decided to give Caralyn their permission since she would be with Derren.

"I can go, Derry."

"Good. I was sweating bullets thinking about running the whole department on my own," he said wiping his brow. "Did you see Tucker before he left?"

She closed her book with a crack. "He stopped by for two seconds, but he talked to Nancy more than me. I kinda got mad and told him to leave."

"Good move, pipsqueak."

"Hush. What time are we leaving?"

"I want to leave around ten Sunday morning."

"I'll be ready."

He picked her up, and she explained her fight with Tucker.

"I shouldn't have raised my voice. The whole thing could have been avoided, but now we aren't talking to each other."

"You can call him next weekend when he gets back," Derren said.

"I suppose I should. I'll make a deal with you, I'll call Tucker and apologize if you call Natalie and patch things up."

"Sounds like a good idea."

They arrived Sunday afternoon, signed in and were assigned housing by the camp director.

"I guess we're stuck working with each other for six weeks, Cara."

"It's okay. I'm sure we will get along all right."

He parked next to her cabin, and Derren grabbed the suitcases as Caralyn headed inside.

"Wow! This is really small, and there are six beds in here."

"Which one do you want? It doesn't look like anyone else has checked in." He set her two suitcases on the floor. "Did you pack clothes or bricks?"

"Books. I want that one." She pointed to one in the corner. "There are two windows, so it should be cooler."

He set the suitcases on her bed. "Do you need anything else, your majesty?"

She giggled and commanded, "Show me your cabin."

He parked next to the rustic cabin with wooden plank siding and a tin roof. She jumped out, dashed up the steps and stepped inside.

"You weren't exaggerating about it being close quarters. This is like a closet."

"It's big enough for two."

"I'll take the top bunk," she teased.

He shook his head. "Not a chance. You have to room with the other brats... I mean camp workers."

Caralyn checked out the bathroom. "There's no way we would both fit in here, Derren. I suppose it doesn't matter since we shouldn't be in there at the same time anyway."

"I think maybe Natalie decided the same thing."

Derren showed her around the camp in the morning. "Some sessions there are more boys than girls, so don't be surprised if some of the older boys hit on you."

"Get out! Really?"

"It could happen."

"I could pretend to be your girlfriend. Nobody would bother me then."

"That might work for a while, but these kids are pretty smart. We might fool them for a few days, but not two weeks."

The campers arrived by noon Monday for a two-week session. After lunch everyone gathered on the softball field. Derren introduced himself and Caralyn to the campers. One of the older boys, Dominick, paid special attention to her.

"Did you bring a one-piece bathing suit, Cara?" Derren asked after dinner. "The guys will be all over you if you wear your skimpy bikini."

"I brought both my one-piece and a modest bikini for when I swim alone."

"I was kidding, but that's a smart move. There is a trail through the woods where you can take the campers running. I'll show you where. It's three miles long with some hills."

"That sounds like fun. Maybe we can kiss and make out since we are a couple," Caralyn teased.

"Yeah, that's never going to happen," Derren said.

After lights out for the campers, the counselors met in the dining hall to talk and get to know each other.

"Caralyn, they think we're a couple," Derren said.

She grinned. "They think I'm fifteen, too."

"Why didn't you tell them we're cousins."

"It will give them something to gossip about."

"Can I talk to you about something?" Caralyn asked after lights out Tuesday as they sat on the dining hall steps.

"Yeah, sure, Cara. What's on your mind?"

"Dominick is trying to get in my pants. Yeah, I know I shouldn't talk like that, but that is the easiest way to explain it. I heard he made a bet with other campers that he would get me in bed before he leaves."

"Am I safe to assume you have no interest in him?"

She poked him in the side. "That would definitely be a safe assumption."

"I don't see the problem. Tell him to leave you alone. If he doesn't, you can tell the camp director, and he will send him home."

"Yeah, I suppose I should, but I kinda wanted to string him along and teach him a lesson."

"Guys like that will never learn, Cara. They only see girls as sex objects to be used and tossed aside like trash."

"He's like a younger Richard."

"Remember Jeremiah..."

"Believe me I will never forget that lesson."

Caralyn chose to string Dominick along. He ran into her before dinner and thought about the money.

"Caralyn, would you like to do something later?"

"What did you have in mind?"

"Maybe a walk. You're not afraid of the dark, are you?"

"Maybe I should be. You might try to seduce me."

"We can get away for a walk and find a secluded place to get to know each other better."

"Okay. I'll meet you at eight outside the dining hall."

"Where have you been the last couple of nights, Cara?" Derren asked after dinner.

"Hiking through the woods with Dominick."

"Why? Do you remember what he is after?"

"I haven't forgotten, but he hasn't tried anything so far."

Derren looked at her and asked, "Do you want to head to the dining hall? Mr. McNaughton made some homemade ice cream."

"That sounds good."

"I thought about telling you to stay away from him, but that would have backfired, right?"

She laughed and answered, "You know me, and I admit I can be stubborn at times."

She and Derren spent a couple of hours at the dining hall with the other counselors and workers.

He walked her back to her cabin and she asked, "Are you still mad at Natalie?"

"I'm not mad at her. She's the one who got mad at me. I never get mad at anyone. I'm too easy going, I guess."

"You'll get back together. I know it."

"I hope so, Cara. I want to marry her."

Friday night the campers had a later lights out time—midnight. Caralyn and Dominick met for their nightly walk.

"Dominick, do you ever do more than kiss a girl?"

"That sounds like an invitation to do more than kiss you, Caralyn, is it?"

"Maybe. You will have to try and see what happens."

Dominick put both hands on her hips, pulled her close and tried to kiss her.

"Dominick, I may lose control of my feelings if I let you kiss me."

"That would be all right with me, Caralyn."

She let him keep his hands where they were until he started to move them toward her butt.

"You should stop now, Dominick. You wouldn't want me to get in trouble, would you?"

"No, of course not. I wouldn't want that at all."

"We should get back before some people start talking about us." Caralyn kissed him once before they headed back to the cabins. "You won't tell anyone about this, will you?"

"No, I promise I won't." As soon as Dominick got back to his cabin, he told his friends the details of his walk.

Dominick surprised Caralyn Monday morning as she came around the corner of the main office. "Hi, Caralyn. How was your weekend?"

"Great. Yours?"

"Okay, but I missed you." He put his hands on her shoulders. "I know a place where we can be alone. We can kiss and make out right in the middle of camp."

"Where?" Caralyn asked backing away. *This has to end right now.*

"The old counselor's lounge. It is locked up and no one uses it anymore. I found a way in and there is a couch in there. What do you say?"

"No. I'm sorry, but this has gone far enough."

He stared at her. "I don't understand. You kissed me."

"I know about the bet, and you've lost. There is no way I am going to kiss you again or anything else."

"But you held my hand and let me touch..."

"And I'm sorry. When I heard about your bet, I wanted to punish you."

"So, you aren't interested in me?"

"Not in that way, but there are girls here who are."

He kicked the ground. "I really blew it, huh?"

She nodded. "You need to learn how to treat girls. I once knew someone who used girls and then tossed them aside. You can be better than that. I hope you will find someone who you really care about and who cares about you."

"I'm really sorry for the bet, and I hope you will forgive me. I was trying to impress the other guys in my cabin."

"I forgive you."

"Did that guy you were talking about use you, Caralyn?"

"Yes, Dominick, he did. He was older than me by several years and used my inexperience to seduce me. That's why I was so upset when I heard about your bet and what you were planning."

Dominick stared at the ground.

"One more thing, Dominick."

"What?" he looked up at her.

"You really are hot, and girls are going to love it if you treat them with respect and are honest with them. You will have your opportunities. I can guarantee that."

"Do you have any plans for after dinner, Cara?"

"No, do you want to do something together?"

"I was thinking about taking a ride into town and checking out a movie," Derren said.

"Do you want to go for a walk instead? It's such a beautiful night, and it's still early. We could stare at the stars and who knows what will happen."

"Caralyn, nothing will happen. You know that, right?"

"I know, but I can still dream," she teased.

"You need to talk to Tucker about your fight."

They ended up sitting by the pool.

"Tuck and I have been fighting so much ever since I met Jeremiah."

"It's because he loves you, and he knew Jeremiah was not the right guy for you."

"I found that out the hard way. He set me up and then used me."

"Cara, you don't have to say anything."

"You know what he did to me, don't you, Derry?"

"Yeah, I know, Cara. He was a jerk."

"At least I didn't get naked for him when he... screwed me."

"Caralyn, you shouldn't talk like that."

"Are you gonna wash my mouth out with soap?"

"I'm not going to do that. It seems kinda funny to hear you swear like that. It's almost like a little kid who uses that word when they have no idea of what it means." He looked at her and she appeared about to cry. "I'm sorry, Cara. I guess you do realize what it means."

She started sobbing as Derren held her.

"Let it all out, Carrie." He held her until she stopped crying. "Are you feeling better now?"

"Yes. Thank you for knowing when to be quiet."

He rubbed her back and asked, "Was it because you were thinking about what he did?"

She nodded.

"You can tell me anything, you know, and I will never tell another soul."

"Since I was with Jeremiah and he used me, I have felt like such a tramp. I lost my self esteem and felt worthless and like someone who would be used by men for their pleasure. I almost let Richard have me. I have been flirting with you, and I tried to make an example of Dominick."

Derren listened to her story quietly. He was confused at times, but listened without interrupting.

"When Dominick wanted me, I wanted to get revenge. I am so sorry I am such a slut." She began crying again.

Derren held her. "You are not a slut, Caralyn. You are still a good person. You don't have to be ashamed about what happened. It wasn't your fault. You were the victim of a predator."

She stopped crying and sat quietly next to him.

"We should get back, Cara."

They headed to her cabin.

"Cara, do you still love Tucker?"

"I'm not sure anymore, Derry. Not in the way you mean and after what I have done, I don't think he will ever love me again. Do you miss Natalie?"

"Yeah, I really do. I know we sometimes fight and her mother drives me nuts, but I still love her."

"I'm sorry if I have spoiled camp for you, Derren. I didn't mean to be such a delinquent."

Derren laughed because he had called her a delinquent before in an affectionate way. "You haven't spoiled camp for me, Cara. It would be so boring without you."

Chapter Eight

One night at dinner Caralyn cut her rib eye into pieces then told Beth, "I think when I get out of school I might move to Chicago or maybe even New York. I like being in a big city where no one knows you or bothers you. Maybe it's youthful innocence and naivety, but I don't feel intimidated in your neighborhood."

"Wrightsville is safer than Gladstone Ridge where I first lived. Ray grew up in the city, so he knows the best areas and which ones to avoid."

"There are areas my friends avoid even during the day," Ray Gardner said. "How's the steak?"

"Perfect, Ray. Thank you," Caralyn said. She noticed his new earring. "Where did you find that?"

He touched his ear lobe. "Beth bought this for me. She found it in Arizona. It's turquoise. Native American original."

"I like it," she said while touching her ears.

"Did I ever tell you I'm part Maricopa?"

"Not that I remember, but you do have a dark complexion."

"One-sixteenth." He took another bite of steak.

Caralyn turned to Beth and asked, "Did you ever live on campus?"

Beth shook her head as she added steak sauce to her rib eye. "I commuted and lived in cheap flats with roommates for a couple years. I was young, foolish and desperate to leave small town U.S.A."

"I am so tired of Stockton Woods where everyone knows everyone's business and secrets."

Beth nodded in agreement. "I got out of there as soon as I could, and I'm so happy I did. You should live with us, Cara."

"Maybe I should. I'll think about it after I get back from France."

"Tell us again why you are spending a semester in Paris. What's the name of the school?"

"Paris-Sorbonne University." Caralyn explained why she was spending a semester abroad.

"I suffered through five hours of tests, and I guess I had the highest percentage. The counselor said I have an innate ability to learn a new language. Grandma taught me French as soon as I could talk."

"I used to laugh because you would switch back and forth between French and English."

"I thought they would choose an older student. The McKays were reluctant to grant permission because of my age. Dad did some research, and they talked several times to the couple where I will be living. They understood what an honor it was to be chosen, and could not deny me the opportunity. Isn't it great?"

"What about Tucker? Have you guys ever been apart for such a long time?"

"No, but he doesn't miss me."

Beth shook her head. "You are fooling yourself if you believe that."

"Maybe. I haven't talked to him all summer. I worked with Derren for six weeks, then came here. Tucker was at basketball camps. The few times he made it home coincided with the time I was in Chicago."

After dinner Caralyn helped Beth with the dishes. Beth caught Caralyn staring out the window and touched her shoulder. "Where are you? You haven't responded to anything I've said. What's up?"

"Sorry, I was thinking about Tucker." She set the plate on the counter. "Do you remember when he was a baby?"

Beth leaned against the counter, looked into Caralyn's eyes and took her hand. "This is a conversation for the couch. Come with me."

They moved to the living room couch. "Cara and I are going to talk," Beth told Ray.

"I need to run to the studio. I'll be back later." He kissed Beth and patted Caralyn's knee.

Beth watched Ray leave then turned to Caralyn. "What do you want to know?"

Caralyn toyed with a lock of hair. "Did you ever babysit for him?"

"I was ten, I think, when he was born, so I didn't until shortly before you were born."

"Then our parents were killed and everything fell apart, huh?"

"Maybe for me, but you had Mrs. McKay and Grandma. I felt lost and didn't know how to express my feelings. I didn't know how to deal with the hurt, so I rebelled. I hung out with the wrong crowd."

"There was a wrong crowd in Stockton Woods?" Caralyn asked. "Where? What part of town?"

"You'd be surprised. It wasn't in some seedy neighborhood, but in normal houses. Anyway, I did drugs, learned to drink and when I was fifteen, I discovered sex."

Caralyn blushed. "I was clueless at fifteen."

Beth put an arm around Caralyn's shoulders and squeezed. "You were the lucky one."

"I always felt loved."

"I could never accept Grandma as an authority figure, and the McKays were simply neighbors." Beth closed her eyes, fought back tears then wiped her face. "Maybe I shouldn't tell you this, but..."

"Tell me, Beth," Caralyn pleaded with her eyes.

"The McKays were supposed to go to the party the night of the accident," Beth said quickly.

Caralyn stared at her with a blank expression.

"Do you know what that means?" Beth asked softly.

Caralyn's lip quivered. Then she nodded.

Beth pulled her sister even closer. "I know you love them as your parents."

Caralyn straightened up. "After Grandma died, did you want me to live with you?"

Beth shook her head. "I wasn't in a place to take care of you. You were... what thirteen?"

"Yes."

"My career was thriving, and I didn't want a young teenager interrupting it. Besides you had your family. You had Tucker and the Stanfields."

"They are your family, too."

"I was never close to any of the Stanfield cousins because of the age difference."

"Derren and I are close. Davey's my age and he's like a brother."

Beth laughed. "I've heard stories about the two of you."

"What?"

"You took baths together when you were little, Do you remember that?"

"Vaguely. What does it matter? I probably took baths with Derren and Tucker, too."

"It doesn't, but Grandma told me about a time when you and Davey got into a fight."

"He tried to touch me," Caralyn said.

Beth waved a hand. "Do you hate me for not taking care of you after Grandma passed?"

"No, I would have resented leaving my family. I'm glad we are friends now."

Beth patted Caralyn's thigh and stood up. "We are more than friends. We are sisters."

Caralyn stood up and hugged Beth. "Thanks for letting me stay with you. I need to get home and pack for France."

"Let me know how it goes, and watch out for the men. They can be devious."

"Mom, do you know when this picture was taken?" Caralyn sat beside her on the couch and held up a small photo of her birth parents.

Mom looked at it. "It had to be at college."

"I know some things about my birth mother, but I don't know much about Douglas Dawson."

"If you have time, I could share what I remember."

"I would like that," Caralyn answered getting comfortable.

65

"What would you like to know?"

"How did she meet him? I know you and Barbara grew up in Stockton Woods."

"We did, and we decided to room together at college. Your father and Doug were roommates, too. I'm not sure, but I think we met in the dining hall one day. Barbara was more outgoing, so she probably talked to them first."

"Did they start dating right away?"

Mom smiled and leaned back against the couch. "Actually, honey, Barbara and your father dated first."

"Do you mean Daddy or... Douglas?"

"Not Douglas," she said with a chuckle. "It's funny talking about both fathers. So, that didn't work out."

"Do you know why?"

"Not sure, but I think Jim was too straitlaced for her. Doug was more adventuresome."

Caralyn grinned. "You don't have to share intimate details."

"Good because she and Doug did some things Florence would have not approved."

"I know you and Daddy went skinny dipping," Caralyn said.

"That was the craziest thing we ever did."

"Did Barbara and Douglas love each other?"

Mom put an arm around Caralyn and squeezed her shoulders. "They were devoted to each other. He asked her to marry him and she wanted to elope, or go to the courthouse to get married. I can't remember exactly."

"Didn't they get married after they graduated?"

"Yes. They got married, and your father and I got married three weeks later. We waited for them to get back from their honeymoon. They traveled out West." Mom stood up. "In fact, I used to have a picture of them by the Grand Canyon. Let me see if I can find it."

Caralyn waited on the couch while Mom searched for the photo. She came back and shook her head. "Sorry, Cara, but it might be in the attic. I didn't throw them away. I know that."

"I don't have anything that belonged to them," Caralyn said. "I wish I did."

Mom smiled and said, "Yes, you do."

"What?"

"You have her smile and his intelligence."

"Thanks, but I meant something tangible."

"I'm sorry. They didn't have many possessions. They had clothes and all the usual stuff, but she didn't collect things like Aunt Mary."

"Do you know what happened to her clothes after the accident?"

"Your grandmother had to sort through everything. She didn't want to keep the clothes, so they were donated to charity."

"Did I ever meet his parents?"

"No, and neither did Barbara. They passed away at an early age."

"Why didn't Grandma Florence ever have another baby? She only had my birth mother, right?"

"Barbara was the only one. Florence had some issues, and she was never able to conceive again. That's why Barbara's death was so hard on her. Your grandfather was gone, and she felt so alone."

Caralyn stood up. "Thanks for telling me. Just because I want to know things doesn't mean I don't love you."

"I know, sweetheart. I'll look for those photos sometime. I'm sure we have them somewhere." Mom sat on the couch and closed her eyes as she thought about her best friend.

Chapter Nine

"Caralyn, we will miss you so much," Mom said as they accompanied Caralyn to the airport security area. "You've never been away for four months before."

"I will miss you guys, too. Say goodbye to Tucker. He left before I could tell him myself."

"Do you have your boarding pass and passport handy?" Dad asked. "You will have to show them again."

"Right here." She held them up. "Henri and Camille will meet me at the airport. I will be fine. They are parents, too. Their children are older, but they understand."

Henri Saucier was a full professor at the university and Camille was an artist with a gallery close to their Latin Quarter home. They met Caralyn at the airport and showed her some of the sights of Paris on the way home.

"I've read stories about Paris my whole life. My grandmother once came to Europe and spent a month here. I've seen photos of her by the Eiffel Tower and Notre Dame."

"We are thrilled to have you, Caralyn. We want you to feel like part of our family," Camille said.

Caralyn met twenty-year-old Laurent Beaufort in one of her classes, and they became study partners.

They were walking to the library one afternoon when Laurent put his hands on her shoulders and said, "I need to tell you I'm gay before you get the wrong idea about our relationship."

Caralyn giggled and said, "Duh. I may be a little naïve and unsophisticated compared to you, but I'm not blind or ignorant."

He took a step back. "So you already knew?"

"Definitely, and it's not a problem for me. I've never known anyone openly gay before. I wonder if any of the guys I know back home are gay but haven't come out yet. Anyway, I don't care if you're gay. We can still be good friends. In a way this is even better because I know you won't try to seduce me." She wrapped a curl around her finger. "You won't, will you?"

He shook his head. "I have known I was gay since I was about twelve. I have never been attracted to girls. Oh, I like to be around pretty girls, but I'm not sexually attracted to them."

"So, if you saw me naked, you wouldn't get excited."

"No, I would enjoy looking at your body, but I wouldn't try to make love to you. Do you plan on testing me?"

"No. I just wondered."

They spent their weekends together. Laurent stayed in the spare bedroom next to her room. He didn't appear in a hurry to start another relationship after breaking up with his partner of three years.

"He looks cute," Caralyn told him whenever she spotted a good looking guy.

"He's not gay though, Caralyn."

"How can you tell so easily?"

"I just can. I can't explain it."

In early October the Sauciers took Caralyn to Nice on the French Riviera for a weekend.

Camille asked, "Are you going to bring Laurent, Caralyn?"

"You don't mind if he comes, do you?"

"Of course not. He is your friend." Camille paused and then asked, "Caralyn, you do know he is gay, right?"

"Oh yes, I know. We're friends, and I like it that way."

"You are allowed to make other friends," Camille said.

"I know, but I'm not planning to get involved while I'm here. That would be awful to fall in love and then leave. This way Laurent and I can be friends and not have to worry about love."

"Or sex either, I assume. I take it you are not ready for a sexual tryst with a sophisticated debonair French student." Camille smiled and her green eyes sparkled. "We promised the McKays we would take good care of you."

She pressed her fingers to her lips, then admitted, "I'm not a virgin, Camille, but I don't want to jump in bed with a boy I don't love. That happened before. I mean I thought I was in love, but he wasn't. He used me one night."

"Americans have such a different view of love and sex. I wouldn't want someone to take advantage of your age and inexperience. I'm glad you and Laurent are friends."

After checking in and having lunch at the hotel, they headed for the beach. Caralyn saw the beach and the blue water of the Mediterranean and gasped. "This is so fantastic. I've never seen anything so beautiful."

They staked out their spot on the beach, and Camille removed the swim dress she had been wearing. She wore a thong and nothing else. Caralyn noticed almost all the females were topless regardless of age or size.

"Laurent, does everyone walk around topless here?"

"Almost. It is no big deal, as you can see. Are you going to keep your top on?"

"I think I will, Laurent. I would be too embarrassed to let you or Henri see me topless."

"If you are uncomfortable, I understand."

"Thanks. Does it phase you at all to see so many topless women?"

"No, I'm used to it. I'm French remember."

"I know. Tucker was my first lover. Did I tell you that already?"

"No, tell me about it."

Caralyn told Laurent about the night she and Tucker made love. Laurent listened and then told Caralyn about his first time.

"Are you concerned about staying in a hotel with me?"

"I think we can stay in connecting rooms for a weekend especially since you are more interested in the pool boy I saw you staring at earlier."

"Would you model my birthday present, Caralyn?"

"No way, Jose! I'm not wearing a thong in front of you."

"Who is Jose?"

"It's an American expression, Laurent. I will try these on, but I am not going to let you see them."

He put a hand to his heart. "My greatest disappointment."

She stepped into the bathroom, slipped on the thong, her pajama pants and returned. "They feel kinda funny but maybe I will get used to them. Do you think my butt is cute?" She wiggled her bottom at him for a second.

"Your butt is cute for a girl."

She smacked his arm. "Are you spending the night?"

"Do you mind if I do?"

"Of course not, I like when you spend the night here. We can talk about boys."

"Will you tell your Tucker friend about me?"

"Maybe, why?"

"Will he be jealous because we talk so openly about sex?"

"I might not mention it, but at least all we do is talk."

"Are you going to get ready for bed now?" he asked.

"Yes, so skedaddle. Just because you bought me underwear doesn't mean anything."

He allowed Caralyn to change and when he came back to her room he was wearing his pajama bottoms. Caralyn let him sit on her bed as they talked about boys.

"Caralyn, have I told you I always sleep in the nude at home?"

"No, have you been sleeping in the nude here?"

"Yes, but I keep some pajamas close in case I need to get up during the night. I wouldn't want to scare you if you happened to see me. Would it upset you if you saw me nude?"

"I don't know. Maybe not, but I guess I won't know unless it happens. Not that I want it to happen."

"Do you ever sleep in the nude?"

"No. Maybe I will try it if you promise not to sneak in my room and look at me."

"Why would I do that?"

"I suppose you wouldn't. I am used to the guys back home. They are always trying to see girls naked. Most of them anyway. All of them actually," she said then giggled.

71

Laurent spent every night at the Saucier home with Caralyn the last week before she had to leave. One night before they got ready for bed she asked, "Will you do my toenails, Laurent?"

"Do you want a foot massage first?"

"Oh yeah, that would feel so good."

He massaged her feet and then painted her toenails pink. "Caralyn, are you trying to seduce me? You don't normally let me see your legs like this."

"I thought letting you see my legs would excite you more than seeing me naked. Is it working?"

"No, not really."

"Well, it was worth a try."

"Caralyn, you are amazing. Most of the time you are so innocent and act like a... what is the American word?"

"Tomboy? That's what the guys used to call me."

"Oh, yeah—tomboy. But then sometimes you can be so sexy without even trying or realizing what you are doing. I know you and I are friends because I am gay."

"I'm not your friend merely because you are gay, Laurent. I would be your friend if you were straight, too. If you remember, we became friends before I knew your sexual orientation. If you were straight, I would be more careful about what I do with you."

"You mean like not letting me paint your toenails?"

"Yes, but the foot massage felt really good. I wish you could teach Tucker how to do that."

Camille took Caralyn to a beauty salon, and Caralyn picked out a new hairstyle from a fashion magazine. "I like that one. What do you think, Camille?"

"It will be so much easier to take care of and you look more mature, Caralyn."

"I love it, Camille," Caralyn said later. She looked in the mirror and shook her head. "It falls right back into place."

They returned home and Henri admired Caralyn's new look. "Camille and I are so proud of you. You will always be welcome in our home. I hope you will come back to visit us."

"Thank you, Henri. You and Camille have made me feel loved. I appreciate how you have treated me as an adult and given me freedom to live my life without a lot of rules."

"We didn't need to force you to obey rules. You are a sensible and upright young lady. Perhaps your parents would be surprised we allowed you to make your own choices as much as we have, but I'm sure they would be proud of you as well for the decisions you have made."

"Laurent and I have became good friends, but I would not have wanted the complications of a sexual relationship while I was here."

Caralyn had one last night to spend with Laurent before she had to leave. They got ready for bed early and Laurent knocked on her bedroom door.

"You can come in, Laurent. I'm decent."

Laurent entered, hugged her then put a hand on his hip and waved his hand while fighting tears. "I didn't mean to cry."

"I will miss you, Laurent. I will miss having you come in to see me at night and keeping me company. I will miss our talks about boys and love." Caralyn smiled and teased him. "You are one of my closest girlfriends."

"I will take that as a compliment."

"I will remember how we would talk half the night."

"You will find a lover back home, Caralyn, and he will keep you warm all night long."

"Maybe."

"I hope you and your lover or friend, I'm not sure how you think of him anymore, resolve your differences and become close again. I know you really love him. You have to figure out how."

"Thank you, Laurent. I do love him, and I've missed him so much. I hope he doesn't hate me for being in Paris so long."

"I'm sure he misses you."

"Laurie dumped him for an older guy, and Mom told me he was dating a girl he dated in high school again. Her name is Nancy Young, and she and I are good friends." She stopped and giggled.

"What is so funny? I am not touching you."

"When Tucker and Nancy dated before, I had to tag along because Nancy's father thought she was too young. Nancy and I had more fun on the dates than Tucker did."

"Americans have some strange customs," he said.

Camille stopped by Caralyn's room the morning before she flew home. "Do you need help with anything, Caralyn?"

"I'm fine, Camille. Laurent will carry my bags to the car."

Before they left for the airport, Caralyn presented a special gift to Henri and Camille.

Camille opened it and said, "We thank you. This is a lovely print, and I will place it in your room to remind me of you. I will think about you every time I see this." She hugged Caralyn and kissed both cheeks.

Caralyn had a gift for Laurent, too. She found a first edition of one of his favorite books. *The Amazing Adventures Of Rex Ford & Clay Horn*.

"Thank you so much, Cara. I love stories about American cowboys and Indians. Where did you find this?"

"I ordered it from the bookstore in Butler. Derren's cousin owns it and he ships rare books all over the world."

Henri, Camille and Laurent took her to the airport.

"Let me hug you first before I start to cry," Henri said.

She grinned and said, "It didn't work, Papa."

"He claims not to be emotional," Camille whispered while squeezing Caralyn, "but you can see he is a true Frenchman."

She hugged Henri and Camille again and then turned to Laurent. They hugged each other tightly and somehow managed not to cry.

"We will see each other again 'mon petit ange'. I know it in my heart."

Chapter Ten

"Do you see her yet, Jim? She should be here by now. Where could she be?" Mom McKay dodged around people as she and Dad McKay waited in the international terminal of St. Louis's Lambert Field for Caralyn's return.

Dad chuckled. "Be patient, Sarah. She will be here soon."

Caralyn spotted them while waiting behind a family of eight. She scooted past them and hurried to her parents.

"Mom, I've missed you so much. You, too, Daddy! I've missed you both more than words can describe. I have so much to tell you. I loved Paris and the school and everything about the city. It's been the most wonderful four months. I loved every minute and the food was great..."

"I think I understand what you are trying to tell us, but could you repeat it in English," Mom teased.

Caralyn put a hand to her mouth then grinned. "Oh, I'm so sorry. I've been speaking nothing but French for so long. Some Italian, too."

Caralyn talked all the way home about her time in France. She told them about Laurent and mentioned he was gay, so they didn't think he was her boyfriend.

"I hope you aren't too tired from the flight, but I invited some people to the house," Mom said after they arrived home.

"I'm not too tired to see my family and friends."

"English, sweetie," Mom urged.

Nancy and Sandy Young were home from college and came to see her. Caralyn pulled Nancy into her bedroom, and they spent some time alone.

"I want you to know how happy I am for you and Tuck."

"Oh, Cara. I was so afraid you would be upset with us."

"I'm not upset. I was at first, but now I realize you and Tuck are meant to be together."

"That means a lot to me," Nancy said. "I wish we could stay longer, but I promised Mom we would see Grandma tonight."

"That's okay. We will have other chances to talk."

When Derren and Richard walked in, she ran to them with open arms. "Derren, I missed you. I have so much to tell you."

Derren held her in his arms, lifted her off her feet and twirled her around. She wrapped her arms around his neck. She kissed Derren's cheeks until he was red with embarrassment.

"Is that what you learned in Paris?" Derren asked.

"Caralyn, I love your hairstyle. When did you get it cut?" Richard asked.

"Just a week ago. Do you really like it, Richard?"

"You look great and more sophisticated."

She hugged and kissed him as well. She looked around the room but didn't see a certain person.

Derren took her aside. "He said he will try to make it later. He wasn't sure if you would want to see him. He thought you might still be mad at him and Nancy, too."

"Oh, Derren. I'm not angry with him. It was all my fault in the first place. I hope he comes. Where will he stay if he doesn't come home for the holidays?"

"He talked about going to Chicago with Richard or staying at school. I'm not sure what he will do tonight."

Ninety minutes passed and most of the guests had gone home when the back door opened. Caralyn was in the living room talking to Derren and Richard when Tucker saw her. He stood by the kitchen door and watched. *You look so grown up now, Carrie. When did that happen?*

Finally, Caralyn turned and saw him standing there. He held his breath as he looked at her. *Cara, you look more lovely than ever.*

She smiled and tentatively, with some apprehension, he approached her.

"Hello, Carrie. It's nice to see you made it home all right."

"Thanks, Tucker. I am glad to be back. I missed everybody so much, including you." She put a hand to her mouth. "Ooops!"

"I don't speak French, but I kinda know what you meant."

They stood in front of each other without invading each other's space. The room was quiet enough that Tucker heard the clock ticking on the wall.

Finally, Richard said, "Kiss her and hug her, you idiot!"

Everyone laughed as Richard broke the tension. Caralyn opened her arms and Tucker picked her up and hugged her tight.

"Oh, Carrie, I'm so sorry for what happened. I have missed you so much and have been afraid you would never like me again."

"Tuck, I'm the one who should be sorry. It was all my fault. I was afraid you would hate me for what I did."

"I could never hate you, Carrie. I love you too much."

Richard asked, "Are you gonna kiss her, or you going to cry like babies all night?"

Tucker kissed Caralyn in front of his parents with more passion than ever before.

"That's more like it now." Richard said with a laugh. *It's a good thing Nancy isn't here.*

"Come on, Richard. Let's see how many stars are in the sky tonight."

"Why? I'd rather stay here and watch them kiss," Richard joked as they left the room.

Mom and Dad stayed with them and hugged them both after they released each other. Dad looked at Mom with confusion.

"I will explain later, dear."

"Do you want to go for a walk, Carrie?"

"Why don't you use the car instead. You can keep warm that way," Dad suggested. "We will see you in the morning. We're going to bed."

"I'm heading home," Derren said. "Are you staying here, Richard?"

He looked at Mrs. McKay.

"Grandma's house is unlocked. Do you need any help?" she asked.

"I'm good. I know where everything is," he answered.

"I don't know how late Tucker and Cara will be out, but I imagine she will stay with you."

77

"I imagine she will. I'm so glad she and Tucker aren't mad at each other anymore. I'll see you in the morning, Mrs. McKay."

"Good night, Richard. I'm glad you came with Derren to welcome Cara home. I know she was so happy to see you both."

Tucker took Caralyn for a ride through the countryside and parked along the country road that led past the east end of Uncle Carlton's field.

"Tucker, can you forgive me for what I did? I know how much I hurt you, and I'm truly sorry."

"I forgive you, Carrie. You did hurt me, but I feel it's partly my fault anyway."

"Why on earth would you feel responsible, Tuck. It was my decision, not yours."

"I feel I forced you into making the decision by giving you an ultimatum to either choose me or else."

"Tuck, you know I have always loved you. Sometimes I loved you as a brother, but mostly not, and I will never regret what we shared that first night. When I met Jeremiah and then continued the relationship after school started again, I did it partly to hurt you for dating Laurie. I was jealous and didn't want you to know it. I never should have spent that night with him."

"Caralyn, I will never hold that against you, and I'm not upset you saw that guy in Carrier Grove. I'm glad you didn't have sex with Richard. That would be harder to deal with."

"Tuck, I told you everything that happened in Carrier Grove. It was a total coincidence I ran into him at the pizza joint."

"I know. I haven't been a saint either."

"Compared to me you have been. I feel like such a slut for some of the things I've done, even though I didn't have sex with anyone except Jeremiah." *If that counts.*

"Do you still hate me for dating Laurie?"

"No, Tuck, I don't hate you for that. I'm sorry she hurt you the way she did, but on the other hand, if she didn't cheat on you, you and Nancy would have never started dating again."

"Maybe. Maybe we would have anyway."

"You and Laurie would probably be engaged or even married by now. You might even be a daddy." Caralyn punched his arm. "I hope you aren't upset Mom told me about you and Nancy. Mom and I talked a lot about you and me when I was in France. She kept me up to date on things. I am happy for you and Nancy. She and Sandy stopped by for a while tonight, but they had to leave to see her grandmother."

"I know. I talked to her before I came home."

"I can't wait to see her again." Caralyn paused and asked, "Does she know about us?"

"She knows, Carrie. It bothered her for several days, and we didn't talk during that time. We almost broke up, but we had a long talk and she is all right with it now. We talk to each other every day, or at least text each other, so she knew you were coming home today. She couldn't wait to see you."

Caralyn told Tucker about Laurent. "He is gay and extraordinarily handsome, and we became good friends. We spent a lot of time together. He even came with us to the French Riviera. We went to a topless beach there. Of course in France a lot of the beaches are topless."

He stared at her. "Did you go topless?"

She poked him in his side. "No, I was too shy. If it had been only me and Laurent I might have. One of these days I will tell you more about Laurent and our relationship."

"Are you sure you want me to know?"

"I don't want to have any secrets from you. I will tell you he was really gay and had never had sex with a girl. Never. Not with any girl. Does that make you feel better?"

"Yeah, I guess so. Did the French guys hit on you a lot?"

"No, not really. I was with Laurent almost all the time."

They headed home. "Do you want me to stay with you tonight? I will if you want, as long as Nancy won't be upset. I know we can't make love, but I would like to stay with you."

"I would like that very much, but do you think we should? What would Mom and Dad think?"

"I think they will understand."

They got to Grandma's house, and Richard woke up when they came in.

"Caralyn, your mom gave me some pajamas for you, if you need them. My words, not hers. She figured you would sleep here, and I told her you probably would. I didn't say what bedroom you would sleep in though. I'm going back to bed. The pajamas are in your grandma's room if you need them."

"Richard, you have a dirty mind sometimes," she said with a grin.

"I know. Remember when you get up, I will be here so don't run around naked. Unless you really want to."

Caralyn blushed and said, "Go back to sleep, Richard, and I'll try to remember not to walk through the house naked."

She and Tucker sat on the new bed in Grandma Florence's old room.

"Are you ready to sleep now?" Tucker asked after they talked for a few minutes.

"Yes. I feel we've moved on from our mistakes, and can still be friends. I was really worried about that."

"So was I. Now we can both rest easier."

She slipped under the covers and fell asleep within minutes. Tucker waited until she was sleeping soundly before quietly moving to the living room couch.

Tucker woke up first, got dressed and tiptoed down the hall to Grandma's room. He stood in the doorway and watched Caralyn as she slept. When she opened her eyes, he sat on the edge of the bed and kissed her cheek.

"Good morning, Carrie. How did you sleep?"

"Like a baby."

She got out of bed but kept her pajamas on. They woke Richard up and headed next door where Mom was making a late breakfast for them.

Mom smiled and said, "I didn't hear the car when you came back. I usually do. Did you stay up all night, or did you get some sleep?"

"We got home around two and tumbled into bed so we got enough sleep," Tucker answered. "The couch is still lumpy. We need a new one."

Caralyn whispered to Mom, "We talked on the bed in Grandma's room until I fell asleep, but we didn't have sex. I hope you will forgive me."

"You want forgiveness for not having sex?" Mom teased.

Caralyn blushed. "I didn't mean it like that."

"Cara, I know you need to sort out your feelings. It must be difficult to grow up with someone and have the feelings you have for each other. At least you still feel you can share things with me."

"Mom, I love you, and I hope I can always tell you anything. Even if I have made a mistake."

"Caralyn, I will love you no matter what you do."

"I'm glad you sent the pj's." She ran a hand along the cotton pajamas. "I like these better than flannel ones."

"Sit down and eat before it gets cold. Did I tell you how much I love your new hairstyle?"

"Thanks, Mom. Camille took me to the place where she gets her hair styled. This morning when we got up all I had to do was shake it and it looks good."

Caralyn continued to talk to Mom about her time in France.

"Caralyn, maybe you shouldn't mention it to your father where you spent last night. He is rather old-fashioned about some things."

"I won't, Mom. I want him to think I am his innocent little girl for a while longer."

Mom shook her head as Caralyn giggled.

"What's so funny?" Dad asked as he walked in the room. "And what's for breakfast, dear?"

"Good morning, Daddy."

"Good morning, Caralyn. It's so good to have my little girl home. Did you sleep well?"

"I slept better than I have for a long time." Caralyn smiled at Mom as she hugged her father.

Chapter Eleven

"Did it seem like the holidays passed faster than normal this year?" Caralyn asked as she sat on the couch at the guys' apartment.

"Are you ever going to remember to speak English and not French?" Richard asked.

"Sorry, I got used to speaking French last semester. Now I do it automatically."

"Whatever."

"How is it possible you only have one semester left?" she asked as Tucker walked by talking to Nancy on the phone.

"Because we are super intelligent," Derren answered.

She turned around and sat on her knees to face the dining table. "Did you find a job yet?"

"I think so. West Memphis looks promising, and Natalie is working in Searsport."

"I got accepted at NYU Law School," Richard said. "Not many people are admitted."

"How will you pay for it?"

"I will find a job with a law firm that will pay off my college loans."

"Good luck with that," she said. She grabbed Tucker's arm as he walked past. "Are you hoping the Bulls draft you?"

"They would be my first choice, but who knows?"

Derren threw a nerf ball at Caralyn. "He should end up as the leading scorer in Midwest Central's history unless he gets hurt."

"You better not get hurt, Tuck."

Caralyn hung out at the apartment more now than ever before. For the first time at college, she had a roommate, and their relationship was strained at best.

"When is Natalie coming to see you, Derren?"

He shrugged. "She's working overtime to save for a house."

"Nancy wants to come up next week, but I don't have the cash," Tucker said.

"I could buy her a train ticket," Caralyn offered.

"Thanks, but we will figure it out."

"I get lonely here," she said. "There aren't any girls to talk to. Even Casanova has cut back."

"Then leave," Richard teased. "Spend more time with Trent. He probably doesn't remember what you look like."

She stuck out her tongue. "I know when I'm not wanted, and Trent is a friend."

"Bye, Caralyn," they shouted.

"It seems ironic that now you have a quiet bed to share, but no one to share it with you," she told Richard one day as she bounced on it while Richard was trying to sleep.

"You're here. Do you want to share my bed?" Richard asked as he moved onto his side.

"You're incorrigible, Richard."

He grabbed her and pulled her onto her back. She smiled at him and thought he was going to kiss her. He started to kiss her, but then touched her side instead.

"Stop it, Richard. I'm too mature now."

"That's bull. You thought I was going to kiss you, didn't you?"

"I didn't think you were going to tickle me. That's for sure."

She lay on her back as he looked at her. He put a hand on her belly and started moving it around.

"What are you doing?"

"I'm looking for your breasts, but I can't find them," he teased.

"They're up here, you goof." She moved his hand.

"Oh, right, here they are. I was looking for something a little bigger."

She smacked his arm, "I should hit you where it will hurt the most."

He moved his hand away, rolled her over and pushed her toward the edge of the bed. "Now get out of here, little girl, before I have my way with you."

She giggled and asked, "Is that a threat or a promise?"

"Stay here for another minute and I'll show you."

"I'm outta here! I don't want to do anything because you would never get over it. You would want me all the time..."

"Show me you what you got, girl."

"No way!" She jumped out of bed before he could touch her again.

"Hey! Anyone seen the delinquent lately?" Richard asked.

"She was here earlier. I didn't know she left," Derren answered. "She got on my case about leaving plates by the TV."

"She can be a nag at times. Doesn't she know guys are supposed to be slobs."

"I heard that." Caralyn walked out of the bathroom carrying a bucket. "Jeremiah was so neat he should have been gay." She stopped and clicked her tongue. "I made a joke about him. I must be getting over how he... you know."

"We try to clean the place every month, Cara," Derren said.

"If I nag you too much it's because I'm getting you ready for when your wife gets on your case for being such pigs."

Richard teased back, "Forget cleaning. You should show us how much sex we will get after we are married."

She smiled wickedly. "I am showing you how much sex you will get after you're married. Absolutely none at all."

"Who told you about last night?" Trent Cussler asked. He looked at his roommate.

Roger Wofford spun his desk chair to face them. "I might have let it slip."

Caralyn giggled and said, "What a crock! You sent me a text then called to make sure I got it."

"Thanks a lot, buddy," Trent said.

Roger turned back to his desk. "What are friends for?"

"I can't believe you hooked up with her," Caralyn said. She poked his ribs as they sat on Trent's bed. "I thought we were going to explore new aspects of our relationship."

Roger spun his chair around again. "I want to see this."

Caralyn twirled a finger and Roger faced his desk.

"We didn't hook up the way you mean it. I kissed her. That's it."

"Okay, so tell me the details."

"Like what?" Trent asked.

"How about an easy question to start. Where did you take her for dinner?" she asked slowly.

"Hey! I'm not Roger. I do have some intelligence."

Roger didn't turn from his desk. "I am right here."

Trent answered that and all her other questions.

"Do you want me to show you how I kissed her?"

Caralyn surprised him. "Show me how you kissed her."

Roger turned around. "I need a break."

Trent put an arm around her and drew her close. They looked at each other then he kissed her.

"Did you kiss her more than once?"

"I am sure I did. Maybe if I kiss you again I will remember how many times I kissed her." He kissed her again and then again. "I'm starting to remember now."

Caralyn giggled and didn't resist as Trent pulled her onto the bed. They had spent time in bed before, but they would be studying or watching TV. She felt safe and comfortable being in his room and even in his bed. He kissed her again.

"Do you want me to show you everything I did, Cara?"

Caralyn realized if she said yes then Trent might take it the wrong way. "Maybe we should slow down a little."

"No, keep going," Roger said. "Where's my camera?"

"Sorry, Cara. I thought you wanted me to... never mind." He started to get up, but she stopped him.

"You don't have to get up, but slow down a little. I'm over that jerk."

One of Trent's legs was on top of her leg and his arm on her chest between her breasts. His hand was touching her cheek as he kissed her. She could feel him moving his hips against her. He stopped for a moment.

"Trent!"

"I'm sorry, Cara. I guess I got carried away."

"It's not your fault. I shouldn't have been teasing you and asking so many questions about your love life."

"He doesn't have a love life," Roger said.

Trent scooted away. They didn't get up, but lay on their sides without touching. He looked into her eyes.

"Have I ever told you how pretty you are, Ms. Dawson?"

"Aw, crap. Here comes the lovey dovey part," Roger said.

"Go away," Caralyn replied.

"I live here, Ms. Dawson," he said sarcastically.

Caralyn turned back to Trent. "Why, no. I don't believe you ever have, Mr. Cussler. Are you trying to tell me you think I am pretty?" Caralyn batted her eyes at him trying to be sexy, but they both laughed because she looked silly instead.

"No. I wanted to make sure I never said you were pretty."

She smacked his chest. "Trent, you are so bad. Don't you think I'm pretty at all?"

"I think you're cute like a puppy dog," Roger answered.

Trent moved on top of her and kissed her. She kissed him back and put her arms around his back. After he kissed her, Trent lifted his head to look at her.

"Ooops! I guess I should get off of you, huh?"

"Do I get a vote?"

"Shut up, Roger," Caralyn said. "I think you should before something happens, Trent," Caralyn said but didn't let go. She wrapped her legs around him. Trent pressed into her and they looked at each other without saying a word.

"Hey. Did you guys freeze up like my crappy computer?" Roger banged on the tower with no effect. "Do something."

Caralyn and Trent waited for the other to make the next move. Trent stayed there for a moment before moving. He sat up on the edge of his bed while Caralyn remained on her back. For a moment they were quiet as they looked at each other. She had her knees in the air. He watched as she moved them back and forth.

"What are we going to do, Cara?"

She chewed her lip then answered, "I'm sorry, but I have some chapters to read."

Trent stood up and pulled Caralyn up to her feet. They stood facing each other, and Trent put his hands on her shoulders. "I have some work to do, too. I'll see you tomorrow, Cara." He kissed her cheek.

She ran across the hall to her room, plopped on her bed and thought about Trent. *How would I have responded if he had actually tried something? I probably would have given in to him. I'm glad we didn't get too carried away. Especially with Roger doing the commentary.*

One weekend Nancy came up from Carrier Grove to visit Tucker, and Caralyn brought Trent on a double date.

"Caralyn, would you come with me to the bathroom?" The girls left the guys sitting at the restaurant table.

Tucker translated for Trent, "Girl speak for I need to talk to you about the guy you're with."

Trent laughed. "Yeah, I caught that. Nancy seems sweet," Trent said but then shook his head. "No, that's not what I mean. I mean she is sweet, but she's pretty, and I can tell she is smart."

"Thanks, Trent. Between you and me though, Carrie is smarter than any of us. Did I tell you she learned to speak Italian and Spanish in four months?"

"I think she learned how to swear in Italian, too. She got mad at some guys and started yelling at them."

"That sounds like her."

Nancy checked her mascara in the bathroom mirror. "Cara, are you and Trent getting serious about each other? I can tell he really likes you."

"I'm not sure," Caralyn said while running her fingers through her hair. "I like him a lot as a friend, but I'm apprehensive about letting our relationship move to the next level."

"Is it because of Jeremiah?"

Caralyn chewed on her lip then said, "I suppose."

"You have to forget about him. Trent is not a Jeremiah. I can tell that already. So you haven't slept with him, huh?"

"No, I haven't spent the night in his room, but I have crashed there a few times. I see him every day, and we study together. We have kissed, but nothing more serious than that. I know stuff about his family, and I haven't been staying at the guys' place as often."

"Trent could be a keeper. Where's he from?"

"I know, but he's from Oregon and will be going back there at the end of the semester. I can't picture ever living so far away from home."

"That's a tough choice. Your heart will tell you what to decide."

"I was waiting for you to make a move, but you didn't," Caralyn told Trent a few days later as they sat on his bed.

"I was hoping you would tell me what you wanted me to do. I didn't want to try something if you weren't ready."

"I think I would have been ready for anything that day."

"Now you tell me," he teased. "It wouldn't have mattered because I didn't have any protection, and you aren't on the pill."

"And I was here," Roger said. "Not that I would have paid any attention."

Caralyn sighed and said, "You're always here. Don't you ever have a class?"

"I do several independent studies," he replied.

Trent moved closer and kissed her. She let him put his hand on her belly. Once again she waited for Trent to make the first move, but he didn't. He was not used to being with a girl like her— a girl he had real feelings for.

Chapter Twelve

"It will be different next year without you guys," Caralyn said one evening. She sat on the couch with Tucker slouched on one side and Derren on the other leaning against the end of the couch. Richard sat in the recliner reading.

"Different in a good way or bad?" Derren asked.

"We won't have to put up with her," Richard said.

Caralyn was quiet and then she began to cry silently. Tucker noticed after a time and sat up.

"Carrie, what's wrong? Why are you crying?"

"I'm not crying. I had something in my eye," she sobbed.

Derren and Richard looked at her, and she kept crying. Tucker put an arm around her shoulder and pulled her close.

"We will still get together, Carrie."

"It won't be the same, Tuck."

Derren patted her knee, and she moved close to him and he hugged her, too.

"I will miss you guys so much."

Richard closed his book and listened.

"The time we have spent here together will be remembered as possibly the best times of our lives," Tucker said. "We have so many memories; some good and others not so good, but we will remember them all the same."

"Wow! That's really deep. Did it take you all semester to think of that?" Richard teased.

Tucker laughed. "Nah. I read it a book somewhere."

"Get out. You haven't read a book in four years," Caralyn teased while standing up.

Tucker grabbed her around the waist before she could get away.

"Leave me alone, or I will tell Nancy you were touching me inappropriately."

"Am I touching her inappropriately?" Tucker asked Derren and Richard.

"Not that I can see," Richard said.

"Derren?" Caralyn asked.

"Sorry, Cara, but his hands are on your hips."

"Fine. I should let you and Richard touch me too."

The guys looked at each other and laughed.

Derren headed to the kitchen. "No thanks, Cara. Natalie would not approve."

"I'll pass on the offer, too." Richard got up and walked toward the bathroom.

"You guys are all creeps, and I won't miss you at all. I'm glad you won't be here to pester me next year."

Two days later Caralyn looked around her dorm room. She knew it wouldn't take her long to pack everything when the time arrived. She heard a knock on the door and let Trent in.

"Have you had dinner yet?"

"Not yet, but I am hungry. Where do you want to eat? Somewhere special or the dining hall?"

"The dining hall. I have money left in my account, and I want to use it up."

"That's okay with me."

At the dining hall they ran into Tucker and Richard.

"Hey, guys. Do you wanna eat with us?" she asked.

"Sure, are you buying?" Richard teased.

They grabbed a table and talked as they ate. When Tucker and Trent returned the trays, Richard asked Caralyn, "How serious is your relationship with Trent? Have you slept with him? I would be happy for you if you have. A little jealous though. But you need to find someone to help you get over Jeremiah."

"We haven't because I'm anxious, and it's because of Jeremiah. I know that, and I'm learning to deal with it."

"Are you coming over tonight, Carrie?" Tucker asked as he sat down.

She looked over her shoulder at Trent, who was talking to a friend, and answered, "I don't think so. I need to finish packing."

"I understand," Tucker said.

She hadn't stayed overnight at the apartment for a week—which was a long time for her. She had been spending the nights alone in her dorm room.

Trent sat on Caralyn's bed and looked at the empty side of the room. "Did your roommate move out for good?"

"She moved in with her boyfriend even though the semester's almost over. I would have waited."

"She was weird, but in a good way. She and Roger should have been roomies."

Caralyn stood up and said, "I know we talk about... you know... but as long as we don't sleep together, we can be friends in the future. I'm afraid it would complicate matters if we do it now."

"I would like to think if we meet ten or twenty years down the road we can look back on these times without any feelings of guilt," Trent said.

"So, should we get naked and screw our brains out?" she asked with a grin.

"Absolutely. I want to do you as often as I can before I have to leave," he said with a smile. "Seriously, Cara. Have you given any thought to moving to Oregon? It's a beautiful state with lots of friendly people. Sexy guys, too," he said threading his hand through her hair. "I'm going to work for my father's construction company. It's stable and offers a secure future."

"I can't make that decision now, Trent." She moved to the edge of her desk. "I have one more year to finish here, and then I want to get my master's right away."

"You could finish your last year at Oregon State. It's in Corvallis and that's only twenty miles from where I live. You could get a master's there, too."

"Trent, I can't leave my family again. I spent four months in France, and I missed them so much."

"It's something to consider, Cara."

"I will think about it, but I'm almost positive I will stay here."

Graduation day arrived and the families came to watch Tucker, Derren and Richard's ceremony. Caralyn sat with Mom and Dad McKay. Later, she took pictures of all the guys and their families and friends. Dad took a picture of her with the three guys.

Richard said, "I remember the first picture I ever saw of you, Cara. It was on Tucker's desk in his old dorm room. I thought you were his little sister, and I thought you were so cute."

"I remember that picture, Richard. Do you still think I'm cute?"

"No."

"What? You don't?"

He smiled and pulled her close. He whispered, "You have become a beautiful young lady."

"Thank you, Richard. You are like a brother to me." She realized that he might take that the wrong way and added, "A very sexy brother though."

He laughed and kissed her cheek. After all the family members were gone, the graduates and Caralyn headed back to the apartment. Richard had finished packing and would be leaving in the morning. Derren and Tucker would be there for a few more days.

In the morning Richard loaded his car as the guys watched.

"Aren't you going to help?" Caralyn asked.

"Why?" Derren asked. "All he has are two suitcases."

"Aren't you going to miss each other?"

Tucker shrugged. Derren yawned.

Caralyn rolled her eyes. "Men. You're afraid to show any emotions. I'm not afraid to hug him." She hugged him firmly and kissed his cheek.

The guys shook hands.

"Drive carefully." Caralyn waved as he pulled away.

Tucker looked at her and asked, "Where are you gonna stay tonight, Carrie?"

"Since we have two more nights here, would you mind if I stay in the dorm tonight?"

They both suspected she might be staying with Trent.

"Will you spend Monday night with us?" Tucker asked.

"Yes, I'll spend the last night in your apartment."

Caralyn and Trent ate dinner and walked around campus before heading back to the dorm. He put an arm around her shoulders as they rode the elevator to their floor. She smiled at him and bumped his hip. The elevator opened and she led him to her room.

Trent took her hand outside her door. "Would it ruin everything if I asked to spend the night? We don't have to have sex, but I want to sleep together at least once."

"Are you sure we can sleep in the same bed and not fool around?" she asked.

"Oh, I want to fool around a bit. I want to kiss and make out and get on top of you one more time."

"Tuck asked me to stay tonight."

"What did he say when you told him?"

"I didn't tell him everything, but he understands. He knows we haven't done it, but he doesn't know how close we have come."

"Are you gonna wear some sexy pajamas?"

"I wasn't going to wear anything," she teased.

They talked until midnight and then got ready for bed. She wore a t-shirt and gym shorts. Trent stripped to his boxers and t-shirt. Once in bed they started kissing until she pushed him away.

"Do you want me to stop?"

"Not really, but I am nervous."

"I sensed that."

"Was it because I was so tentative?" she asked softly.

"You kept pushing my hands away, but then you moved them back. It is somewhat confusing."

"I'm sorry." She looked at him and gradually grinned. "Are you going to touch me under my t-shirt? You can if you promise not to get all out of control and try to undress me."

"I think I can control my animal urges somehow."

Trent slid a hand under her t-shirt, but kept it on her belly.

"You can move your hand up higher tonight, Trent," she whispered.

He slowly moved his hand. She didn't stop him when he moved her t-shirt up higher than ever.

"You look so perfect, Cara."

After a few minutes, she made him stop and fixed her t-shirt.

"Are you afraid I will go too far?" he asked while staring.

"No, but I'm not sure I will want to stop." *If it happens, it happens.*

He slipped his t-shirt over his head, and they looked at each other.

"I didn't bring anything, Cara. I'm sorry."

"It's okay. I thought about going ahead, but it would be too risky right now." She saw her teddy bear on the dresser and whispered, "We can cuddle."

"Is that a euphemism for sex?" he asked. "If not, I should put my shirt on."

He did. She sat up against the wall, looked into his eyes and said, "I hate to spoil the mood, but I have given it a lot of thought. I can't relocate to Oregon, Trent. I just can't. I'm sorry."

"I understand, Cara. I wish we had gotten to know each other better before this year. Maybe your answer would be different."

"I don't intend to be hurtful, but it wouldn't change."

The next afternoon Tucker and Derren loaded the van for her. She didn't have much stuff to pack, but the last two things in the room were a couple of teddy bears. She carried them to the van herself. She said goodbye to a couple of friends and saw Trent in the lobby.

"I have to say goodbye," she told Tucker.

"Go ahead, Cara."

She hugged Trent. "Do you hate me for last night?"

"If you're talking about the answer about Oregon, no, but if you're asking about the sex..."

"The lack of sex you mean."

"Yes. Then I hate you."

"I know you're kidding. Will you stay in touch even though I'm such a tease."

"I promise, and maybe you'll change your mind about Oregon someday. It's a beautiful state."

"With sexy men. I remember," she said playing with her hair. "I'm sorry I made you go back to your room."

He left for his flight to Portland thirty minutes later.

"Should we order pizza for our last night?" Tucker asked as Derren returned.

Derren nodded. "Pizza would be good. That's my last trip tonight. All I have to load tomorrow is my duffel bag."

"Can we order the Supremo?" Caralyn asked.

"Are you buying?" Derren asked.

"Have I ever paid for my food?" she asked.

The guys shrugged.

"Let's have it delivered," Tucker said.

They sat on the couch, ate the pizza and talked about the last three years.

Later, Derren looked at her, "Kinda like old times, huh, Tuck?"

Tucker looked at Caralyn and smiled. "Yeah, just like when she was a kid."

Tucker picked her up and carried her into the bedroom. He gently lay her on the squeak-free new bed. She woke up for a brief moment.

"Good night, Carrie. Go back to sleep."

"Did you put me in bed?"

"Yes, but I think I strained my back," he teased.

"Good night, Bubby, I love you."

Tucker waited by her side for a few moments watching her until she fell back asleep. "I love you, too, Tarry," he whispered with a tear in his eye. "I always will."

After breakfast at the Pancake Palace, they walked back to the apartment. Caralyn took one last look around and headed downstairs. Derren and Tucker checked to make sure they had everything. Tucker tossed the envelope with all the keys on the dining table which seemed much larger now since it was not covered in books. Derren stepped out into the hall, and then Tucker followed. He turned off the light and closed the door.

"Well, that's it, I guess." Tucker made sure the door was locked.

They looked at each other realizing they would never be roommates again.

Tucker chuckled, "That was a quick four years. It's been a blast, hasn't it?"

"Sure has." Derren slapped Tucker on the back. "See you back home. Drive safely and don't let the delinquent distract you."

Derren and Tucker headed downstairs where Caralyn waited impatiently next to the van.

"Took you guys long enough. Did you get all weepy and stuff?"

Derren shook his head. "Yeah, I'm gonna miss her. Like a high ankle sprain."

"At least you don't have to live with her all summer."

"You're going to be playing basketball all summer, Tucker. I doubt if I see you. When you're home you will be at Nancy's."

"You could always tie her on top, Tuck. That way you wouldn't have to listen to her."

"I thought about that. Do you have any rope handy?"

He shrugged. "Sorry, but I don't."

"I could run to Ace Hardware and buy some bungee cords."

Caralyn stood with her hands on her hips and listened to the guys.

"Guess you'll have to let her ride inside."

Caralyn stuck her tongue out at them. Tucker and Derren looked at each other, "I guess she will never grow up, Tuck."

"Yeah." He smiled back at Derren. "I sure hope not."

Chapter Thirteen

"Hello, Mr. Green. Are you busy?"

He looked up from his desk and smiled. "Never too busy to see you, Ms. Dawson. How are you? How has college been? Have you been home long?"

"I got home three days ago, and college has been a memorable experience so far."

"I was reading some essays, but they're rather boring. I was about to head home."

"Would you like to get something to eat or drink?" she asked suddenly.

"Where?" he asked without thinking. "I do have to eat."

"The Curve, or we could run into Butler if you give me a ride. I walked here."

"Butler, huh?" He tapped his chin. "We can ride together. Give me a second, and I will join you."

She waited in the hallway at the top of the stairs and looked at the banister. She saw him coming and said, "I'm tempted to take one more ride."

"Please don't. I would have to give you a detention," he said with a chuckle.

She looked at Mr. Green and smiled.

He drove to Butler and they grabbed a table near the front door of the Jennings Sisters restaurant and ordered Cokes.

"Did I hear correctly? You spent a semester at the Paris-Sorbonne University," he asked while reading the menu.

"I did. That was unbelievable. I polished my French and learned Italian and Spanish in four weeks."

He replaced the menu next to the mustard bottle and asked, "What else have you done?"

"I lost my virginity."

He choked on his Coke

"Oh, my God!" She put a hand to her mouth. "I can't believe I actually told you that. I am so sorry, Mr. Green."

"It will be our secret, Caralyn."

The waitress returned and they ordered burgers and fries.

"Do you need to get home?" he asked after they ate.

"I probably should, Mr. Green. I don't want to take up your time. You probably have things you need to do."

"Not really, Caralyn. Nothing important. It is more interesting talking to you."

"You mean like me telling you I'm not a virgin?"

"That is not something I hear from former students every day and never from a female student. You were always interesting, Caralyn."

"I have always thought you were so handsome, Mr. Green, and I had such a crush on you. I hope that doesn't embarrass you."

He looked at her and pictured her first days in his class.

"Would it be wrong if I wanted to kiss you?" she asked.

"It would only be wrong if you followed through. The desire in itself is not wrong until you act on it."

"Maybe, but that's not they taught us at church."

He put his hand on her leg. She felt an electric charge.

"I'm familiar with the Bible," he said. "Simply having impure thoughts about a woman is considered a sin."

She grinned and said, "I'll try not to cause you to have impure thoughts."

He jerked his hand away. "Caralyn, I know you are a grown up young lady now and even prettier than ever, but I'm not going to kiss you."

"I want to kiss you, Mr. Green. I know that much. I know a place where we could have absolute privacy."

He shook his head. "Caralyn, I think you are a charming young lady, but I should take you home."

"Please, Mr. Green, I'm not ready to head home. Could we go to the park for a while? I won't mention kissing again."

He thought about for a moment. "Sure. You can tell me more about Midwest Central. Aren't Tucker and Derren in school there, too?"

"They graduated. We spent a lot of time together. I'm going to miss them next year."

He drove to the park, and they meandered along the path watching young mothers with their children. They walked past the town swimming pool and listened to laughter and splashing. They passed the ball diamond where a group of teenagers where playing baseball.

"So, you want to be a writer. You always showed natural talent."

"I remember other students would complain whenever we had to write essays in your class, but I enjoyed that more than anything."

"Here's a bench. Would you mind if we sit?"

"Are you getting tired, Mr. Green?"

"Not tired. But my knee bothers me. I'm getting old."

"You don't look old to me. I think you are still handsome."

"Thank you, Ms. Dawson. I appreciate the compliment."

They sat on the bench and talked. Caralyn moved close to Mr. Green and touched his arm. They looked into each others eyes.

"Caralyn, how old are you now?"

"I'm nineteen, Mr. Green. How old are you?"

"Much too old for you to be interested in me."

"Please tell me."

"Thirty-four. Are you always going to call me Mr. Green? You could call me Tom, if you want."

"I will always think of you as Mr. Green no matter how old I am."

Two cyclists rode past and Mr. Green waved. "We should get going, Caralyn. I have papers to read tonight."

They talked a few more minutes before leaving Butler.

"Could you drop me off by the grocery store, Mr. Green. I need to pick up a couple things for dinner tonight."

"Sure, should I wait for you?"

"No need. I can walk. It's only a couple of blocks." She put a finger to her mouth and asked, "Are you busy tomorrow?"

"No, I don't have anything planned."

"Would you like to take a drive? I could show you where Grandma and Grandpa live."

"I already know where they live."

"I know, but we could take a ride anyway and maybe go for a hike again." She raised a hand. " No kissing. I swear."

He chuckled and nodded. "Okay, Caralyn. That sounds all right. I like to torture my knee."

"I'll see you tomorrow after school."

"I'll be better prepared, I promise."

That evening at dinner Mom asked, "Caralyn, why are you so nervous and fidgety? You haven't been able to sit still for a second since you got back from wherever you were."

"I know. I can't seem to settle down. I should probably run for an hour and use up some of my energy." She knew the real reason was because of what she was planning to do the next day. "When are Tucker and Dad coming home?"

"They will be home Saturday, dear. Do you miss them?"

"I do." She added gravy to her mashed potatoes then said, "I miss them both, and I know you miss Daddy a lot."

"Have you talked to Nancy lately?"

"I talked to her a couple days ago. She and Sandy were going to visit their other grandmother in Ohio for a few days. She sent me a text and some pictures of her holding her cousin's baby girl. Nancy looks so happy. I know she is going to want to have several kids when she gets married."

"Do you ever want to have kids, Caralyn?" Mom asked. "I don't know that I've ever heard you mention children."

"I do, but then I see mothers deal with screaming babies, and I wouldn't have the patience for that. I know I want to write books and maybe work for a publishing house."

"I know you love to write, and I have kept all the stories you gave me from school."

"I didn't know you kept them."

"Yes, I have all of them, even the ones Grandma Florence had. Someday I will give them all back to you, honey, and maybe you can read them to your little girls."

The next day Caralyn kept busy to avoid looking at the clock. She helped Mom clean the house, and they ran a few errands together. She even dusted Grandma's house to pass the time. Finally, it was time to leave.

"I'm not sure when I will be back, Mom."

"Okay, dear. Have a good time."

After the bell rang dismissing the last class, Caralyn knocked on Mr. Green's door.

"I'll be ready in a minute, Caralyn," he said.

"I will wait outside by your car."

She saw two other teachers she knew and stopped to say hi. Then she hurried outside.

"Would you mind if I stop by the house, Caralyn? If we are going to hike for any length of time I need to change."

"I don't mind."

"It will only take a minute."

They stopped at his place, and he invited her in. She waited in his living room while he changed clothes. She inspected his collection of books and pulled out a few that looked interesting.

"I'm ready," he said walking into the room.

She smiled at him. "You look much more comfortable now. I've never seen you in shorts. I like your place. It looks like it belongs to a teacher."

"Thanks, Caralyn, I think."

"The McKays are teachers, and I mean it as a compliment. I like it that you have a lot of books, and your table is covered with books and papers."

They got in his red Mustang GT and headed to the farm.

"Can you lower the top, Mr. Green? I want to feel the wind on my face."

He put the top down, and she sat on her knees in the seat.

"I have never been for a ride like this before. This feels so good."

"I love owning a convertible." He watched as she let the wind blow her hair.

As he turned onto the highway, she sat down and buckled her seat belt. When they got to the farm, Caralyn hopped out and opened the gate. They parked next to the big white barn.

"Do you want to see the pond, Mr. Green? It's not real big, but we used to swim there when we were kids."

Caralyn climbed over the gate like a tomboy, but then she opened it to let Mr. Green walk through. They walked through the pear orchard to the pond. Caralyn ran ahead of him. She waited for him by the edge of the pond.

"We used to fish here all the time. Daddy taught me how to fish. I would dig for my own worms and everything."

"You always were a real tomboy, Caralyn. I bet you haven't changed too much."

"I still feel more comfortable in jeans than a dress."

She skipped a rock across the pond as they walked to the bank at the west end.

"When I was younger I went skinny dipping here. One time Tucker and Derren caught me. They saw me totally naked. Does that surprise you, Mr. Green?"

He looked at her and imagined the scene. "Yes and no. Lots of kids in the country do that. I used to when I was a kid."

"Really? Did you ever go swimming with a girlfriend, Mr. Green?"

He smiled at her. "Can you keep a secret?"

She nodded.

"I did, and after we finished swimming we made love."

"Mr. Green! I didn't expect you to tell me anything so personal."

"I didn't tell you her name or anything."

"Was that your first time?" Caralyn grinned.

"It was the first time with that girl," he said then laughed.

"Mr. Green, you are so naughty. Did you seduce a lot of girls before you were married?"

"Only two, and that is more than I should be telling you."

Caralyn moved close and reached up to kiss him. He put a hand on her shoulder and moved a curl off her face.

102

"Caralyn, you are too young for me, and, besides, I still think of you as a student."

"I still think of you as my teacher, Mr. Green. I don't want to cause you any trouble, but I think we can be friends. Out of all my teachers in high school, you are the one who influenced and encouraged me the most. You taught me how to think. You saw potential in my writing and showed me ways to improve. Thank you."

"That means a lot to me, and we can certainly be friends."

"You can call me Cara if you want, Mr. Green. All my friends do."

They walked to the southern side of the pond, through the woods to a clearing and she pointed to a tree.

"We used to come here and eat the walnuts when I was a kid."

"Do you mean last year, Cara?"

She poked his side. "No. When I was really a kid. I'm not a little kid anymore, Mr. Green."

"I can see that," he said.

She walked close to him. When they got near the barn, he picked her up by the waist and set her on the gate. She put her hands on his shoulders as they talked.

"Can I ask you something personal?"

"You can ask me anything. Doesn't mean I will answer."

"Is it true your wife left you because she found you in bed with one of your students? That's the story I heard at school."

He shook his head and took a step back. "That's not true. She left because I caught her with a college student. I walked in on them as they were... in the act, so to speak, by the kitchen table. The first thing I saw was his bare butt, and then I saw the rest."

"The kitchen table! I am so sorry. Did you and your wife ever use the table for sex?"

He didn't answer, but Caralyn noticed him grimace.

"Sorry. That wasn't an appropriate question. You don't need to answer. I would die if I ever caught Mom and Dad McKay doing that. Anywhere, for that matter."

103

"Your parents are not that old. I'm sure they still make love." He moved closer and touched her knees.

She looked into his eyes. She put her hands on his shoulders, leaned forward and wanted to be kissed.

"Caralyn, I know it would be incredibly sweet to taste your lips on mine but..."

Caralyn kissed him quickly. "I'm sorry, Mr. Green. I'm sorry. Are you going to give me a detention?"

"You were warned about the banister, Ms. Dawson."

"Oh, right. I forgot about that. I was thinking of the time you gave me a detention for swearing at Johnny Bowser."

Mr. Green remembered and laughed. "That was so funny, Caralyn. If I remember correctly, you were a sophomore. I heard a commotion and then I heard you swearing at him using words that would embarrass a marine."

Caralyn blushed as she remembered the incident.

"I warned him not to touch my butt, but he wouldn't leave me alone, so I smacked him and called him a few names."

"It was all I could do to keep from laughing. I'm sorry I had to give you that detention, and had I known what precipitated the outburst, I would never have punished you."

"You are sounding like my teacher again, Mr. Green." She jumped down from the gate and stood up in front of him.

"Are you hungry, Caralyn?"

"Hungry and thirsty. Wanna run into Butler and get something to eat?"

"Where? Anyplace is all right with me."

They drove into town, ordered hamburgers and fries at the Salty Dogs drive-in and sat in the car to eat.

"We could watch the baseball game if you want, Mr. Green. I like to watch, and it's so pleasant today."

"Are you sure you want to be seen with me?"

"I don't mind as long as you won't get in trouble for being with me."

"People will talk sometimes, but maybe we won't see anyone who knows us."

104

"Mr. Green, everyone knows you and most everyone knows me, too. One of the 'benefits' of living in a small town."

"At least it's Butler. If we were in Stockton Woods, we would be the talk of the town."

They watched the game for a time and then took a drive through the countryside.

"I want to show you something, Mr. Green."

She gave him directions to Uncle Alton's lake. He parked near the old shed and they walked to the top of the hill.

"At night you can get great views of the sunset from here. Not too many people know this lake is here."

"I never would have guessed. It's a man-made lake, right?"

"Yes, but it's been here a long time. We used to come out here and have picnics, and Tuck and I would swim."

Mr. Green looked at her with a sly grin.

She bumped his hip. "Swimming with Mom and Dad along. I kept my bathing suit on."

"I'm sorry. I was thinking about what you told me earlier."

"That's all right, Mr. Green. You can imagine me skinny dipping if you want. I won't be embarrassed."

"I shouldn't be thinking of you in that way, even though I'm sure you would look very sexy."

She hooked her hand through his arm as they looked at the calm water of the lake. "We had a good time today, didn't we?"

"It was enjoyable, Caralyn. I appreciated your tour of the countryside."

He looked at her and put his hands on her shoulders. She didn't feel the slightest bit shy to be with him now.

"We should get going," he whispered.

"I suppose so. You have school in the morning."

He dropped her off at home. She got out and blew him a kiss before running in the house.

Chapter Fourteen

"Caralyn, I saved your supper in the fridge."

"Thanks, Mom, but I'm not hungry right now. I got something in Butler."

"Who did you go with, honey?"

"I got a ride with Mr. Green, and we watched a game with some friends and grabbed some food at the drive-in. I'm sorry I forgot to let you know I was going to get something."

The landline rang, Mom answered then handed the phone to Caralyn. "It's Nancy."

"I'll take it to my room, Mom. Thanks."

"Hi, Nancy. What's up?"

"I've been calling your phone all afternoon. Where have you been?"

"Sorry, I must have turned it off."

"Sandy and I are going to hang out at The Curve. Wanna join us? We might catch a movie."

"Sure, I'll meet you there in a half hour." She got ready and told Mom, "I'm meeting Nancy and Sandy at The Curve. We might run to Butler and watch a movie. Don't wait up for me if you get tired. See you later, Mom. I love you."

"I love you too, honey. Do you need some money?"

"Thanks, but I've got a few dollars."

She walked to The Curve and met the Young sisters. They ordered Cokes and caught up on school. Caralyn didn't mention being with Mr. Green earlier that day. Later, Sandy was the first to notice Mr. Green pull up in his car and get out. He ordered a hot fudge sundae and sat at the table next to them.

"Would you like to sit with us, Mr. Green?" Sandy asked. "Or we could sit with you."

"I'll sit with you. How is everyone doing? How is college treating you?"

The girls talked about school while he finished his ice cream. Caralyn sat next to Mr. Green, slurped her pop and exchanged secretive smiles.

Nancy asked, "Would you like to catch a movie, Mr. Green? I know it's a school night and you have to be up early."

"I'm not that old. I can stay out at night and still get up in the morning. I'm only thirty-four."

"Wow! That's really old, Mr. Green," Caralyn and Nancy said together as they giggled.

"Don't act so childish," Sandy scowled.

"I'll go to a movie, and we can take my car. I'll put the top down and we can count the stars."

They left Sandy's car at the McKay house. Caralyn sat in the back with Nancy. They giggled and whispered to each other as they talked about Tucker. Caralyn caught Mr. Green looking at her in the rear-view mirror. She smiled and stuck out her tongue. He smiled back and wondered how she could be an innocent schoolgirl with her friends and be so sexy with him.

"I want to teach school after I graduate," Sandy said. "I would prefer first or second grade."

"Make sure you pick the age group that best fits you," he said. "I feel old because you are still calling me 'Mr. Green.' My name is Tom, and I don't mind if you call me that. You are not my students anymore."

Sandy called him Tom, but Caralyn and Nancy still called him 'Mr. Green' to tease him. They headed to Butler's outdoor theater, the only one left in the county, to watch the movie.

"Do you have a boyfriend, Sandy?" Mr. Green asked.

"Yes, his name is Lloyd Waters, and he just graduated."

Nancy piped up from the backseat, "Sandy and Lloyd are in love, and he's going to propose to her soon."

"Is that true?" Mr. Green asked.

"Yes, we are in love, and I hope he proposes soon, but Nancy has a big mouth."

"I wish you and Lloyd the best." He looked in the mirror at Caralyn, grinned and said, "He is a lucky man to have such a pretty and mature lady for a fiancee."

Nancy and Caralyn giggled in the backseat. Sandy turned around to give them a dirty look.

107

"You will have to forgive Caralyn. She is the youngest person here and needs to grow up. She acts like she is still in high school most of the time," Sandy said.

"I do not act like an immature high school kid," Caralyn protested.

"Yes, you do. Do you still sleep with that stuffed bear?" Sandy asked trying to embarrass her.

"I keep him on the dresser and not in bed with me."

"Since when?"

"For several weeks if you must know."

"Sandy, quit teasing her," Nancy said defending Caralyn.

"It's all right, Nancy. I don't care if Mr. Green knows I have a favorite stuffed bear. It's not like he is going to see my bedroom anytime soon."

She smiled at him in a teasing fashion. *Unless you want to see my bedroom. I'll show you all my stuffed animals.*

The movie ended, and Mr. Green brought them back to the McKay house. Sandy and Nancy left while Mr. Green waited for a moment.

"Thanks for taking us to the movie, Mr. Green, and for driving your car. It was fun to watch the show with the top down." She got out but waited by his car. "You should close the top because it looks like we're in for a storm."

"It was my pleasure, Caralyn. Do you need to get inside right away?"

"Not really."

He hit the button to close the top and got out. He walked to the passenger side and leaned against the door. "The house is dark."

"I'm sure Mom is already in bed, and Dad and Tucker are gone for the week."

"Where are they?"

"A basketball camp somewhere in Kentucky. They will be home Saturday afternoon."

He looked at Caralyn and smiled.

"Why are you looking at me like that, Mr. Green?" She shifted her weight back and forth.

"I was thinking about your stuffed bear. Do you really have one on your dresser?"

"Yes, and sometimes I have him on the bed with me. Does that make me seem like a child?"

"No, it doesn't. It makes you even more interesting than before. You are grown up, but not afraid to hang on to some of your childhood memories. Are you really younger than the Young sisters?"

"Sandy is almost two years older than me, and Nancy is eleven months older. If you remember, I skipped a grade and my birthday is November 30, so I would have been the youngest kid in my class anyway. Skipping a year meant I was even younger."

"That is why you were in Sandy's class and Nancy graduated a year later."

"Sandy was born in early December so she was almost exactly two years older than me. Tucker dated her for a while, but found that he liked Nancy better. They are still friends. Sandy and Tucker, I mean. Tucker and Nancy are a couple again. Do you date much, Mr. Green? Is that too personal a question?"

"Caralyn, after today I think you are allowed to ask me anything you want. Are you always going to call me Mr. Green?"

"Yes, it would seem weird to call you Tom."

"Do you regret spending time with me the last couple days?"

"Not at all. I enjoyed your company, and I think we are friends now. I realize we will always think of each other as student and teacher in a way, but we can be friends, too. Are you sorry about anything, Mr. Green?"

"I don't regret a thing. I'm glad you came to see me. It's been what, three years since we saw each other."

"I think so unless I saw you at a game."

He looked at the sky, felt a few drops of rain as the wind picked up. "I should tell you I have taken a position with another school."

109

"Mr. Green! You're leaving?" She moved close enough to touch his arm.

"I'm afraid so. I've been here too long. I applied for a position with the Fremont school district. I will be teaching at Fremont Central next year."

Lightning flashed and she jumped.

"Are you all right?" he asked as the thunder boomed.

"That caught me off guard." She reached out her hand. "I can feel rain."

He felt more drops on his face. "You should hurry inside before it starts pouring."

"In a minute. We will miss you, Mr. Green, but you will probably make more money there."

"Quite a bit more. Housing is more expensive, but I am renting a place in the country for now."

"Maybe we can do something before you leave. How soon are you going to be moving?"

"I will be leaving two weeks after school ends. I'm going to Colorado to see my sister and maybe head to Rocky Mountain National Park."

She didn't jump when another streak of lightning lit the night sky and the thunder shook the ground.

"That should be fun. I've never been there, but I've seen pictures and the mountains look beautiful. We will miss you. Does everybody know, or is it a secret?"

"The teachers and administration know already. I haven't told the students."

"We will have to go to another movie, Mr. Green, and maybe something else."

"We can do something before I leave."

The sprinkles intensified into a steady rain.

"I better go in the house before I get soaked."

"Yes, and I need to leave."

She moved next to him as the lightning flashed again.

"Did you feel that?" she asked.

"I did."

"Maybe it was a sign we're supposed to be together," she said before running into the house.

He ran to the driver's side and got in the car. "It was just the storm, Caralyn," he said as he started the engine. "We are not meant to be together in the way you'd like."

Dad and Tucker returned home Saturday and Caralyn greeted them as if she hadn't seen them for a year. "How was your trip?" she asked Tucker as she sat on his bed while he unpacked.

"Good, but the competition was fierce. There were so many great athletes there."

"I bet you were still the best player."

"Not even close, Carrie. There were players there who were so much bigger and stronger."

"But they weren't point guards, were they? I bet you were the best point guard there."

"You're only saying that because you're biased."

"Yeah. So what? I can't think my best friend was the best player?"

Tucker smiled and told her, "I missed you, Carrie. Do you want to get something to eat. I'm starving."

"Sure. I could eat. Did you know Mr. Green is moving to Fremont?"

"Yeah, Dad told me he got a new job. It's got to pay a lot better than here. Why did you ask?"

"I saw him at school, and he told me he was leaving. I thought he was a good teacher."

She didn't reveal anything to Tucker about her recent time spent with Mr. Green, or her crush on him through the years.

"I think he is tired of living in here. He will be able to meet more people in Fremont. Maybe he will get married again."

"Yeah, I suppose. Come on. Let's eat."

"Caralyn, I need to talk to you about Grandma's house," Dad said after Sunday dinner. "The pork chops were very tender, Sarah. Did you get them at Heppner's shop?"

"I did. They were on sale. I added apple juice. Could you tell?"

"Yes." He looked at Caralyn, who was trying to slap Tucker's hands. "The house."

"Yes, Daddy, I'm listening. I talked to Beth. She has no intention of ever living here again."

"Tucker will be living in whatever NBA city drafts him."

She grinned at Tucker and said, "If any team is that desperate."

Dad continued, "You only have one year left at Midwest."

"And graduate school," she added.

"The house will be empty. Would you consider selling it, or renting it?"

"I can't sell Grandma's house. Couldn't we keep it for when Tuck and I are home."

"That might not happen often," Mom said.

Caralyn looked at Tucker for support.

"It's not my house, Carrie. You and Beth need to decide."

"Beth doesn't need the money, and I will have my trust when I turn twenty-one. We couldn't sell it for much. No one wants a two-bedroom house anymore."

"You don't have to decide right away, but it is something to consider. Empty houses deteriorate faster."

"I'll think about it, but unless Beth changes my mind, I can't imagine selling it. He and Nancy will have lots of babies, and they will need the house."

Tucker looked at her and asked, "Do you know something I don't?"

"You will marry Nancy one of these days, and she wants six kids."

Chapter Fifteen

A week after the school year ended, Caralyn saw Mr. Green getting his mail.

"Hi, Mr. Green. What are you up to today?"

"Not much, Caralyn." He sorted through the mail. "Nothing but junk." He looked at Caralyn. "I finished packing, the movers are coming in the morning and tomorrow I'm heading to Fremont. From there I am heading to Colorado for my vacation. What are you doing?"

"Nothing special. Would you like to take a ride?"

"I would love to. Anywhere special you want to go?" he asked with a grin.

"I know the perfect spot. Would you like to have a picnic by the lake?

"That would be nice. Give me a few minutes to get ready and we can go. Would you like to help me in the kitchen?"

She ran in the house with him.

"I made some sandwiches earlier, and I have some bottled water in the fridge. If you want, we can take them."

"Sure."

He noticed her faded jean shorts, pink tennis shoes and white socks and said, "You don't act much different than my students." He tapped his chin and said, "You're only a year older than the seniors I taught this year."

"But I have more life experience. I've studied in France, and I told you about my love life."

"Let me change, and I'll be ready."

They headed to the lake, but as they got close, Caralyn cried out, "Oh no! Keep going, Mr. Green. Please don't stop."

"Is that Uncle Alton and Uncle Carlton?"

"Yes, it is. We can't stop there today. I hope they didn't see me in the car with you. They would tell Mom they saw us together, and she might get the wrong idea about us."

"I'm sure they didn't see you, Caralyn. They were busy working. We could have our picnic in Butler if you want."

"I guess we can do that. Are you disappointed we can't have a picnic by the lake?"

"Yes, but we can still have fun."

They stopped in Butler and spent an hour at the park. Mr. Green told her where he grew up, and how he met his wife.

"I'm so sorry that she cheated on you, Mr. Green. I will never cheat on my husband."

He shrugged and said, "Nobody gets married and expects to cheat. At least, I hope they don't. Why get married in the first place if you aren't going to be faithful?"

She turned onto her stomach and lifted her feet in the air and moved them back and forth. Suddenly, she turned over and caught Mr. Green looking at her legs.

"I was looking forward to having a picnic by the lake. Could we check and see if my uncles are gone."

He coughed and said, "If you want. We have time."

They gathered up the picnic basket and the blanket and headed back to the lake.

"They are gone. Do you want to sit by the lake. Maybe we could go swimming?"

"I didn't bring my trunks, Caralyn."

She grinned and put a finger to her mouth.

He saw the look and shook his head. "No way, Ms. Dawson. Listening to you talk about skinny dipping and your sex life is bad enough, but I will not be a party to that."

"We could swim in our underwear."

"Do I need to take you home?"

"Now you sound like my father." She sighed and said, "I promise not to take my clothes off and go swimming in front of you."

"Not working, Caralyn."

"I tried."

He parked the car by the shed, and they hiked to the lake. When they got there, Caralyn removed her shoes and socks and walked into the water's edge.

"How's the water?" he asked.

She grinned and said, "Nice and warm. You should try it."

"I might take off my shoes and socks, but nothing else."

She splashed water at him and giggled.

"Caralyn."

"Will you splash me?"

"I thought we were going to sit by the lake and talk."

She waded back to him. "Can we talk about love?"

"Sure. I love the Cardinals."

"I didn't mean baseball. You're worse than Tucker and Daddy."

He sat and patted the grass next to him.

She sat down and asked, "Do you want to fall in love again, Mr. Green?"

He looked at her. "I suppose that is a safe question. Yes."

She waited for more. "Is that it?"

"Ask a better question."

"Could you fall in love with a younger woman?"

"No."

"Mr. Green!"

He laughed and noticed a scar on her knee. "Is that from basketball?"

She touched the scar. "I can't remember. It might have been from volleyball. I played all three sports at school. I was good enough for Stockton Woods, but not college. Did you play any sport?"

"Yes." He grinned and she wrinkled her nose. "Okay, I'm through acting like a jerk. I played baseball in high school for three years. Then I hurt my shoulder and decided to be a teacher instead of the Cardinals' ace starter."

"Tuck is going to play for the Bulls."

"He's the best player to ever come out of Stockton Woods."

He kept the conversation on sports for twenty minutes.

"Caralyn, you are so interesting to be with. I hope we remain friends and stay in touch through the years."

"I hope so too, Mr. Green."

"It's getting late."

"It's the afternoon," she said with a giggle. "It's okay. I promised Mom I would help with supper. We are making meat loaf, and she is teaching me how to put it together."

Mr. Green started laughing.

Caralyn looked at him perplexed. "What is so funny?"

"You are so innocent, Caralyn, and so sexy, too. Were you planning on spending an afternoon with me, and then making meat loaf with your mother like it's no big deal."

"I wasn't going to tell Mom about my afternoon unless she asked. We haven't done anything wrong. We had a picnic. I tried to get you to go swimming, but you wouldn't. You haven't even kissed me."

"Caralyn."

"Mom knows I'm not a virgin, but she hasn't told Daddy. I will certainly never tell him."

Mr. Green smiled at her for a moment. "I was thinking about something. You have always gone by Dawson and not McKay."

"That's because the McKays never formally adopted me. Grandma Florence was my legal guardian, even though I lived most of my life with the McKays. I don't think about it much. I think of them as Mom and Dad, and they think of me as their daughter."

"Do you think of Tucker as your brother, Caralyn?"

Caralyn turned red and looked away. Mr. Green could tell she didn't think of Tucker as her brother now if she ever did.

Caralyn saw Mom working on her flower beds as Mr. Green dropped her off. She hopped out of the car as Mom waved to Mr. Green.

"Hello, Tom."

"Hello, Sarah. How are you today?"

"I'm fine. It's not as humid today."

Mom learned he was leaving in the morning and asked, "Would you like to have dinner with us? We're having meat loaf, and Caralyn is going to help me cook."

116

"I would love to have dinner. What time should I be here? Should I bring anything?"

"We'll probably eat around six, but you can come earlier if you want. You don't have to bring anything."

Caralyn saw Tucker shooting baskets in the backyard and raced to join him after waving goodbye to Mr. Green.

"Hey, Carrie. Where have you been?"

"With Mr. Green," she said then waited for his reaction.

"Where did you guys go?" Tucker didn't seem surprised.

"We drove to Butler and had a picnic at the city park, and then we headed to Uncle Alton's lake and talked."

Tucker smiled at her, and she got a little embarrassed. "Please don't tell Daddy."

"I won't. I know you've always had a crush on him even though you tried to pretend you didn't."

"You knew? You never teased me about it."

"I was saving it for today."

"Cara," Mom called. "We need to get started on dinner."

"You're lucky, Carrie. I had some good material."

"Save it for later."

When Mr. Green arrived at six, Caralyn ran to answer the door even though Dad and Tucker were in the living room. "Come in. Dinner is almost ready."

"Hello, everyone," He shook hands with Mr. McKay and Tucker and turned to Caralyn. "What's the occasion? You're dressed up."

Tucker snickered because she had showered, shaved her legs and changed into a sundress.

She shrugged and said, "It's just an old dress." She put her hands behind her back and twisted back and forth.

The conversation during dinner centered on school and sports and everyone was almost too busy talking to eat.

Mom asked Dad, "What do you think of the meat loaf tonight, dear?"

"It's delicious as always."

117

Caralyn smiled proudly. "I made it, Daddy. Mom watched, but I put it together." Caralyn looked at Mr. Green and blushed as she realized she sounded like a child looking for praise from her father.

"You did a good job, honey. It tastes as good as Mom's."

Tucker grinned at Caralyn because he could tell she was blushing because Mr. Green was listening. "That was the best meat loaf I've eaten all day, Carrie."

She looked at him and was about to smack his arm, but stopped because it might seem childish to Mr. Green.

"Thank you, Tuck. Maybe you can have a sandwich tomorrow if you ask me politely."

After dinner Caralyn helped Mom in the kitchen while the guys sat in the living room and talked about sports. Caralyn fidgeted as she kept trying to listen to their conversation.

"Cara, honey, you don't have to worry. Your father knows you and Tom are friends and have spent time together."

"Did you tell, Daddy?"

"Yes, dear, I did. I wanted him to hear it from me, and not from someone in town. You still call him Mr. Green."

"Yes, I'll always think of him as Mr. Green."

"That's all right. He will probably always remember you as his student. Do you remember telling me about the first day in his class and how he startled you?"

"I remember. He seemed so intimidating especially since I wasn't even a teenager."

Caralyn and Mom finished the dishes and joined everyone in the living room. Mom sat on the couch with Dad and Mr. Green sat in the newer recliner, so Caralyn sat on the arm of the older recliner next to Tucker.

"I really must get home," Mr. Green said a short time later. He shook hands with everyone except Caralyn.

"I will walk you to your car, Mr. Green."

She walked beside him, and they stopped to talk as he leaned against the driver's door.

"You have my email address to stay in touch."

"I will let you know how school goes this year. Have a great vacation in Colorado. If you think about it, you could send me some pictures of your trip."

"I'll do that. I should be going. I want to get an early start."

He looked at Caralyn and neither one of them knew how to say good night. Finally Caralyn moved close and hugged him.

"I will miss you, Mr. Green."

"I will keep in touch, Caralyn." He held her for a moment and then got in the car and backed out of the driveway. They waved at each other as he drove away.

Tucker came outside, walked up behind her and put his hands on her shoulders. "Fremont is not that far away, Carrie. Maybe we can visit him someday."

"He was my favorite teacher ever, Tuck, and it's not because I had a crush on him, either. So don't get the wrong idea."

Tucker walked beside her toward the house, but she told him, "Let's sit on Grandma's porch. We can sit in the swing and talk. Did you really like my meat loaf?"

"God no." He sprinted to the porch. "It was the worst tasting stuff I ever had to swallow. It was all I could do not to puke."

"You're going to get it. Come back here so I can punch you." Caralyn laughed and said, "I know you're kidding because you ate two helpings and would have eaten the whole thing if Mom hadn't put it away."

Chapter Sixteen

Tucker marched into Caralyn's bedroom and stood at the side of her bed. "I really need to talk to you."

"What's up, Tuck?" Caralyn asked as she lay on her stomach reading a book. She looked up at Tucker. "Whoa. That's your serious face. You and Nancy have a fight? Did she dump you? What did you do?"

"No. This is seriously serious, Cara."

She sat up and motioned for him to sit next to her on the bed. He did and looked at her face. He could smell strawberry because she had recently showered.

"What is so serious, Tuck? You look kinda scared."

He sighed and then told her, "I'm going to ask Nancy to marry me."

"Tuck! You are?"

He nodded and she tackled him to the floor.

"Let me up, Carrie." He picked her up and deposited her back on the bed. "Was that a happy tackle, or..."

"I am so happy for you. Do you have a ring?" She sat on her knees.

"Not yet. I would like you to help me pick it out. Would you do that for me?"

"Of course. When can we go shopping?"

"How about now?"

"All right. Let's go." She jumped off the bed and hugged him. "I can't believe you're going to ask her. Do you think she'll say yes?"

"I sure hope so."

"Hey!" She punched his arm. "She's not pregnant, is she? If she is, it's been nice knowin' ya. Her father will kill you."

"No. She's not pregnant." He frowned. "We haven't... you know."

"Just making sure. Let's go. I know the perfect place to shop." She chuckled. *As if there's a choice in Butler.*

They headed to the only jewelry store in Butler. Caralyn browsed the display cases as Tucker talked to the clerk. Tucker told him how much he could afford, and the clerk showed him several rings.

"Cara, come and look at these."

She looked and held Tucker's hand. She realized the clerk assumed the ring was for her.

"I like that one on the end, Tuck." She pointed to one that was neither the most expensive nor the cheapest in the case.

"Would you like to try it on, Miss?"

"Yes, please." The clerk handed the ring to her and she slipped it on her finger. "Look, Tuck. It fits perfectly."

The clerk left them to answer the phone.

"Do you think Nancy will like it, Cara?"

"She will love it. When are you going to give it to her?"

"I'm going to ask her after dinner tomorrow night."

"I'm going to be there, too. Is that all right?"

"Yes. I planned it that way. I need you to be there for moral support."

The clerk returned and Tucker negotiated with him on the price as Caralyn looked around the store. Tucker took out his wallet and paid cash. The clerk placed it in a ring box and congratulated Caralyn and Tucker on their engagement.

"It's not for..."

Caralyn stopped Tucker by kissing him on the mouth.

"I love the ring, and I love you so, so much," she said after breaking off the kiss.

"You're a stinker," Tucker said as they left the store. "That clerk thinks the ring is for you."

"I know. I want him to think that for now. I am going to pretend I am engaged to you today. You have to buy me lunch and treat me special since I helped you pick it out."

"All right. You are so spoiled, Carrie. God help the guy who marries you."

Caralyn tried to hold hands with Tucker as much as she could as they ate lunch and did some more shopping.

"I know you have a lot of money left in your wallet since you didn't have to pay as much for Nancy's ring as you thought. You have to buy me a new dress. I want to look nice when you propose to her."

"I suppose I can buy you a new dress." He checked his wallet again. "As long as it's not over a hundred dollars. And doesn't look like that certain one."

"Which one could you possibly mean?"

"You know the one."

"Oh! The 'One.'" She loved making him blush.

They walked to the Steinmark Dress Shop, and Caralyn made Tucker watch as she modeled several new dresses.

"I like the second one you tried on, Cara."

"You like that one because it's the cheapest."

After trying on five dresses, Caralyn chose the second one. "Will you wipe that silly grin off your mug? I didn't choose it because of the price."

Tucker grinned at her.

"Men. You don't know anything about fashion. This dress fits the best, and I have shoes that will match perfectly."

They passed the jewelry store on the way to the car. Caralyn saw the clerk and waved.

"Carrie, what are you doing?"

"I think you should invite him to the wedding. I want to see the look on his face when he realizes you are marrying Nancy and not me."

"Caralyn, you are so devious."

She smiled at him, "I know. But you still love me, right?"

"If I have to," he said.

"Don't be so nervous, Tuck. You know she will say yes." Caralyn told him the next morning as they ate pancakes.

"I hope so, Cara." He poured more syrup on his plate.

"Don't be silly. She will say yes, but if she has lost her mind for some reason and refuses, then I will marry you."

"Why?"

"Because I really like that ring. In fact I'm going to pretend we are engaged for the rest of the day."

Tucker smiled as she radiated happiness. She pretended to show the ring to imaginary people and Tucker laughed at her goofiness as they worked around the house.

"Oh, hello. Did I tell you I'm engaged to Tucker McKay, the famous basketball player? We're getting married next month and spending our honeymoon in bed having sex."

Tucker rolled his eyes.

"That's everything on Mom's list, Cara," Tucker said later. "We should get cleaned up."

Tucker showered and dressed at Grandma Florence's house while Caralyn got ready at home. He came back and paced as Caralyn finished getting ready. Mom braided her hair, which had grown back enough from her short hairstyle in Paris.

"Mom, do you think I look okay?"

"Caralyn, you look beautiful. Why?"

"I want to look good for tonight."

Mom looked at Caralyn and wondered. "Are you wishing it was you instead of Nancy, honey?"

"Maybe a tiny bit, Mom, but I know Tuck loves Nancy, and she loves him, too. I am happy for them."

"Stand up and let me see how you look."

Caralyn stood up and let Mom took a good look at her. Mom pictured her as a little girl with skinned up knees and a ribbon in her hair.

"You will be the prettiest girl there tonight. Someday a boy will ask you to marry him, and I will be so happy for you."

Caralyn gave Mom a hug and a kiss. "Tell Tuck I will be ready in a minute."

Mom told Tucker, who waited anxiously in the living room with Dad, "She will be out in a minute, guys."

Caralyn appeared a couple minutes later, and Dad and Tucker stood up to get a better look.

"Sweetheart, you look like a princess," Dad said with pride.

"Do you like the way Mom fixed my hair?"

"Yes, it looks... adorable," he said then shrugged.

"Oh, Daddy, you don't even know what she did." Caralyn turned around and pointed to her hair. "She braided it the way she used to when I was younger."

"I knew that," Dad tried to fool her. *To me you still look like a little girl, but I'm smart enough not to say that out loud. I am a college professor, after all.*

Tucker was sweating profusely but still managed to compliment her. "Carrie, you look amazing. A whole lot better than you did when we were working in the garage and you had dirt on your face and smelled like sweat."

"Thank you for such a nice compliment, Tuck. You cleaned up nicely, too."

It normally took two minutes to drive to the Young house but not this night.

"Did you remember to bring the ring, Tuck? Do you know what you are going to say?"

"I've got the ring. Actually you've got it. I put it in your purse."

"What purse? I didn't bring a purse."

"Oh crap! I put it in that purse you usually carry. I thought you would bring it."

"Turn around, and I will run in and get it." She ran in the house and hollered on the run, "Forgot something important." She showed Mom and Dad the box holding the ring. "He's such a basket case tonight. He's lucky to have me with him."

This time they made it to the Young home. Tucker kept rather quiet during the meal. Mr. Young knew what Tucker had planned because he asked him for Nancy's hand earlier that week.

"I will bring out the dessert if everyone's ready," Mrs. Young said.

Caralyn kicked Tucker under the table.

"Ow! That hurt, Cara."

"Do you have something you need to do?"

Tucker frowned at her, stood up and walked around the dining room table to Nancy. He wiped his brow with the back of his hand then knelt beside her. Caralyn looked at Mr. Young and noticed he had tears in his eyes.

This better be good, Tucker James. Caralyn thought.

"Nancy Young, will you marry me sometime? Your Dad said it was okay."

Caralyn rolled her eyes. *Oh my God! That has to be the worst proposal in the history of marriage proposals. You're lucky I can't reach you because I would smack you.*

Through her tears Nancy said, "Yes, I will, Tucker McKay. I will marry you whenever you want."

Tucker slipped the ring on her finger. He stood up, hugged Nancy and gave her a long kiss. Mr. and Mrs. Young hugged as they watched with pride. They were crying. In fact everyone had tears in their eyes except Caralyn. She smiled, beaming with pride at her Bubby. Mr. Young shook Tucker's hand and Nancy showed her mom the ring.

"Caralyn, look at the ring. Isn't it perfect."

"It is beautiful, Nancy. I'm so happy for you." Caralyn and Nancy hugged tightly.

"Did you know he was going to ask me tonight?"

"Yes I did, and I even helped him pick out the ring. I hope you like it."

"Oh, Cara. I love it."

"I almost forgot. We have apple pie and ice cream for dessert," Mrs. Young reminded everyone.

Nancy twisted the ring as she admired it. "Now I know why Daddy insisted I wear a dress."

After they ate dessert, They moved to the living room. Tucker sat on the couch with Nancy on one side and Caralyn on the other side to watch a movie.

"Stop it!" Caralyn dug her elbow into Tuck's ribs.

He threw his hands in the air. "What did I do?"

"You've got your arms around us. You're hugging Nancy and pulling on my hair."

125

"Should I switch?" He glanced back and forth at the girls.

Nancy leaned against him. "You shouldn't tease Cara so much. She helped you pick out my beautiful ring."

When it was finally time to leave, Caralyn said, "I'll wait outside while you guys kiss. I'm happy for you." She hugged Nancy and dashed outside.

"I wish I could stay longer, but your father was checking his watch. I can't wait until you are my wife."

Caralyn sat on the car's fender as she waited for Tucker. He said good night and kissed Nancy on the front porch. He walked toward the car and finally noticed Caralyn's sneakers.

"That dress really looks great with those shoes, Caralyn. Now I see why you picked it." He shook his head.

She kicked her feet back and forth. "Hey. I said it matched my shoes. I didn't specify any particular pair."

When they pulled into the driveway, Caralyn jumped out and ran into the house. Mom and Dad were on the couch.

"We're back," Caralyn hollered. "Tucker is a twerp."

"How did it go, son?" Mom asked.

"She said..."

"I had to kick him under the table and remind him to ask Nancy the big question," Caralyn interrupted. "He was so quiet during dinner, and I was afraid he was going to chicken out."

"We are so happy for you, son. Have you and Nancy set a date?"

"We were thinking maybe late next summer, but we haven't thought about a specific date."

After a while Mom and Dad headed off the bed.

"Night, Mom. Good night, Daddy. I am going to stay up for a while. I'm too keyed up to sleep."

"Don't stay up all night, Cara. We have to run into Butler in the morning."

"I remember, Mom. I think I will stay at Grandma's tonight so we don't keep you guys up. I'm sure Tucker is too excited to sleep."

Mom saw Tucker yawn and said, "Are you sure it's Tucker who's too keyed up? Good night, sweetie."

"I'm going to put my pajamas on so I'll be ready for bed in case I fall asleep," Caralyn said as she and Tucker walked to Grandma's house.

"I kinda screwed up the proposal, huh?"

"No, I thought it was so romantic." She put her hands together as if praying. "By the way, Nancy, if you're not busy next summer, would you like to get hitched. Your dad doesn't care."

He nudged her side. "That's not what I said."

"You sounded like you were ordering a burger from The Curve."

"I'll do better the next time."

"You're a blockhead. You only get to propose one time."

She got ready for bed and they watched TV.

"That's it for me," she said later.

"Good night, Cara. He looked at her as she stood before him. "Did I tell you how pretty you looked tonight, Cara?"

"Maybe. But you can tell me again."

"You looked as pretty as an angel."

She looked puzzled. "Are angels pretty?"

"I don't know, but that's all I could think of."

She grinned at him. "You think I'm pretty."

"You are in deep trouble, Caralyn."

Tucker picked her up and carried her into Grandma's room and tossed her on the bed. He sat on the edge of the bed as Caralyn lay on the covers looking at him.

"Are you going to give me a good night kiss, Tuck?"

He leaned over and blew a raspberry her cheek.

"You are such a cretin."

"Go to sleep, delinquent," he said then grinned.

She giggled as she slipped under the covers. "I've seen that look before. You're planning something devious. Spill it."

"I texted Nancy. We're going to sneak out for a ride. She can't sleep either."

She sat up. "Really? Are you going to make love?"

127

"None of your business, pipsqueak," he answered.

She giggled and said, "Don't let Mr. Young catch you. He'll fill you full of holes."

"We will be careful. I won't be out all night. I love you, Carrie."

"I love you, too, Bubby."

"Are your parents asleep?" Tucker asked when Nancy got into the car. "Caralyn guessed what we're doing."

"They are sound asleep. Daddy wouldn't wake up in a hurricane, and Mom didn't hear me."

"What about Sandy?"

"Her door was closed, and I didn't step on the squeaky board. We can stay out all night if you want, Tuck."

He started the car but didn't turn on the lights until he was at the corner. "Where should we go?"

"You choose."

He grinned and drove toward Grandma's farm.

Caralyn dreamed about a wedding where she was the bride. She could never see the groom's face, but his build looked familiar.

Chapter Seventeen

"Beth, can I talk to you?" Caralyn asked.

"What about?" Beth asked as she read the instructions on a frozen pizza.

"Grad school. I can't decide. New York would be great because of all the publishing houses, but Chicago would be closer to home."

"You have family here. Tucker won't be home much, but Ray and I are here." She set the oven to 425 degrees.

"At least I have time to decide."

"Where is Tucker going to live now that he's a member of the Chicago Bulls?" Beth asked. "He was drafted in the second round. Not bad for someone from Stockton Woods."

"And he signed a three-year contract with a bonus. He found an apartment in Holland Park. It's not real close to the stadium, but the practice facility isn't too far."

Beth searched for a pizza cutter as she asked, "What are the other guys doing?"

"Derren is teaching history and coaching baseball at West Memphis High School. That's in the St. Louis area. He and Natalie live in a two-story house only two blocks from the school. She's still working for an insurance company in Searsport. Their wedding is set for late June."

"Isn't Tucker getting married about then?"

"Three weeks later." Caralyn picked up a pizza cutter from the sink. "Are you looking for this?"

"Thanks."

"Richard is living in Queens and going to NYU law school. He wants me to come to New York sometime."

"Are you going to miss them?" Beth asked.

"Yeah, but I plan to see Tucker once in a while, and I can visit Nancy, too."

"Where is she going to school?"

"She graduated from Kilkenny and is going to SWU like our parents. Sandy goes there."

"Who?"

Sandy is Nancy's sister. Don't you know anything about Stockton Woods?"

"Not much."

"Did I tell you I agreed to be a teaching assistant for Professor McBride. He's published five books already, and he promised to critique my writing."

"What kind of class?"

Caralyn grinned. "His erotic lit class. It's an independent study with fifteen students who meet once a week."

"What do you know about eroticism?" Beth asked.

"I know a little about love. Thanks for helping with the rent. I didn't want to spend another year in the dorm."

"You can pay me back when you are older, and don't argue with me," Beth insisted. "I'm glad you found a furnished flat."

"Thanks, Beth. I will pay you back with interest."

"You're only nineteen. I can wait until you are twenty-one. You need to be careful when you start using the money from your trust."

"I will. I'm not going to spend it foolishly."

"Would you like to fly out here and spend a weekend, or even longer?" Trent Cussler asked on the phone one Sunday morning. "You could check out the graduate program at Oregon State." He kept in touch with Caralyn through emails mostly, but they did talk on the phone occasionally.

"I did check it out, but I kinda eliminated it. Sorry, Trent. I'm going to get my masters in either Chicago or New York, but I haven't decided which city, yet."

"Too bad," Trent sighed.

"Just because I'm not going to school in Oregon doesn't mean I wouldn't like to come out to see you," she said. "I do miss you and our little sessions."

His mood brightened. "I miss them, too."

"I could fly out for a weekend sometime, but that wouldn't give us much time to be together."

"It would be better than not seeing you at all, but I have a better idea."

"What might that be? And I can see your grin even on the phone."

"I'm pretty sure my father would give me a couple days off if I wanted to come back for the Homecoming game."

"You could stay with me."

"That sounds really good," he said.

"I have a spare bedroom..."

"Oh, that kinda burst my balloon."

"I didn't say you would have to use it," Caralyn teased. "If you come here for Homecoming, maybe I could visit you during the holiday break."

"That would give us plenty of time to visit."

"Would I have my own room, or would we have to share?"

"I guess that would depend on how things work out at Homecoming. My parents have several empty bedrooms now that everyone is married except for me."

They checked their schedules and set in motion a plan for her to visit.

Caralyn found she was going to be busy even with her light class load. Professor McBride's erotic journalism independent study required more time than she expected. She was surprised to see the name Jamie Wilton on the class roster.

"I noticed you are from Meyersdale, Wisconsin. Do you know a Jeremiah Wilton?" she asked after class.

"He's my older brother. Do you know him?"

"I knew him briefly when I was younger. What is he doing now?" *This sucks! He probably knows about us.*

"He works for an accounting company in Meyersdale. He's married and has a young son named Clayton. His wife works at the same firm, and they have a house outside of town."

"That's great." Caralyn realized Jeremiah had achieved many of his goals in life already.

"He lords it over us," Jamie said.

She could see a family resemblance, but Jamie was shorter and heavier than Jeremiah. *I will die if you know about my relationship with your brother.*

One day Jamie stayed after class because he needed some help with an assignment. They talked about the assignment and then Caralyn asked, "Are you and your brother close?"

"Which brother?"

"I didn't realize you had more than one."

"I have two brothers. Jeremiah is the oldest and Jackson is one year older than me. He is a junior at Wisconsin State. I didn't want to go there so I ended up here."

"I guess I meant Jeremiah. Do you have any sisters?"

"No sisters."

"Why do you all have names that start with 'J'?"

"My father's name is Jerome and Mom's name is Jennifer."

"I take it you are much closer to Jackson than Jeremiah."

"Oh yeah. Jackson and I are close. I suppose neither one of us is really close to Jeremiah."

"So Jeremiah didn't share his deepest secrets with you," Caralyn mentioned casually as she continued to read through his lame story about dinosaurs in love.

"Naw, there was too big of an age gap, I guess."

"How old are you, Jamie?" she asked.

"I'm twenty."

"So, Jeremiah must be twenty-six or so, right?"

Jamie laughed. "He may try to look twenty-six, but he turned thirty-one on his birthday."

Caralyn gasped and put a hand to her heart. "What? That can't be. He said he was twenty-five when..." She paused then asked, "What year was he born?"

"Jeremiah?" Jamie asked.

She nodded.

"Let's see." He scratched his ear. "I was born in 1987. Jackson in 1986 and Jeremiah's ten years older than him." He held out his fingers..."

132

"He was born in 1976. How can that be?" She balled her hands into fists. "He lied to me. He was actually thirty when I met him."

"What?"

"Nothing. What is his wife's name?"

"Which one? He's married to Anna now, but..."

"How many times has he been married?"

"Technically, twice," Jamie said with a puzzled look. "Why does it matter?"

"I'm curious. When I met him, he was rather reticent about his past. You said technically. What did you mean exactly?"

"I guess it doesn't matter if I tell you. It's not a big secret in Meyersdale. When he was in high school, he had a thing for his English teacher. She was thirty or so, and after he graduated, they had a brief affair. It was quite a scandal in the family. She had moved to a small town close to the Upper Peninsula by then."

"How long did this affair last?" she asked. *I can't believe what I'm hearing.*

Several months. She broke it off and threatened to call the police because he kept stalking her. That's how I would describe it. Anyway, after that debacle..." He paused and stared at her.

"What?"

"It's funny, but I just realized something."

"Go on."

"Her name was Carol. She had darker hair, but you and Carol are about the same size. From the back you would look similar. She had the same kind of hairstyle, and your eyes look like hers. Not only was she his teacher, but she babysat him for years."

Caralyn stared at Jamie. "You mentioned a first wife."

"Frances. That only lasted a few months. He was probably twenty-four. Give or take. I don't remember exactly. It was after he came back from the army..."

"He was in the army?"

"Several years. After he was discharged, he started college. He almost seemed normal after that."

"How so?"

"He never talked about being in the army, but he was different when he returned. More serious about life." Jamie chuckled. "He was never what you could call carefree. He became single-minded about what he wanted in life. He met Anna, and they got engaged soon after. Then she dumped him for a younger man. He was in college. Graduate classes, I believe. He went mental for a while, but his psychiatrist worked wonders. Now he's a typical, boring banker. Investment consultant. You get the picture." He waved a hand.

"I'm beginning to see him more clearly."

Caralyn waited for Trent at the New Lebanon airport Thursday evening. *I hope this weekend doesn't turn into a disaster. It could make or break our relationship.* She paced back and forth by the exit of Gate 4 until she spotted him. He saw her right away, and they smiled at each other.

"How was the flight?" she asked nervously.

He dropped his carry-on bag. "Now that I see you, I can't even remember being on the plane," he said as he held her close and kissed her.

"That's quite a line. I like it." She melted into his embrace. *I don't think you will be using the spare room.*

He kissed her again. They only stopped because she ran out of breath.

"Do you have to wait for your luggage?" she asked.

"Nope. I didn't check anything. I like to travel light. I'm ready to go."

"Are you hungry? Did you eat anything on the plane?" She smiled at him. *You let your hair grow out. I like.*

"I had a snack, but I would love a sandwich from Nico's. I miss eating there."

"Oh, yeah. I'm gonna miss Nico's when I leave. It's a one-of-a-kind place not like those chain restaurants that dominate the country. I've got pop and bottled water at home."

He placed his arm around her shoulders and asked, "How have your classes gone so far?"

134

She explained about her lighter class load and the amount of time she spent working as Professor McBride's assistant.

"It sounds like you are keeping busy."

"There's my car," she pointed. "Tucker gave me his old Civic. It still runs great and the gas mileage is super."

Trent tossed his bag in the backseat and got in. "Do you like living in an apartment better than the dorm?"

"Without a doubt. I have more privacy, and I can have guests without the whole floor knowing. The downside is I have to do my own cooking."

"Couldn't you buy a meal plan?"

"I could, but since I have a small kitchen, I figured I might as well cook for myself. I usually grab lunch somewhere, but I make my own dinner. Unless I order out."

"Have you had many guests stay with you so far?" he asked.

"Are you asking if I have a new boyfriend and has he spent the night?"

"I suppose so."

"Tucker came to see me one weekend, but he's engaged. Did I tell you that already?"

"You mentioned it. A girl from back home, right?"

Caralyn explained more about Nancy. They stopped at Nico's and ordered sandwiches and fries.

"They always give you a ton of fries," she said as she started munching on them before they got back in her car.

He opened the bag to take in the aroma. "I haven't had a beef sandwich this good since graduation and their fries are the best in town."

"This is it, Aspen Commons. It's only five blocks from the dorm." She pulled into the parking lot in front of the building. "I'm in 203A. We have assigned parking so that's a bonus. Plus, I have a washer and dryer. I don't have to use the laundromat anymore." She used her key to open the front door. "The security is better than most of the other complexes. The McKays really liked that."

"No elevator though," he mentioned.

"There are only three floors. The floors and ceilings are concrete or something. I can't hear anything from the apartment above me, or on either side. It's really quiet."

"You must be paying quite a bit for rent."

They climbed the stairs and she opened the door. "Actually, my sister is paying the rent. I will pay her back after I turn twenty-one. It's even more because it's furnished."

"Oh, the trust fund thing, right? You told me a little about that. That's got to feel good to know you have that money." He slapped his forehead. "I'm sorry, Cara. I know you lost your parents in that accident."

"It's okay. I don't have any memory of them. I do have photographs, but the McKays are the only parents I have."

He dropped his bag and looked around. "I like it. This part is open and I'm assuming those are the bedrooms and bathrooms there."

"I rarely use the guest bathroom, but it's nice to have it. We could both shower at the same time." She said it innocently, but then realized how it sounded.

"I know another way we could shower at the same time." He put his hands on her waist and pulled her close.

"You have to behave for now, Trent." She broke away and giggled as she walked into the kitchen. "We don't want our fries to get cold." She opened the fridge. "I have Coke and Dr Pepper."

"Coke for me, please." He set the food on the kitchen counter. "Do you usually eat at the counter?"

"Yeah, I sit at the barstool because I can see the TV from there. I only use the dining table to study."

They caught up on news as they ate.

As she tossed the trash away, Trent made himself at home on the couch. "What should we do tonight, Cara? Do you want to go out? See a movie? Go bowling? Watch a chess match?"

She plopped down next to him. "I thought we could hang out here. I have two classes tomorrow morning, but then I am free for the weekend."

"I've got friends I could visit in the morning. I have our tickets for the game, but I didn't know if you would want to attend any of the other activities. Do you?"

"Would it be all right if we didn't?" Caralyn moved closer to him.

"Fine with me. I'd rather spend the time with you." He gazed into her eyes and then pulled her close and kissed her.

"Are we going to wait until later?"

"Wait for?" he asked slowly.

"To finish what we're starting." She scooted away and pulled her knees up to her chest as she faced him. "You know all about my love life. Nothing has changed since you left."

"I haven't been on a single date, Cara. In fact, I haven't been out with anyone since we started getting more serious." He looked at her and almost frowned. "Oh, I get it. You're still afraid to totally trust a guy because of that jerk in Wisconsin. I'm sorry, Cara. Is there anything I can do?"

"No, it's my problem. I trust you, and I think you know how I feel... about sex." She grinned. "You've had your hands on me so I know you know how I feel."

"You're funny, Cara."

Two hours later, they were ready for bed.

"Here is a towel and a washcloth." She handed them to him. "I'm sure you can figure out how to use the shower."

He scratched his head and tried to look confused. "I might need some help with that. Could you show me?"

She poked his arm. "Maybe tomorrow. Give me a chance to shower before you come to my room, okay?"

"I will be waiting patiently." He kissed her and put a hand on her hip.

After her shower Caralyn dried and brushed her hair. She opened her drawer and tried to decide what to wear. She pulled out a thin nightgown and then a long t-shirt with a university logo on the front. *I guess it doesn't really matter since it will be dark, and I might not have it on for long.* She chose the t-shirt.

137

Five minutes later Trent knocked. "Are you decent?"

She giggled and said, "Yes, but you can come in anyway."

He opened the door and stuck his head inside. "You are decent. Hah! I've got a t-shirt exactly like that one, but it doesn't look like a dress on me."

"It was either this or a nightgown." She grinned nervously. "Which side do you want?" She pointed at the queen-size bed.

He lifted her into his arms and carried her to the bed. "I want the middle with you underneath me."

"Oooh! That sounded so romantic," she teased. "Put me down so I can pull back the covers."

He set her down and watched as she arranged the bedding. He glanced at the dresser and saw her teddy bear. "Will teddy be jealous that I get to share the bed tonight?"

She turned to look at him. "Maybe." She got into bed and scooted to one side and sat up. "Do you...?"

"Be right back. They're in my bag." He sprinted to the other bedroom and grabbed his bag. He found the condoms in the second compartment he tried. He hurried back to Cara's room and held them up. "Found them!"

"You don't have to show me, silly." She grinned and patted the empty spot next to her.

"Should I turn off the light?"

"Yes, please," she said as she moved onto her back. "Can you put it on in the dark?"

"Yes. I'm almost an expert like your friend Richard," he teased as he turned off the light and slipped in next to her.

She woke up and checked the clock. *Eight o'clock already. I need to get up.* She reached to touch Trent, but no one was there. She stretched her arms over her head, thought about last night and sighed. *There weren't any candles, but it was amazing for our first time.* She leaned over the side of the bed and saw her t-shirt. She threw back the covers and slipped out of bed. She heard the fridge door close and quickly put on the t-shirt. She walked out to the kitchen and leaned against the counter, facing into the kitchen.

138

"Hi."

Trent smiled. "Hi, yourself. I thought I would make breakfast. Are eggs okay?"

"Sure. Scrambled, please."

"Your request is my command, or however that old saying goes." He bowed. "What time do you have to be at class?"

"Not until nine." *Are we not going to talk about last night?*

He got the eggs started and then walked over and hugged her. "Are you all right? Last night meant a lot to me."

"Oh, Trent. It meant a lot to me, too. Now I feel like I can put the thing with Jeremiah behind me. You were so sweet and loving."

"Cara, you did scream a little, and I think you scratched my back."

"I did not."

"It's a good thing the walls are soundproof."

"You shouldn't have made me feel so good."

"Which time?" he asked with a straight face.

"I can't remember."

After dinner that evening, Caralyn's cell phone rang.

"It's Mom. I need to take this," she told Trent who was sitting next to her on the couch.

"Hi, Mom. What's up?"

"I wanted to let you know we have tickets to the game tomorrow and wondered if we could spend the night with you. Would that be all right?"

Caralyn looked at Trent. "You're always welcome to stay here." Caralyn talked to Mom McKay for ten minutes. She ended the call and looked at Trent.

"I can stay with a friend, Cara. It's no big deal."

"Do you think it's silly for me to try to hide my love life from them?"

"Not at all. Mr. McKay thinks of you as his little girl."

"Mom knows I'm not a virgin, but I don't know if Daddy does. I'd hate for him to be disappointed with me."

139

They made plans for Saturday. They would watch the game with her parents, and Trent would spend the night with a friend.

"Are you going to wear that nightgown tonight, Cara?" Trent asked as they got ready for bed.

"Should I even bother?" she asked from her bathroom.

"I'll turn out the light. I know you are still shy about letting me see you naked. You can wear it if you want."

"Don't turn off the light yet," she said as she turned off the bathroom light and stepped into the bedroom.

He smiled. "You look fantastic, Cara."

She stood by the bed with a finger to her mouth. "Do I really?"

"Yes. You are so beautiful."

"I'm still embarrassed letting you see me this way. I feel almost naked."

Trent laughed and replied, "That's because you are naked except for your socks."

She looked down. "My feet get cold at night."

Trent helped her clean the apartment in the morning. The McKays arrived shortly after eleven and Caralyn hugged them.

"This is Trent..."

"Hi! I'm Trent Cussler." He shook hands with the McKays. "I graduated last year. Caralyn and I were neighbors. My dorm room was right across the hall..." He explained that he lived in Oregon and flew back for Homecoming. He made it seem like he and Caralyn were merely friends.

"It's a pleasure to meet you, Trent." Mr. McKay shook his hand. They sat on the couch and started talking about football.

Mom looked at Trent and then back at Caralyn and mouthed, "It's okay, honey. I won't tell your father."

There were no more complications the rest of the day. Everyone went to the game and then out for dinner later. Trent left to stay with his friend and the McKays stayed in the spare room.

"Thanks for breakfast, sweetie," Dad said. "You're getting better at creating interesting meals."

"Oh, Daddy. I'm sorry I burned your toast."

"We will buy a new toaster for your birthday," he said.

"I love how you've decorated the place," Mom said. "Where did you find the bookcase?"

"In a local second-hand shop. I refinished it."

"We need to hit the road, Sarah," Dad said checking the time. "I need to prepare for this week's classes."

Mom hugged Caralyn and whispered, "Keep me informed about Trent. I like him."

"They're gone," Caralyn called Trent ten minutes after her parents left. "Are you coming back?"

"I'll be there in fifteen."

They ate lunch at Nico's. At three Caralyn drove him back to the airport.

"I'm pretty sure I will be able to come to Oregon after Christmas. I could stay for a whole week if you can put up with me."

"An entire week, huh? That's a long time," he teased.

"You're so mean to me."

"I wish you could stay forever, Cara." He hugged and kissed her and then headed for the check-in counter.

She waited until he disappeared and then drove home.

Chapter Eighteen

"Happy birthday, Carrie. How does it feel to not be a teenager?" Tucker asked Sunday night.

She closed her laptop, set it on the floor and moved onto her back with her feet dangling over the arm of the couch. "I feel so mature. It's like totally awesome," she said using her Valley Girl voice.

"Yeah, you sound like it. Did you do anything special this weekend? I'm sorry I couldn't call earlier."

"I didn't go anywhere. Mom and Dad called. Beth texted me. Derren and Richard sent cards."

"You sound bored."

"A little."

"Did you talk to Trent?"

She sat up and stepped on her laptop. "He's just a close friend, Tucker."

"If you say so, but he should call you on your birthday."

"He called yesterday. He's in Alaska right now. Something to do with work, and he might have sent a dozen red roses," she added softly.

"Roses, huh? Nice friend."

"Hush."

"Mom said you drove home for Thanksgiving."

"I did, but your car sounded funny."

"Funny how?"

She shrugged. "I don't know. It was running rough."

"It might need a tune-up. Can you take care of it for me?"

"Do I look like a mechanic?"

He laughed and answered, "No, take it somewhere. John Greenwood knows how to fix cars."

"The guy we know from home?"

"Yeah, he's the best mechanic in Stockton Woods."

"He's the only one you mean."

"That, too," he said with a chuckle. "Did I tell you we have a game Christmas Day in Boston?"

She moved onto her back again. "Yes, and it sucks. What did Nancy say when you told her?"

"She whined but understood. I am coming home for a couple days before Christmas. Will you be there?"

"Where else would I go?"

"Nowhere, I suppose. Did you finish your shopping?"

"Yes, but I didn't buy you anything. I gave Nancy a couple ideas."

"Like what?"

Caralyn giggled and said, "I told her you needed new boxers with teddy bears or basketballs on them."

"You aren't any more mature than when you turned thirteen."

"I need to go. I'll see you soon.

"Oh, should I pick you up when I drive home?" he asked.

"No, because you have to leave before I do, and it will be a chance to get your old car fixed. Did you give it to me because you knew it was falling apart?"

"Sure. Why would I keep it?"

"You're a stinker, Tucker McKay."

"Nancy, should I come to your house, or do you want to come here?" Caralyn asked upon arriving in Stockton Woods.

"I'll come there. Sandy and Lloyd are here, and she's fussing to Mom about the wedding plans. Oh, Daddy is making them sleep in different rooms."

Caralyn giggled and said, "At least he can stay in the same house. When I was bringing Jeremiah home to meet my parents, Daddy was going to make him stay at a motel in Vernon Heights."

"It's good to hear you laugh about him now, Cara. I'll be there in ten."

Nancy knocked on the door an hour later and Caralyn let her in.

"Sorry, but it's like total chaos at home. I had to act as a peacemaker."

"Come back to my room. I want to show you something."

143

Nancy followed and looked for something different. "What am I supposed to see?"

"Do you see any stuffed animals?"

Nancy looked again. "No. Why?"

"I put them away because I'm a big girl now," Caralyn said with a childish voice.

"You're silly, Cara. No one cares if you have your teddy on the dresser."

"I thought since I'm twenty, I should... never mind. Are you and Tuck doing anything tomorrow?"

"He's coming for dinner because he won't be here for Christmas. We could do something during the day."

"It's weird this year," Caralyn said as she sat on the edge of her bed.

Nancy sat at the desk. "How so?"

"I'm used to seeing the guys. Richard lives in New York. He's flying to Chicago to see his parents, but I won't see him. Derren and Natalie are going to stay home and see her parents and his on Christmas Day."

"I ran into Davey in Butler yesterday," Nancy said. "He was with a girl."

"Probably Melissa. It better have been Melissa, I mean. I will ask him when I see him. He promised to come over while he's here."

"Where does he work?"

"He works for a machine shop in Butler. He went to Kilkenny for two years, but that was it. He's doing okay."

"I'm home!" Tucker hollered as he walked into the utility room.

"We're in the kitchen, son," Mom said. "How were the roads?"

He dropped his Chicago Bulls duffel in the utility room. "Not bad. There was a little snow around New Lebanon." He kissed his mother's cheek and patted his father's back. "Where's the delinquent?"

"She left to pick up Davey. Apparently, the four of you are spending the afternoon together."

"Did Nancy go with?" Tucker asked. He opened the fridge and pulled out a Coke.

"Not sure, but probably. Caralyn got a tune-up on your Civic and expects you to pay for it."

Tucker took a drink, laughed and said, "She's so cheap. She could buy a new car if she opened her purse."

"Tucker McKay, why did you park in my spot?" Caralyn hollered as she flung her gloves and coat at the couch. "If I'm stuck in the snow, you have to dig me out."

"Nice to see you, too, Caralyn," Tucker said. He moved past her and hugged Nancy. They kissed as everyone watched.

"Merry Christmas, everyone," Davey said. "Mom and Dad said to say hi. They drove to West Memphis this morning to see Derren."

"Tell your father I need to talk to him and Alton about Mom and Dad."

"What did Grandpa do now?" Davey asked. He sat on a kitchen chair and picked a cookie from the platter.

"He insists he can work in the machine shop in this cold."

"I thought Dad and Uncle Alton installed a gas heater in there."

"They did, but your grandfather refuses to turn it on. He claims it costs too much," Dad McKay said. He grabbed a cookie, too.

"Hey! I made those for later," Caralyn said.

Davey looked at her and his cookie. "You made these?"

Caralyn wrinkled her nose at him. "Yes, and I put rat poison in yours."

He tool another bite. "Doesn't matter. I'm not a rat."

"I hear we are going somewhere this afternoon," Tucker said as he and Nancy stood in the doorway. He had his arm around her waist as he ran a hand through her long hair. "Do I have a choice in where we go?"

145

"I suppose," Caralyn said. "What do you want to do?"

"I want to drive..."

"No way," Caralyn said. "We're going to the farm and going sledding. There has to be a foot of snow on Bilek's Hill."

Mom looked at Caralyn then at her husband.

Caralyn caught the look and said, "Yes, I know that's where the accident happened. It's okay. I've driven over it plenty of times."

Tucker looked at Nancy. "Are you interested?"

"If it's not too cold, it could be fun."

Tucker loaded his Jeep Wrangler with two plastic discs and they drove to the Stanfield farm.

"Why couldn't you park closer?" Caralyn asked. "Now we have to walk half a mile."

Tucker handed her a disc and said, "There's no shoulder, remember?"

"Right." She turned to Davey. "Will you give me a piggyback ride?"

He laughed and answered, "You aren't a kid anymore. Do I look like a pack mule?"

"No, but you kinda smell like one," she teased.

"Carrie, you better watch it," Tucker said. "He might decide to throw you in the pond since we have to walk right past it."

"Good idea, Tucker." He tried to grab her, but she darted away.

Ten minutes later after tramping through the deep snow, they were at the top of Bilek's Hill.

"We can't use the road, but the east side of the hill is better anyway," Tucker said. "Make sure you don't hit that tree and stop before the creek. There's ice on top, but it might not be thick enough to hold us."

Caralyn snickered. "It would have to be ten inches thick to hold Davey."

"You will pay for that, Cara." He grabbed her and sat on the disc. "Hang on, brat."

He pushed off and the disc started to spin. They avoided the tree, but couldn't stop. Seconds before they would have flown over the bank of the creek, Davey held onto Caralyn and rolled off into the snow. They tumbled over each other, but stopped in time.

"Are you okay, Cara?"

She giggled and said, "Let's do it again. That was more fun than..." She paused and bit her lip.

"What were you going to say?" Davey asked.

She grinned and answered, "It was better than sex."

He laughed, jumped down the bank, retrieved the disc and they walked up the hill.

"Are you all right?" Nancy asked. "I don't want to crash like that."

"Tucker will hold on to you. He isn't as reckless as Davey."

An hour later, Caralyn took off her gloves and stocking cap. "These are soaked, and it's too hot to wear them, but too cold not to."

"We should head home," Tucker said. "We have to clean up for dinner."

He drove through the two foot high snowdrift in Uncle Carlton's driveway and parked behind the house.

"Thanks for the ride, Tucker." He smiled at Caralyn. "I hope you're not too sore from crashing so many times."

"I don't care. That was the best part. See you later. Call me if you want to go again."

Mom waved from the porch. "Drive carefully, Tucker."

Caralyn wrapped her arms around her chest and hollered, "Thanks for my charm, and you better win the game on Christmas."

"You're welcome, Carrie, and I want to lose the game." He made a snowball and threw it at her.

"You cretin! You could have hit me."

"That was the idea."

She jumped from the porch, compacted enough snow to make a softball-sized projectile and threw it at him.

147

He grinned as the snowball missed. "You throw like a girl."

Dad laughed and put an arm around Sarah. "I hope the kids can always be here for Christmas. It would be boring without them."

"Merry Christmas, Tucker," Richard said as they shook hands in the lobby. "Well, it will be in a couple days."

"Merry Christmas, Richard. Did you see your parents already?"

He looked up. "Yeah, their condo is on the fourteenth floor. It's small so I'm crashing on the couch."

"You could crash at my place," Tucker offered.

"Thanks, but you're leaving tonight. I don't mind the couch. It's only for one more night." He rolled his shoulders to relieve a kink. "Did you make it home at all?"

"Got back this morning. Nancy understood why I couldn't be home on Christmas, but Caralyn was mad. She threatened to write a nasty letter to the Bulls' ownership and boycott all our games."

"Sounds like the Caralyn I know."

"How is it living in New York?" Tucker asked.

"Expensive! A dollar burger costs five bucks."

"You should tell Caralyn how expensive it is because she is thinking of doing her graduate work there."

"I'll let her know. Is she really thinking of living in New York? She would love the city."

"Yeah, she's considering it and Chicago. I'd rather she stay in Illinois, but if she does end up by you, would you keep an eye on her?"

"Of course I will. Maybe it would work out that she could share the apartment with me. There are two bedrooms. They are tiny, but everything is so expensive. There's only one bathroom, but there was only one bathroom in the old place, and it never seemed to be a problem. Of course she wasn't there every night. I'm sure we would get along."

148

"I haven't told your father the whole truth about Trent," Mom mentioned as she and Caralyn sat in the kitchen Saturday morning two days after Christmas. "Do you think it's time to tell him?"

"Do I have to?"

"He will want to know why you are spending a week in Oregon."

"I don't think I can, Mom. He will be so disappointed with me."

"Caralyn Ann Dawson! Do you think your father will stop loving you because you are growing up?"

"No, Mom, but will he understand?"

"He has old-fashioned ideas about some things, but I will make him understand."

Mom explained everything that night to her husband.

"A week in Oregon is a long time to be gone."

"Jim, have you forgotten she spent four months in France? She will be all right. She will be staying with her friend and his family."

He looked at Sarah for a moment and then sighed. "Okay. I guess she's not a little girl anymore, and I have to respect her desire to make her own way in the world. At least this Trent guy doesn't seem to be another Jeremiah."

"She is older and wiser."

Chapter Nineteen

Two days after New Year's Caralyn flew to Portland where Trent picked her up.

"Is this all you brought?" Trent asked taking her carry-on bag.

"I pack light. I learned from a friend."

He smiled and asked, "How was the flight?"

"Not bad, but I think the pilot got lost over the mountains. He would zigzag this way and that."

"Very funny, Cara." He kissed her cheek and opened the door.

"Will it take long to get to your parents' house?"

"Thirty minutes tops. They actually live in Dallas, but if I tell that to people they assume I mean Dallas, Texas. Dad's company is headquartered outside of Portland."

He pointed out some of the sites along the way. "A lot of people don't know the state capital is Salem."

"There's a Salem about fifty miles from Stockton Woods," Caralyn mentioned. "Trent, I'm kinda nervous about meeting your family. Have you told them much about me?"

"I told them you were very pretty and very good in bed."

She put a hand to her heart. "You didn't?"

"Sure. Why wouldn't I? You are good in bed." He kept a straight face the whole time.

Finally, she caught on to his joke. "You're so mean."

"Mom asked if we wanted to share a room."

"What did you tell her?"

"I told her I would let you decide. She knows we have been intimate, Cara."

"How does she know? Did you tell her?"

"Moms know things like that. She doesn't think less of you. I should warn you the whole family will get together for Sunday lunch. My sisters will check you out. They've always been rather protective of me since I'm the baby of the family. But you don't have to worry. They will love you."

"Do you love me, Trent?"

He grinned and answered, "Sure. Of course I do."

"I'm serious. We've never told each other that. Not in so many words. I tell my parents and Tucker that I love them all the time."

"I guess maybe we don't say that a lot in my family. We let our actions speak louder than our words."

She stared out the window and thought about his statement.

"This is it," Trent said pulling into a wide asphalt driveway. "Are you ready to meet Mom? Dad won't be home until ten or so."

"Is it too late to back out?" she asked getting out of the car.

"Too late now." He pointed to the front door. "There's Mom."

Caralyn took a deep breath and attempted to smile. *You never told me your mom wouldn't fit through the door.*

Trent retrieved her bag from the trunk and squeezed her hand. "Don't be nervous. Mom won't eat you."

She looks like she might. Caralyn thought as she noticed the snowman in the yard.

"Come inside, child, before you catch a cold," Mrs. Cussler said opening the door.

Caralyn walked inside and was immediately smothered by Trent's mother.

"Mom, this is Caralyn Dawson."

"I would know you anywhere. Trent has your picture on his desk." Mrs. Cussler continued to smother Caralyn.

"Thanks for letting me stay, Mrs. Cussler," Caralyn said as soon as she could breathe.

"You are welcome, and you have to call me Eileen. Everyone does."

"Okay," she said looking up at Trent.

"Oh, the bathroom's the first door on the right."

She walked into the bathroom, closed the door and her jaw dropped. "Wow! This is the pinkest room I've ever seen." She touched the ceramic tile. "The tile, the vanity top and even the tub and toilet are pink." She came out and saw Trent in the hall.

151

He grinned and said, "It's a little much, huh?"

"You could say that. Do you have to use it?"

"No, the bedrooms are upstairs and those bathrooms have been updated. I took the liberty of dropping your bag in my room, but you can always use one of the others."

"I'll decide later, okay?"

He nodded. "Mom doesn't cook Saturday nights, so we can go out or order something. There's a decent pizza place that delivers."

"Sounds good. I'd rather not go out in the cold again. I probably should have worn a heavier coat."

"I'd offer one of Mom's but it would obviously be too big."

Trent ordered pizza, and they ate in the family room with his parents and watched TV.

"Trent, you should make some popcorn," his mother said. "Add extra butter to my bowl."

"Do you need help?" Caralyn asked.

"Sure, I can show you the kitchen."

"It's not pink, is it?" she asked following him.

"Nope. It's yellow."

She stopped in the doorway and covered her eyes. "That's bright."

"I have a pair of shades if you need them."

She grinned and walked up to the island. "Is this granite?" she asked running her hand along the surface."

"Yes, and somehow the black granite reminds me of something."

She giggled and whispered, "A bumble bee maybe?"

He kissed her cheek and said, "If it's any consolation, Dad hates it."

Though she felt a bit uncomfortable about it, Caralyn decided to share a room with Trent. When he kissed her in bed that night, she didn't respond like she would normally.

"Could we not do anything tonight? It feels kinda awkward to be sharing a room with your parents across the hall."

152

"We can cuddle. My parents are used to it though."

"What do you mean? Have you had lots of girls share your room?" Caralyn asked as she scooted to the edge of the bed.

"Only Belinda has been here. You know that. But my brothers and sisters all lived together before they eventually married. My parents didn't mind them sharing a room when they visited."

"Dare I ask what color your parents' room is?"

He grinned and answered, "Peach. Dad threatened to move into the basement if Mom painted it pink or something."

"My sisters are on their way, Cara," Trent said shortly after noon. "They will grill you and make comparisons to people they know. Don't pay any attention to what they say."

"Okay, should I have an attorney present?"

He rubbed his jaw. "I could see if our neighbor's home. He's a judge."

She stared at him then said, "I want to go home."

"Too late. They're here. Oh, don't pay any attention to my nieces if they talk about my old girlfriends."

"Where is Trent Michael's new girlfriend," one of the sisters shouted upon entering. She saw Caralyn standing next to him. "There you are. I'm Rosalie. His favorite and that's Shelby."

"I'm really his favorite sister," Shelby said. She waddled across the room and pinched Trent's cheek. "He hates it when I do that. Are you enjoying our fine weather, honey?" She looked at Trent. "What is her name again? I forgot."

"It's Caralyn Dawson, and she can hear you, Shelby."

Caralyn turned her attention to the front door as three teenage girls entered followed by who she assumed to be their fathers.

"This is Uncle Trent's new girlfriend," Rosalie hollered to be heard above the racket. "Her name is Caroline, so be nice to her."

"It's Caralyn, actually," Trent said.

The girls glanced at her then ran down the hallway.

"So much for that," Trent said. "They are attached to their phones. At least they looked at you."

"Dinner will be ready in fifteen," Mrs. Cussler said. She pointed to her husband. "Albert, will you grab two chairs?"

He smiled at Caralyn and whispered as he passed, "Don't listen to anyone. I like you a lot, and Trent has finally brought home a keeper."

She grinned and tucked a curl behind her ear.

During dinner, Caralyn listened to the conversation which ranged from local politics to the price of real estate in a new subdivision in Dallas to the latest gossip about the local TV news anchor's latest affair.

Trent whispered, "They will eventually start eating."

Caralyn looked at the sisters. *They don't look like they have ever missed a meal.* She looked at Trent again. *How can you be related?* She glanced at Mr. Cussler. *Oh, you have your father's genes.*

After dinner Trent showed Caralyn his father's library.

"Your father has almost as many books as Uncle Carlton." She checked one shelf and turned to Trent. "Someone must like Derek Pitt books."

Trent pulled one off the shelf. "Grandpa wrote these. Didn't I ever tell you?"

She shook her head.

"He wrote several books, but he passed away last spring."

"I'm so sorry, Trent."

"How would you like to spend the rest of the day?"

"Will your mother and sisters allow us to escape?"

He replaced the book, grinned and whispered, "We can escape while they're gossiping and comparing you to my numerous other girlfriends."

"I thought you only had two before me."

"Yes, but they remember every girl I dated in high school."

"How do I compare?"

He looked up and down her body, shrugged, scratched his ear and said, "In the middle."

She slugged his arm and walked away.

He grabbed a belt loop of her jeans and stopped her. He turned her around and saw her grin. "You can be such a tease, Cara." He kissed her until she couldn't breathe.

Since Trent had to work Monday, Caralyn got to know his mother better. She helped make dinner and even had time to write.

"Did you and my mother get along," Trent asked that evening?

"We did. She is hilarious."

"I don't have to work until Thursday morning. I have to attend a mandatory meeting. Otherwise, I am all yours."

"Good. I want to see the city."

The first glitch occurred when Caralyn overheard his mother talking to the neighbor about how she favored Trent's former girlfriend, Belinda, over her.

Well, Mr. Cussler likes me. Should I ignore what she said, or should I mention it to Trent? Caralyn toyed with a lock of her hair. *I won't say anything for now.*

The second glitch happened after Friday's dinner when Trent asked her to move to Oregon when the school year ended. It was practically an ultimatum.

Caralyn faced him with hands in her jean pockets. "If I don't move to Oregon, are you going to get back together with Belinda? I know she works with you."

"She does work for Dad's company, but I almost never see her. She also happens to be married and is expecting a baby." Trent raised his voice for the first time ever with her.

"Oh, I didn't know that."

"There's something else I should tell you. This was only finalized last week. Dad bought a company in Alaska, and he asked me to run it for a year."

"How thrilling for you."

"I will have to live there. I thought if you were living here, I could at least see you once a month or so."

"I can't move to Alaska. I can't move to Oregon, either," Caralyn said. "I won't accept seeing you once a month."

That night she slept in her own room.

"I'm sorry I can't be what you want, Trent, but I can't abandon my family any more than you could yours," Caralyn said on the way to the airport. "Everything has changed. We still like each other, but you would never move to Stockton Woods, and I would never ask you to."

"I was wrong to ask. Maybe I can move," he said.

"You would never move to Chicago or New York which is where I will end up living." She paused and took a breath. "I really loved our time together, and I don't regret sleeping with you."

"I don't regret that, either," Trent said with a grin.

She poked his arm. "You're so bad. You just had to come to my room last night even though we both knew it was over."

"You didn't make me leave."

"No, but I shouldn't have let you do those things again."

"Are we still going to be friends? I know you thought sex would change that."

"It has changed things, but it hasn't ruined our friendship the way I thought it would. Who knows? Maybe I won't ever get married, and we can find a way to run into each other a couple of times a year."

"That would be nice, but I think you will find the perfect guy and get married. I think in ten years you will have three kids, two dogs, one cat and a white picket fence on a farm in upstate New York."

She grinned and said, "No cat, please."

Chapter Twenty

"How are things at Midwest Central?" Tucker asked over the phone. "Are you slacking off since it's your final semester?"

She slumped on her couch with her feet over the arm and sighed. "I wish. My classes aren't cupcakes like the ones you took. What was that one?" She tapped her chin. "Oh, yeah. The art of spinning a basketball on your finger while signing autographs for junior high wannabe teens."

He laughed and said, "I got an A+ in that one."

She rolled her eyes then asked, "Where should I get my masters? Chicago or New York?"

"I take it Oregon State is not a contender, huh?"

She chewed on her lip before answering, "It's over."

"I'm sorry, Carrie."

"Thanks. I really like Trent, but neither of us is willing to relocate. At least we are stills friends."

"If I have a vote, it would obviously be Chicago. Not that I want to see you, but New York's too far away."

"You're no help. I can't decide. Both cities have advantages. I talked to Richard and agreed to fly in for a weekend. He offered to show me around the city."

"He loves it there, but he complained about the cost of living."

"Yeah, he said something about hamburgers costing more than a whole cow in Stockton Woods."

"You know your way around Chicago, and Beth is here. Plus me as long as I don't get traded."

"You better not."

"Thanks, Carrie."

"What other team wants a skinny runt like you if they could have Jacob LeBron for a point guard."

"Let me know what happens when you visit Richard."

"He will probably tease me about moving in and having sex all the time."

"Richard, if I came here for school and we lived together, how would we handle it if you brought a girl home?" She knocked on the wall behind her. "The walls are so thin we can hear each other breathing. I don't want to listen to you having sex."

Richard raised his bushy eyebrows. "How do you mean that?"

"I know you are a sex magnet," she teased.

"That is my cross to bear," he replied. "Well, then maybe I won't bring home any girls since there will be one here already."

"Richard! I didn't mean to imply that you and I would become lovers."

"I didn't mean that's what would happen, Cara. I have been so busy that I haven't been on a date for three months, and I haven't brought a girl here for even longer."

"You poor baby. Such a sacrifice. How have you survived?"

"Okay, I deserve it. You were right about my fear of commitment."

Caralyn realized living with Richard would be more complicated than she wanted.

"I decided to come to Chicago to do my graduate work," she told Tucker when she landed at Midway.

He took her carry-on bag and rolled it behind him. "I'm glad to hear it. Nancy will be thrilled to have you close," Tucker said.

"How about you?"

"Chicago's a big city. I might never have to see you."

She made a face at him. "Same here, dweeb brain. Have you seen Richard's place?"

"No, but he described it to me. I could never live in a closet," he said with a chuckle. "How are you getting home?"

"There's this new invention called a train."

"You're a stinker. Call me sometime. There's a new invention called a telephone."

"Cara, we are so proud of you," Mom said after the graduation ceremony. "You are only twenty and already have a degree. Two degrees, right?"

Caralyn looked at Tucker and grinned. "Yes, journalism and foreign languages. That might not be as useful as a degree in throwing a round ball through an orange metal hoop since that pays so well, but I might be able to land a job as a fry cook at The Curve."

"Go ahead, Caralyn. Take your best shots," he grinned and added, "Best shots. Get it? Shots. Basketball."

She rolled her eyes. "I hope you get traded to Tokyo or somewhere."

"Well, Sarah, what are we going to do now? Both kids have college degrees," Dad McKay asked as they headed home.

Sarah answered, "I know I am going to retire in three more years. By that time we might have to start taking care of grandbabies."

"Tucker and Nancy might have a baby right away, but I don't think Caralyn will settle down that soon. She isn't even going out with anyone right now."

"No, but her relationship with Trent proved to her that she could find someone."

Dad shrugged. "I don't understand. I thought they were friends. Do you think she let him kiss her?"

"You're right, dear. She is still your innocent little girl."

He grinned. *I am a college professor and not totally clueless about love.*

Chapter Twenty-One

Caralyn and Mr. McKay checked the addresses as they walked along the cracked sidewalk.

"There's Beth," Caralyn hollered. She waved and hurried toward her sister.

Beth waved back. "I'm glad you found it. It's hard to find parking in this neighborhood."

"We parked a block over. Thanks for meeting us, and searching online for possible apartments. You know the city better than me," Caralyn said.

"No problem. Hello, Mr. McKay. How was the drive? Did Caralyn drive you nuts?"

"I'm not a pest anymore," Caralyn insisted.

"Smooth sailing. We didn't stop until we got into the city."

"We're staying with Tucker," Caralyn said. "He's got a nice place."

"Good." Beth looked at the commonplace building. "Well, this is the first apartment I thought would work for you. I feel like a real estate agent taking clients out to buy an apartment. This place is only two blocks from the bus. It might be too far to walk to school, but the neighborhood is decent. Changing, but safe."

They walked through the small one-bedroom apartment. Caralyn heard the patter of feet from the apartment above her.

"What do you think?" Beth asked.

"It's clean, but..." Caralyn said.

"Yeah, I agree. It's too small and the neighbors would be a distraction. That's all right. There are plenty of other apartments to see."

"I really like this place, Daddy. It's close to school, and I would feel safe here. We've checked out six units in different neighborhoods, but this is the best one."

"What about the rent? It's pretty steep."

"I'm going to have to rely on Beth until I turn twenty-one. But I will pay her back every penny."

160

"The landlord wants a cosigner."

"I could ask Beth. I don't want you to cosign for me."

Dad suggested, "Why don't you have Tucker cosign for you instead of Beth. The landlord might be more impressed since he already lives here."

"He won't want to help me out. I don't think he really wants me to live in the same building he does."

"He wouldn't have told you about the apartment if he felt that way. Let's ask him."

They walked outside and talked to him.

"You can tell me if you don't want me to live here, Tuck. I'll find another apartment somewhere."

"That's not it at all," he assured her. "I didn't think you would want to live this close to me and Nancy."

"It will be perfect since she wants to finish her degree in the city. Maybe she will be accepted into McCormick University. Will you cosign the lease for me?"

"Are you absolutely sure about this place?"

"It's the best apartment I've seen. The location is perfect. I suppose I'll have to adjust to the neighbors above me, but maybe the couple on my floor will be normal," she teased.

"Little stinker," he teased back. "Sure, why not?"

When the landlord realized his celebrity tenant, Tucker McKay of the Chicago Bulls, was her cosigner, he gladly accepted Caralyn. For once Caralyn didn't make a fuss about being too young to do something on her own.

"Caralyn, you need to keep in touch with Tucker so we know you are all right," Dad insisted.

"I will, Daddy. I will pester him all the time." She smiled at Tucker and stuck out her tongue.

"Can I shoot her?" Tucker asked. "This is Chicago."

"You have to put up with me until I can bring what little furniture I own to Chicago. Now I see the disadvantage of living in a furnished apartment."

"Are you going to borrow the van?" Tucker asked.

"Since basketball season's over, will you help me move out of my apartment?" She put her hands together to ask. "I'll bake you a cake if you do."

Tucker grinned at his father. "What do you think, Dad? Should I eat a cake she makes?"

Dad shrugged and said, "That's entirely up to you, son. At least there are plenty of good hospitals in the city."

"Forget it, Tuck! I'll load everything in the Civic and make a dozen trips."

Dad listened to them bickering in a good-natured way.

Tucker looked at her and groaned. "Why did I even mention this apartment to you, Carrie?"

"Because you love me, and will love having me live right below you. We will have so much fun together. I can't wait to tell Nancy. She can spend weekends with me and not you." Caralyn realized maybe she shouldn't have said that, but it was too late. "Oh, Daddy. It's okay. They are engaged."

"I didn't hear anything." Mr. McKay coughed and looked down the alley. "I'm still not used to you being all grown up." He held out his arms. "Give me a hug, so I can head home. I want to be out of Chicago before rush hour. Let me know when you need the van. I will meet you in New Lebanon."

"I want to move in as soon as possible," she said. "That way I don't have to sleep in his spare bedroom. He found the mattress in the alley and is too cheap to buy a new one."

Tucker shook his head and muttered, "She's got quite an imagination. Could you do me a huge favor and take her back to Stockton Woods?"

Dad patted Tucker's back and said, "Sorry, son, but she's living in the city now. Deal with it."

"I'm so glad to see you." Caralyn stepped aside to allow Nancy and Tucker inside. "Welcome to my humble abode."

Nancy noticed the peach-colored walls and brown leather couch. "It's different than Tucker's apartment even though it's probably the same size."

162

"The basic floor plan is the same, but I don't have a porch like his." She grinned at Tucker. "He has to let me use his if I want to grill out or work on my tan."

"Where did you find the couch and the end tables?"

"Ray and Beth took me shopping. I know the styles clash, but I was more concerned about price."

"How is your sister doing? They don't live too far away, do they?" Nancy asked as she looked into the bedrooms, bathroom and stopped in the kitchen. "I like the openness."

"Ray's photography business is flourishing, and Beth works at Premier Talent. That's a booking agency for models. They still live in a condo in Wrightsville and are even talking about getting married in a year or two."

Tucker snorted. "I can't see Ray getting married."

"He would if Beth wants a baby," Caralyn replied. "Beth can't wait much longer."

"How are the neighbors?" Nancy asked. She opened the cabinets, ran a hand along the surface then opened the fridge. "Is that a bottle of wine?"

"Beth bought it as a housewarming gift." Caralyn sat on one of the wooden barstools. "Tucker introduced me to them. They're from Iran and have a young son. I rarely seen them and never hear a peep from their place."

"Do you have a favorite restaurant already?"

Tucker plopped onto the couch and answered, "I took her to Tito's Casa. She loved it and wants to eat there all the time."

"It's a great neighborhood for restaurants. There are so many choices within walking distance."

Nancy joined Tucker on the couch and Caralyn swiveled on her stool to face them. "I haven't use my car for a week. It's been in the garage the whole time."

"We're fortunate to have a garage," Tucker said. "It means we don't have a yard, but I wouldn't have time for a yard anyway."

"Where do you do the grocery shopping?" Nancy asked. "There aren't any supermarkets in the area."

"There's a mom and pop style store on the corner."

"That's convenient."

"It's really limited, but the owners cater to the locals. It's great. They already know my name, and the wife treats me like a daughter. She suggests recipes and give me tips for cooking. Tuck and I shop together most of the time. He doesn't want me walking by myself because he thinks I'm a baby."

"It's a safe neighborhood, but you still need to use common sense. It is Chicago and not Stockton Woods," Tucker said.

"Have you heard from any Chicago colleges?" Caralyn asked. "You cannot spend one more year at Southern Wesleyan."

Nancy crossed her fingers and said, "I haven't heard back, but I think I have a good chance of being accepted to McCormick University."

"Nancy, that would be perfect. You could live here with me, and we could walk to school together. I'm sure Tucker wouldn't mind having you so close either."

"Caralyn, you do realize after Tucker and I get married, I will be living with him, right?"

"Oh right, I almost forgot about that. Are you sure you want to live with him? He can be a slob at times."

"I know, but I still think we will live in the same apartment," Nancy said. "We might even share a bedroom."

"Well, at least we will be in the same building."

Nancy jumped up, pulled Caralyn off the barstool, hugged her and told her, "Sometimes you can be so goofy, Cara, but I love you even more because of it. I feel closer to you than Sandy, and you know how much I love Sandy."

Caralyn was quiet for a moment.

"What are you thinking?"

"I was thinking if the McKays adopted me when I was little then we would be sisters when you and Tucker get married."

"We can pretend we are sisters-in-law. I don't think anyone will care."

Caralyn bounced on her toes. "This is going to be so much fun. I can't wait for school to start. It will be like we are finally college roommates."

"Cara, you never told me any details about your trip to Oregon. Tuck said you and Trent broke up, but... why? What happened?" Nancy asked. She looked at Tucker. "Cover your ears. This is girl talk."

"I'm going home. You can gossip all you want."

The girls waited until he left the apartment.

"He wanted me to drop my life here and move out there. I couldn't do that, and he couldn't move back here."

"Why did he ever go to college here and not in Oregon if his whole family is there?"

"His grandfather graduated from Midwest Central and paid for Trent to attend. I think there might be more to the story, but that's all he ever told me. Oh, his grandfather was a famous author. I didn't know until I saw his books in Trent's father's library."

Nancy grinned sheepishly.

"What is it?" Caralyn asked. "I know that look. You want to ask something personal."

"Did you guys ever take that final step?"

Caralyn grinned and nodded. "At Homecoming last fall."

"Didn't the McKays come up for Homecoming?"

"Yes, but Trent stayed with a friend that night. Mom knew, but Daddy didn't think we were more than good friends."

"Fathers can be so clueless and old-fashioned at times." Nancy rolled her eyes, but then wanted to know more. "So how was it?"

"Are you asking how he compared to Tuck? You know it was awful with Jeremiah."

"I thought you never wanted to use or hear his name again."

Caralyn waved a hand then shrugged. "Oh, I'm over it. I don't think about him often, and I don't gag every time I hear his name anymore."

"So tell me," Nancy giggled and her eyes blazed with excitement.

"Trent was very considerate..."

"Caralyn! Tell me!"

165

"He really rocked me. Tuck was amazing and incredibly tender, but we were both virgins. We kinda learned as we did it. You know we haven't..."

"I know. Tuck always makes sure I know you guys still love each other, but you don't... you know."

"Trent had a lot more experience. He and Belinda were together for a year. I feel like there is so much more to learn."

"Tuck is... maybe I shouldn't tell you. You might tease him."

"I tease him about his sex life anyway. Go ahead. I want to know all the juicy details."

"Originally, he was totally conservative. He liked to be on top all the time."

Caralyn chuckled. "Yeah, he was like that with me, too."

"Now he is more willing to experiment," Nancy said then blushed.

"Did you have oral sex?" Caralyn's eyes opened wide. "We were always too chicken to try that."

"He did, but it was under the covers and dark. He... he... needs more practice," Nancy admitted.

"Beth told me a lot of guys aren't very good at it. Trent knew what to do though. The last night we were together at his parents' house he gave me such an intense orgasm. I think his parents heard me. I was so embarrassed to face them the next morning."

"I would die if Dad McKay, or my Daddy, heard me having an orgasm."

"I think Dad finally realizes I'm not a virgin, but he won't ever talk about it. He's always going to think of me as a baby."

"Fathers." They both sighed and then giggled.

Chapter Twenty-Two

"I don't like that one, Nancy. Sorry, but green doesn't work for you. It doesn't fit your brown eyes or your skin tone." Caralyn checked out the latest dress Nancy was trying on. "Are you surprised Natalie didn't ask either one of us to be in the wedding?"

"Not really." Nancy smoothed out the front of the dress. "She's best friends with Connie. They roomed together so I figured she would be the maid of honor. Are you sure about the color?"

Caralyn nodded.

"Too bad. It fits perfectly. Do you know either of her other friends from college?"

"I can't recall ever meeting them." Caralyn picked another dress for Nancy to try. "This one is a better color for you."

"I'm glad Derren chose Tucker to be his best man rather than David," Nancy said as Caralyn waited outside the dressing room. "I know you like Davey, but he and I have never gotten along."

"That's because he made a pass at you. He used to try that with me, but I knew how to handle him."

"You and Davey are the same age, right?" Nancy asked as she zipped up the new dress.

"He's three months older. You know Davey and Richard are the groomsmen, right? You might have to dance with him."

"No way! I'm not going to let him grope me like you do."

"I do not," Caralyn insisted but then giggled. "We tease each other. Not as much as when we were in high school though. Hurry up. I want to see that dress and then I want to show you one I like."

After trying on several dresses, they each found one they liked.

"Tucker will like this. It's shorter than what I would have worn before." She looked at Caralyn's dress. "My father would get after me if I wore a dress that short," Nancy lamented. "He would make me wear a sweater so no one could see my cleavage. Won't Mr. McKay get after you?"

"I might not let him see this one until the day of the wedding. Then he won't be able to complain."

"Make sure you don't lean over too much."

Caralyn grinned and said, "I'll be wearing a bra, Nancy. No one will see me."

"Would you be willing to help with the guest book?" Natalie asked Caralyn and Nancy at the rehearsal. "I'm sorry for the late notice, but the girls who were supposed to take care of it aren't going to be here. I'm so mad at them."

"We don't mind helping, Natty." Caralyn used a nickname she knew Natalie's mother used. Caralyn also knew how much Natalie despised the nickname. "It will give us something to do since we will be there anyway."

"They walked out because Mother told them how to make sure everyone signed the guestbook." Natalie sighed, looked at her mother and whispered, "I would elope if I could. She is driving me to a nervous breakdown. Derren tunes her out and won't get involved. He avoids talking to her now."

Richard listened to Mrs. Bledsoe, nudged Tucker and asked, "Why is Natalie's mother such a control freak? If she were my future mother-in-law, I would join a monastery, but it doesn't seem to faze Derren."

"He's known her long enough to tune her out. Please don't say anything about her."

"I won't, but it's kinda funny." He laughed as Mrs. Bledsoe instructed one of the bridesmaids how to stand. "I'm never getting married."

"Natalie, would you introduce your friends to the guys, please?" Derren asked.

"I'm sorry. I wasn't thinking." She introduced her friends and Derren introduced the guys.

Richard smiled and offered a hand to Natalie's blonde roommate. "It's a pleasure to meet you, Connie. It's a shame your football team didn't win a game last year." He flirted with the ladies until Natalie's mother insisted they begin the rehearsal.

Richard did an about-face and found Caralyn staring at him with her hands on her hips. "Do you have to flirt with every female you meet?"

He threw his hands in the air and said, "I was only trying to break the ice. Natalie's bridesmaids are snobs. Attractive ones though."

"Just remember who you came to the rehearsal with, blockhead." She put a hand to his chest.

"Who?"

She smacked his arm. "Me!"

He smirked and whispered, "Are you asking to spend the night with me?"

"In your dreams, bucko." She turned and walked away.

Derren chose to have the rehearsal dinner at Tony's Pizza in Butler because they had a private room.

"Richard, eat as much as you want," Caralyn said. "It's free pizza."

"It's not free," Tucker said. "Uncle Carlton is paying for every slice you eat."

"I've already eaten four slices, and Natalie is still nibbling on her first." Caralyn pointed at her. "Poor Derry. Mrs. Bledsoe is trying to rearrange the chunks of pepperoni on his slice."

Nancy whispered, "I heard Natalie complaining of a nervous stomach to Connie. I can see why. Her mother would drive my mom to violence."

Caralyn laughed. "Your mom is the sweetest person I know. She wouldn't step on a bug."

Because Natalie had introduced Tucker and Caralyn to her bridesmaids as Derren's cousins, the ladies thought Tucker and Caralyn were brother and sister.

Caralyn looked at Tucker. "Do you want to tell them we aren't related, or should I?"

He sighed and shook his head. "I'm tired of explaining it, Cara. I wouldn't bother since we'll never seen them after tomorrow."

169

"I heard one of them say Richard and I looked good as a couple."

"A couple what?" Tucker teased.

"Keep it up, buddy. You are getting married soon, and I might embarrass you."

"How? You going to wear sneakers?"

"I'll think of something."

The Bledsoe family had been members of the Butler Lutheran church for many years, so Natalie's mother insisted the ceremony be held there. Derren and Natalie decided to take pictures beforehand as much as possible. The ceremony started at two, and Caralyn and Nancy didn't need to be there until 1:30. After the ceremony, Mrs. Bledsoe insisted on more pictures of the wedding party.

"Nancy, let's go home. The reception isn't until six and I don't want to listen to Natalie's mom all afternoon."

"I'm with you, Cara. I feel sorry for Natalie. Her mother's antagonizing everyone."

"I wonder how much she paid the wedding planner?"

"Don't know, but Mr. Bledsoe is on the board of the Butler Country Club, so he probably can afford it."

"Did Derren have a choice of where to have the reception?"

"Are you kidding?" Nancy laughed. "I doubt if she let him choose his boxers for today."

Caralyn grinned and asked, "How do you know he wears boxers?"

Nancy poked Caralyn's arm. "I don't, but I… never mind. Let's get out of here before she tries to show us how to redo our nails."

Natalie's family kept the two bartenders busy as they took advantage of the open bar. After the meal, the speeches and everything else that happened at wedding receptions were finally finished, the DJ started the dance music.

170

"Richard, you have to dance with me," Caralyn pulled him onto the dance floor.

"Okay, you don't need to yank my arm out of the socket."

"Did you hear Mrs. Bledsoe telling the bartenders how to make a martini?"

"I heard her talking to Derren's mom about how much they were spending on the reception."

"I don't think Grandma and Grandpa Stanfield are having any fun. Grandpa is sitting with his arms over his chest and Grandma keeps putting her hands on her ears."

"It is loud in here," Richard said putting his hands on her waist. "Have you always been this skinny?"

"Maybe. Why?"

"If my hands were as large as Tucker's, I could stretch them all the way around you."

"Is that supposed to be a compliment?"

He shrugged. "It's just a fact."

"Make sure your hands stay there, bucko."

Few of Derren's family danced except for Mom and Dad McKay. They enjoyed dancing to the slow songs. The people from Natalie's family were drinking, dancing and talking loudly.

"I'm going to have another beer," Richard said. "Would you like one, Cara?"

"I can't with Dad here. He might not care if I have some champagne though."

"I'll sneak some over for you. You can tell him you thought it was 7-Up."

Derren's brother, David, didn't dance except for the time the whole wedding party danced as a group. At least until Caralyn dragged him to the floor.

"Come on, Davey. You can dance with me. I won't bite."

"Cara, I don't know how to dance."

"It doesn't matter. All you have to do is hold me close like we're wrestling and move your feet a bit." She grinned to ease his embarrassment. "You can look down my dress all you want. You can't see anything."

171

At first he held her awkwardly, but she got him to relax and he ended up enjoying it so much he asked her to dance again later.

"Can we try it again, Cara? I kinda liked the last one."

"Sure, but this time try not to squeeze me so tight. I could barely breath before."

He smiled at her as they danced at the edge of the crowd.

"This isn't so bad, is it?" Caralyn asked.

"I need the practice. I may have to dance again pretty soon."

"Why is that?" She twirled and he bumped into her and stepped on her foot.

"Melissa and I may get married sooner than we planned," he admitted.

"What have you been doing?" Caralyn asked as she moved closer to him.

"Nothing you need to know about. She needs to finish college first," he answered. "You're dancing pretty close to me, Cara."

"Oh, was I? I'm sorry." She put her arms around his neck and pressed into him.

"Stop it. You're teasing me."

"That's what dancing is for. If Melissa was here, would you let her dance this close?"

"That's different. She's not my cousin," he said trying to back up.

"We're second cousins if you want to get technical."

Tucker and Richard took turns dancing with Nancy and Caralyn.

"Tucker, do you know where they are spending the night?" Caralyn asked as they danced later.

"I told you I know, but I've been sworn to secrecy."

"I promise I won't say a word to a soul."

"Carrie, I can't."

"I'll tell Mom you and Nancy were fooling around."

"I'm not giving in to blackmail."

"Fine, be that way."

172

Finally, the DJ announced the final song. Caralyn pulled Tucker onto the dance floor.

"What time did Mom and Dad leave? I didn't see them go."

"They left an hour ago with Derren's parents."

They both glanced to the right as they heard a loud crash.

Caralyn laughed. "That's one of Natalie's uncles. He fell off his chair. What a drunk! They're so opposite of Derren's family."

Tucker laughed. "I hope Derren can put up with them."

The song ended and Tucker looked for Nancy. "I'm going to take Nancy home. Do you want to ride with us? I'll probably hang out at her house for a while."

Caralyn spotted Richard. "Do you mind if I pass? I think I'll see if Richard wants to do something."

Tucker frowned.

"Not that!" Caralyn grinned.

"Sorry. I should know better. I'll see you in the morning."

Richard walked up behind Caralyn and put his hands on her shoulders. "Are you ready to leave? I can give you a ride."

"I'm not ready to go home. Do you mind if we stop at Uncle Alton's shed?"

"I'm not sure what that is, but I'll stop. I'm not ready to call it a night, either."

"Nancy, are you ready to go?" Tucker asked. "I said goodbye to Derren."

"I'm ready. Can you stay? Sandy and Lloyd are back from their honeymoon, and I want to talk to her."

"Will your parents be up?"

"Maybe. Why?"

He shrugged.

"Tucker McKay! We are getting married in three weeks. You can't let Daddy intimidate you. He likes you and Mom loves you."

"I'm not afraid of your father, but he won't let me sit by you when I come over."

Nancy grinned. "That's because he wants you to wait until we are married."

Chapter Twenty-Three

Caralyn directed Richard to Uncle Alton's old shed. They sat on the edge of the roof and gazed at the twinkling lights.

"I've always liked coming here at night. You can see so many stars." Caralyn leaned back and used her hands for balance.

"Did I mention I grabbed a bottle of a particularly fine Merlot from the reception?"

"Did you bring any glasses?"

"I brought two plastic glasses with me, and I happen to have a corkscrew in the car. I might be persuaded to share if you're interested."

"And what would I have to do in order to share this wine?"

"I would need a kiss at the very least," he said while grinning.

"It seems like you have planned this pretty well, Rickey." She called him by his nickname, which she recently learned his sisters called him. "Do you always have a corkscrew in the car?"

"No, I stole it, too. I admit I did plan to try to get you alone tonight. I hoped to get you drunk and make a pass at you. Hopefully, you will be too drunk to realize what you are doing, and we can make love under the stars."

"Did you bring a blanket?"

"There happen to be a couple of them in the trunk. My father keeps them there because of the harsh winters in Chicago. I checked to make sure they were still there before I drove down."

"You have been a devious boy, haven't you?"

"You know I was kidding about getting you drunk, right?"

"Oh, too bad. I was hoping to get plastered so you could ravage my body," she teased. "It's been so long since I've enjoyed a decent ravage."

He looked at her trying to decide if she was serious.

"Well? Are you going to get the wine and blankets, or do I have to?"

"I'll do it, Cara."

"Thanks, Rickey."

"You can sit here and watch the stars." He brought the wine and blankets back with him and also a jacket in case she might get cold. "Do you want to stay here, Cara, or should we move to the ground which might be softer?"

"We can stay here for the time being."

Richard opened the wine and filled the glasses for them while Caralyn arranged the blankets on the sloping tin roof. He made a toast to the night sky, and they began drinking the red wine.

"Richard, you know I won't have sex with you, don't you?"

"I know, Cara, but we can kiss a little bit. I won't try to undress you unless you insist."

"You should have brought another bottle if you expect to accomplish that."

She knew this bottle was more than enough to get her drunk if she drank much of it. Richard also knew it. They moved close to each other.

"Tell me about the first time you had sex, Rickey."

"Well, I was ten and..."

"Tell me the truth, Richard, or else I won't let you kiss me."

"All right. I was thirteen."

Caralyn looked at him still not sure if he was telling the truth.

"Okay, I was eighteen and a senior in high school. Her name was Tessa Rodriguez and we went to prom together. The next day we drove to the sand dunes in Indiana, and on the way home we stopped at a park and did it. It was over in a couple of minutes, and that was the only time we were together. Are you going to tell me about your first time?"

"You know my first time was with Tuck the weekend you and Derren were gone."

"What about details?"

"I'm not giving you all the details, but I will tell you it lasted more than a couple minutes, and we... let me say it was rather comical because we were so nervous." She smiled as she shared these intimate details. "It took a few minutes to get it right."

"TMI. Can I kiss you now, Cara?"

"As long as you don't try to stick your tongue down my throat."

He turned to kiss her as she turned toward him. They shared a kiss that lasted longer than Richard anticipated. Caralyn allowed him to kiss her again. They stopped and she began asking about his girlfriends again.

"Which one was the best lover, Richard? Do you even remember?"

"I remember all right. It was Lonnie without a doubt."

"Which one was she?"

"She was part Chinese and part Venezuelan."

"I remember her now. She was kinda short with long black hair and a great smile. She's the one you insisted you never took on a date. You claimed she only wanted to have sex and not be bothered by all the other stuff."

He nodded. "She was very flexible, too."

"Did you guys do it in a lot of different positions?"

"More ways than I can remember, Cara. We were lovers for a year before she left for California. She was born there and ended up graduating from Stanford. We still keep in touch by email."

She had another glass of wine and told Richard, "I haven't done it in many different ways. Just the normal ones I guess."

Richard looked at her and asked, "Do you want me to show you some of the ways Lonnie and I did it?"

"I'll pass."

After they finished the bottle of wine, Caralyn took Richard by the hand, and they walked over the hill to the small lake.

"Are you a good swimmer, Richard?"

"Pretty good. Why?"

Caralyn looked at the lake and then at Richard.

"Are you thinking what I think you are?"

"It might be cold."

"I'm willing to if you are, Cara."

"You aren't too drunk to swim are you?"

"Maybe."

176

"Too bad. Maybe another night." She did an about-face and headed to the car.

"Wait." He chased after her. "Are you saying you would go swimming in your... you know... naked?"

"No! I haven't gone swimming here for years." She stopped, pivoted and faced the lake. "Tucker and I used to swim here a lot when we were kids. Mom and Dad would bring us out here and watch us. I wasn't allowed to swim here by myself. Tucker wasn't supposed to either now that I think about it. Dad was always worried something might happen to us like it did to his friend."

"What happened, Cara?"

"One of Daddy's friends drowned while swimming alone. Not here, but in a lake close to where he lived. His name was Tucker Anderson. That's who Tuck is named after."

"It must have happened a long time ago."

"Yeah, I can't remember how long ago, but I think Daddy was still in high school."

Richard looked at her.

"Stop leering at me. We are not swimming naked."

"I would probably drown. I should take you home. It's getting late."

They gathered the blankets, the empty wine bottle and tossed them in the trunk. Then he drove back into town.

"Thanks for showing me the lake. Maybe we can hang out there again," Richard said. He kissed her cheek and walked across the yard to Grandma's house.

She fell into bed and was out in five minutes.

She woke up and rubbed her temples. *I must have drank more wine than I thought. If this is how it feels to have a hangover, I never want to drink again.* She walked into the kitchen where Tucker and Richard sat at the table eating cold cereal.

"About time you got up, sleepyhead."

She plopped onto a chair. "What time is it?"

"Ten thirty."

177

"I feel like crap." She put her hands and head on the table and closed her eyes.

"You look like crap. How late were you out?"

"I don't remember exactly. I know it was really late though."

Tucker looked at Richard. "Where did you guys go after you left the reception?"

"To Uncle Alton's shed," Richard answered.

"What were you doing out there?"

Caralyn lifted her head and rubbed her temples. "Richard brought a bottle of wine with him from the reception, and we drank that."

Richard told Tucker, "Actually, I drank most of it. Caralyn only had a little bit."

"It was enough to give her a hangover. Did you go by the lake?"

Caralyn blushed and was embarrassed by the question, and Tucker could tell.

"You did. Why are you blushing, Cara?" He waited for an answer and when she didn't he knew. "You went skinny dipping."

"No! I thought about it for a second, but we didn't go swimming at all."

Tucker didn't know if he should be angry or happy for her. He didn't say anything for a moment.

"It really doesn't matter, Cara."

Chapter Twenty-Four

"You will love living in Holland Park. I've told you about the restaurants and shops within walking distance." Caralyn took Nancy on a tour like Tucker had taken her. "I'm glad you're staying with me for the week."

"I wanted to get used to the area before I moved in for good."

"I'm glad there's three weeks between your wedding and Derren's. I need the time to recover," Caralyn said.

"Tuck told me you and Richard drank a whole bottle of wine that night. You won't be mad at him for telling me, will you?"

"Of course not. Don't tell Mom and Dad. They might get upset with me, and Richard drank most of it."

Nancy blurted out, "I want to go skinny dipping with Tuck someday, but I couldn't do that with anyone else around."

"Could I go with you?" Caralyn asked with a giggle.

Nancy blushed then said, "I suppose you could, but no other guys. "Oh! Did I tell you I heard from the university?"

"No. You didn't tell me." Caralyn grabbed Nancy's arm. "Please tell me you got accepted."

Nancy grinned. "I did!"

"That will be so awesome. We haven't been together since high school."

Nancy bounced on her toes. "Just think, Cara. In two weeks I will be Mrs. Tucker McKay."

"I'm so happy for you guys," Caralyn said tugging at her earring.

With the ceremony only four days away now, Tucker and Caralyn headed home to help with the final arrangements.

"Do you remember the time we were going home and... you know?" Caralyn asked as they passed the exit to New Lebanon.

"Could you be a little more specific? We journeyed home a hundred times or more."

"If I said 'organizer,' would that help?"

He nodded and glanced over his shoulder to switch lanes to pass a truck. "I remember. Why?"

"I was trying to act so mature. Then you teased me about my underwear."

"Pink polka dots or something, right?"

"I think so. You swore that's what I was wearing because it was in my organizer."

He laughed and said, "And you showed me I was wrong."

"I did, but what I remember most was you got me to laugh at myself."

"I knew the old Carrie was still alive deep inside."

She squeezed his arm. "I guess that's one of the good memories from that time."

Tucker's cell phone rang.

"Should I get that since you're driving?"

"Sure. Who is it?"

She looked. "It's Nancy."

Tucker nodded and Caralyn answered.

"Where are you guys?" Nancy asked.

"About two hours out, I guess. Are you calling because you miss him?"

"I haven't seen him for a week," Nancy answered.

"It's Tuesday. Do you think you can hold out until Saturday to 'see' him." Caralyn used air quotes.

"It's not that."

"Yeah, right. How are the details coming along?"

"Everything is set. The flowers are finally figured out. They will be delivered Saturday morning."

"Speaking of Saturday, are you still not going to see Tuck until the ceremony?"

"That's how I want it. Do you think that's old-fashioned?"

"I wouldn't want to see him either if I was marrying him," she teased.

Tucker ignored her.

"But it's your decision, Nancy."

"I'm glad we decided to keep it simple. Only three girls and three guys in the wedding party," Nancy said. "The church will be packed as it is."

"It's a good thing Derren's back from his honeymoon."

"Cara, are you disappointed I chose Sandy to be my maid of honor?"

"She's your sister."

"Matron of honor," Tucker said.

"What?" Caralyn asked.

"She's married, so it's matron of honor."

"Whatever." Caralyn rolled her eyes. "I'm happy to be a bridesmaid, Nancy. Can I call you when we get home?"

"Tell Tucker Mom's making his favorite dinner."

"I will."

Caralyn interrupted the rehearsal Friday evening by continually teasing Tucker.

Tucker asked Derren, "Can you do something? Tie her up. Lock her in a closet. I don't care. Just make her behave."

"How am I suppose to make her behave?"

"I'll make her behave," Richard said. He walked up to Caralyn and whispered, "If you don't behave, I'm going to tell your father about the speeding ticket you got, and how you tried to flirt your way out of it."

"Fine! I'm ready to be serious," she said to Tucker. She frowned at Richard. "It was your fault. You were... never mind."

Tucker chose Tony's Pizza for the rehearsal dinner, but this time no alcohol was served.

"Hey, Tuck. Natalie and I are going to head home," Derren said. "I know it's early, but she wants to get home. We'll see you in the morning."

"See you later," Tucker waved.

Caralyn stood beside him as Derren and Natalie left. "Is it just me, or does Natty try to control everything he does? I get the feeling she doesn't want him to hang out with us anymore."

"You're right. Nothing we can do about it," Tucker said.

"It's still early, and I'm too wound up to sleep," Caralyn said. "Let's go to Uncle Alton's lake."

Tucker and Richard gave her dirty looks.

"We can talk. I wasn't suggesting we go swimming."

"I like to swim," Nancy said.

"Not the way Caralyn goes swimming," Tucker replied.

"Oh, right." Nancy blushed. "I'm not going skinny dipping the night before my wedding with another man along."

Caralyn asked, "Are you saying you would go skinny dipping if it was only Tucker and me?"

"Yeah, I can't get naked in front of Richard."

"Richard, you need to make yourself scarce," Caralyn said.

"Why?" Richard asked. "It won't bother me if you and Nancy go swimming."

"Nancy, I didn't get naked in front of Richard. We didn't go swimming. We drank some wine. Didn't I tell you this before?"

"Right. You did tell me. Sorry, I was thinking about being naked."

"Well, are we going to the lake or not?" Tucker wanted to know since he was driving. "Nancy, what do you want to do?"

"Let's drive to the lake, but no swimming. Okay? No skinny dipping tonight, Cara."

"I guess you and Richard will have to wait until tomorrow night," Tucker teased.

"I'm going to smack you so hard, Tuck. You won't be able to have sex for a month. Sorry, Nancy, but you will have to wait before you have sex."

They got to the lake and found something new.

"Hey. Where did this picnic table come from? It wasn't here last week."

"I don't know. Maybe Uncle Alton put it here. It is his property you know. He talked about adding a boat dock soon."

"Too bad we don't have anything to drink."

"Who says we don't? I stashed some pop and water in the trunk beforehand," Richard said.

"Do you happen to have a blanket in there, too, Rickey?" Caralyn asked. "Or some bug spray. They are thick tonight, and we're wearing shorts. I don't want my legs to look horrible." She swatted a mosquito on her calf. "I'm getting attacked."

"It so happens that I do. Not the bug spray though."

"You are a wicked boy."

"If I was really wicked, I would have brought two blankets and a six pack of beer."

They sat on the picnic table and drank the pop and water. Tucker and Nancy talked quietly to each other. Richard and Caralyn decided to take a walk around the lake.

"We aren't going to do anything. You don't have to leave us alone," Tucker said.

"Maybe we want to make love, and we don't want you two to watch," Caralyn teased him. She took Richard's hand and they set off on their walk. Soon they were out of sight.

"Cara, why did you tell Tucker we were going to make love?" He stopped, took off a sandal and shook it. "I had a rock in it."

"I wanted to tease him. You know we can't do that."

He shrugged. "I figured, but I wanted to double check."

She lightly punched his arm.

"Do you want to go skinny dipping tomorrow night, Cara?"

"We did have fun the night of Derren's wedding."

"That doesn't answer my question."

"Richard, you know I love you like a brother. No wait, I love you as a friend. I would never do what I have done with you with a brother. Am I making any sense?"

"None whatsoever. I think we should come back here tomorrow night and bring a couple of sleeping bags and some beer or maybe a bottle of wine. Maybe some cheese and crackers. We could have a nighttime picnic and sleep under the stars. After we go skinny dipping of course, and tomorrow night I will not be a gentleman. I will undress you myself if I have to so I can see you naked. I mean totally naked. Then we can share a sleeping bag and make love until the sun comes up."

183

Caralyn looked at him then extended her middle finger.

"Or maybe not. We could play it by ear and see what happens."

Caralyn smiled at him. "You are never going to quit trying, are you, Richard?"

"I don't suppose I will, but you know I have never given it a hundred percent effort."

Soon they were back at the picnic table but didn't see Tucker or Nancy.

"Where do you suppose they are?" Caralyn asked.

"Maybe they went swimming."

"I don't think Nancy would do that with us around."

"Well, then where are they?" Richard asked.

"Maybe Nancy got cold, and they hightailed it to the car. I'll look. You stay here and keep looking for them." Caralyn checked the car, but they weren't there. She came back to the picnic table.

She and Richard sat down to wait, and, in a couple of minutes, Tucker and Nancy reappeared.

"Where were you guys? I was starting to get worried."

"Nancy had to use the bathroom."

"Where? There aren't any bathrooms out here," Richard said.

"Sure there are. They are all around you," Caralyn said waving her arms.

He looked puzzled.

"The trees, dweeb brain. Haven't you ever taken a leak outdoors?" Caralyn jumped down and pointed to the trees.

"Never. I grew up in the city, remember? We have indoor plumbing and everything. Besides how can Nancy use a tree. She's a girl."

"You are such a city boy. Girls can pee outdoors like guys do. We just drop our shorts and underwear and squat. Should I show you?"

"Will you stop talking about peeing and behave?" Tucker scolded. He and Nancy sat on the table. "Are you getting chilled?"

"A little," she admitted.

Tucker wrapped the blanket around her shoulders.

They were quiet for a time until Richard announced, "All right I need to take a leak." He got up.

Caralyn asked, "Do you need help finding a bathroom, city boy?"

"I think I can find one by myself, Daisy Mae."

Caralyn watched him as he walked up to a tree. "Not that one!" she shouted.

"Why not? What does it matter which tree I use?"

"That's an elm tree, and they are poisonous. If you piss on it, it will send a toxin up the stream into your thing. You will get a urinary tract infection and won't be able to get an erection for a month," Caralyn said with a straight face.

He looked at the tree then back at Caralyn. "Tucker, is she yanking my chain, or is she telling the truth? I don't want to take a chance."

Tucker shrugged.

"Caralyn, are you getting back at me for threatening you earlier?"

"No, I'm concerned about your health."

Richard didn't know what to do, but he moved to another tree. He emptied his bladder and came back. He stood in front of Caralyn. She couldn't keep a straight face any longer.

"I was kidding about the tree."

"You brat. I'm going to toss you in the lake for that."

"Try it, city boy, and you will die a slow painful death."

Richard grabbed her and slung her over his shoulder.

She cried out, "Tucker, stop him. He's going to throw me in the lake."

"Sounds like a good idea to me." Tucker and Nancy were both laughing as Richard carried her along the bank.

"Richard, if you throw me in the lake, I swear to God I will never speak to you again."

"I'm not going to throw you in the lake, Cara."

"Good."

185

"I'm going to heave you into the lake because you are so big and fat."

He tossed her into the lake. She screamed as she hit the water. He lost his balance and fell in after her. She stood up, spit out some lake water then started swearing like a sailor.

"If I don't stop laughing, I'm going to cry," Nancy said as she and Tucker stood at the edge of the shallow end of the lake listening.

Soon Caralyn stopped swearing and started laughing. "The water actually feels good."

She faced Richard and splashed him.

"Hey! Watch it." He moved behind her, grabbed her and picked her up.

"Put me down, you cretin," she yelled and kicked her legs as Richard carried her into the shallow end of the lake.

He set her down, and they kept playing in the water. Richard chased her, and she kept trying to get away, but never strayed too far.

"Let's go in the water, Tuck," Nancy said removing her sandals and stepping into the water. "It doesn't matter if we get wet."

She splashed Tucker so he splashed her back.

"Are you going to join me?" Nancy asked.

Tucker shook his head. They stopped splashing each other and watched Cara and Richard, who were still in the water.

Nancy looked at Tucker and whispered, "It looks like foreplay. She is letting him grab her, then she runs away and then she comes back. Do you think they have ever made love?"

"I don't think so."

Caralyn ran up to Tucker and tried to hide behind him. "Make him stop, Tuck. He wants to go swimming tomorrow."

"You are big enough to fight your own battles, Carrie. That's what you always tell me anyway."

Caralyn waited for Richard, and they walked toward the table. "Did you enjoy getting my underwear wet?" Caralyn asked.

"Always."

Nancy looked at Caralyn and Richard as they were still teasing each other.

"Quit touching me." Caralyn slapped his hand away.

"I will if you stop trying to grab me."

Nancy looked at Tucker and whispered, "Foreplay."

"Who knows, Nancy? Maybe you are right."

Soon Caralyn got cold because she was still soaking wet. Richard wrapped the blanket around her.

"We should get back." Tucker said. "I have to take Nancy home. She is supposed to be somewhere tomorrow."

Tucker dropped Richard and Caralyn off then took Nancy home. He returned to find Richard and Caralyn sitting at opposite ends of the couch bickering.

"What are you fighting about?"

"He won't say he's sorry for throwing me in the lake."

"Well, maybe he's not sorry. Did you ever think of that?"

She stuck her tongue out at Tucker.

"You guys looked like you were having fun. Nancy said it looked like foreplay."

Caralyn was speechless for a few seconds. "It was not! How can you say that, Tucker McKay? Take it back."

"I didn't say it, Nancy did, and I think you are protesting too much. What is that old saying? Something about when someone protests too much about something, it must be true."

Caralyn threw a pillow at Tucker. She turned red because she knew Nancy was partly right.

Tucker said, "I'm going to bed. You can stay up all night if you want, but I have something to do in the morning."

Ten minutes later Caralyn said, "I'm going to bed. Where are you going to sleep?"

Richard followed her down the hall. She put a finger to her lip as he stood outside the bedroom door.

He took a deep breath then said, "Good night, Cara. See you in the morning. I'm used to sleeping on the couch."

She retreated into Grandma's room without a kiss.

Chapter Twenty-Five

Caralyn heard the guys outside when she woke up. She looked out the window and saw them playing basketball. She threw on some clothes and ran out to watch.

"We could use another player, Cara. Are you interested?"

"Only if I can be on your side, Tuck. I want to be on the winning team."

"We'll see about that, Caralyn," Derren answered.

A couple of minutes later Mom stood outside the back door. "Caralyn Ann! What are you doing?"

"Playing ball with the guys, Mom."

"You are too short to be playing with the guys, honey."

"Mom!"

"I said too short, not too young. They are so much bigger than you. I'm afraid you will get hurt."

"We're being careful, Mom. We won't run over her."

"Don't forget you have a wedding today, son."

"Is that today? I thought it was tomorrow."

Mom shook her head and withdrew into the house to cook breakfast. The guys and Caralyn kept playing until Mom announced breakfast was ready.

"Caralyn, you need to eat and then take your shower. What time do you have to be at Nancy's?"

"Eleven. She wants me to help her get ready."

"Why do you have to be there so early, Carrie?" Tucker asked with a sly grin. "You only need a couple of minutes to get ready."

"I only need a couple minutes, but Nancy needs more time. It is kind of a special day for her, even if you guys would rather be playing ball."

They finished breakfast quickly and Mom cleared the table. "You guys can do whatever you want, but Cara needs to get ready. Leave her alone and stay out of the house."

Caralyn got ready to head to Nancy's. She came out the back door while the guys were still playing ball.

"Where's your fancy dress, Cara? I thought you were going to put it on," Richard asked.

"Not until later. It's at Nancy's house. I'll see you guys at the church around one. Derren, make sure he gets there on time and in his tux. Heads will roll if you guys are late." She threatened as she smiled.

She arrived at the Young house to a scene of chaos.

"Caralyn, I'm so glad you're here. Nancy is so upset. Please see if you can calm her down."

"Certainly, Mrs. Young." Caralyn ran upstairs to Nancy's room. She found Nancy and Sandy bickering. "What's going on? Why are you guys arguing?"

"Sandy won't give a toast at the reception. She claims she would be too nervous and screw everything up."

"That's no reason to be arguing. If Sandy doesn't feel she can make a toast, then I will. How hard can it be?"

"You would do that, Cara?"

"Of course I would. That will give me a chance to tell everyone about all your dirty secrets."

"You better not."

"I won't, Nancy. Maybe only one or two of them." They laughed and the situation was resolved. "Now come on. We have to get you ready for your big day."

Mrs. Young hollered up the stairs later. "Come on, girls. It's 12:45. We have to leave."

Mr. Young drove them to the church, and they arrived with five minutes to spare.

Caralyn asked Mom, "Is Tucker here? Does he look okay?"

"The guys are here, and they look great. They will be waiting for you girls up front with the preacher. Let me fix your sleeve, honey." Mom adjusted the sleeve and smiled. "There. You look so pretty, Caralyn."

"Thanks, Mom. You look very pretty, too. It's time for you to be seated."

The guys waited at the front. Derren tugged at his tight collar. Richard kept buttoning his jacket and then would unbutton it. Tucker wrung his hands without realizing it. Soon it was time for Caralyn to head down the aisle. She looked around the old Methodist church and admired the scenes depicted in the stained-glass windows. She turned her attention to the front and looked first at Richard, then Derren and then at Tucker. He didn't seem to be nervous at all—if you ignored the sweat on his brow. She smiled at him, and he smiled back.

He winked and whispered as she walked past, "You cleaned up nicely today, Carrie."

Sandy made it down the aisle, and then Nancy waited with her father. Tucker saw her in her wedding dress for the first time.

"Wow! She looks better than ever," Derren whispered.

"Tell me," Richard said.

Tucker smiled.

The ceremony lasted long enough for plenty of tears to be shed. Caralyn nearly made it through the ceremony without crying, but shed a few tears near the end.

"I saw the tears, Cara. Were they tears of joy or regret?"

"Both, Rickey, both."

Richard didn't mention the tears again. He took her arm and they walked down the aisle and then outside to join the reception line. She hugged Nancy and kissed her cheek. She turned to Tucker and hugged him quickly.

"Is that all I get, Carrie?" he asked.

She looked up at him and nearly broke into tears. "You will get your hugs and kisses from Nancy from now on."

"Oh, Carrie, you know I still love you." He hugged her tightly while they had a moment before the crowd was ushered out to greet them.

"I know, but it's different now."

He kissed her cheek tenderly and Nancy smiled. She understood their deep feelings for each other.

190

After standing in the reception line to greet everyone, Caralyn stayed close to Richard when they weren't needed for pictures. They laughed and teased each other about what he wanted to do after the reception.

"There are two sleeping bags and food and beverages in the trunk. Even bug spray. We can build a campfire. The only thing I don't have is a tent in case it rains, but otherwise I have everything we need to spend the night under the stars."

Caralyn smiled at him and thought it might be a fun way to spend the night. At least he had two sleeping bags. After an hour and a half the photographer finished.

Richard looked at his watch. "We still have two hours before the reception, Cara. What are we supposed to do now?"

"We are going to ride around town, and then we have to see Grandma and Grandpa. Tucker wants some pictures taken at the farm. That will eat up time."

Richard looked at Caralyn and smiled. "You look even prettier than the bride and Nancy looks absolutely gorgeous."

"Thank you, Richard. You look all right yourself."

"Would you be upset if I kissed you right now?"

"I don't know. Maybe you should try it and see."

Richard kissed her, and she didn't smack him. "That was nice, Cara, and you didn't slug me so I take it you didn't mind."

"Don't kiss me in front of Daddy, okay?"

"Whatever you say, Cara."

Now she slugged his arm.

"What was that for?"

"That was for what you will try later tonight."

"Does that mean you want to go to the lake again?"

She looked at him. "I still haven't completely made up my mind. It might be a huge mistake, but I'm thinking it might be a nice way to spend the night. If it's not raining."

"Yes!" Richard pumped his fist.

"Just because I said maybe does not mean we were going to make love, so wipe that silly grin off your face before I decide to go home and sleep in my comfortable bed with my teddy."

191

Richard knew her well enough to know she had already made up her mind, but wasn't going to tell him what she wanted to do until later. She rode with Richard out to the farm. Tucker and Nancy were driven to the farm by Derren and Natalie. On the way out of town, they were stopped by a train.

Nancy covered her ears. "I hate trains. The whistle hurts my ears."

Tucker watched the Illinois Central train zooming past and said, "It was loud, but it sounds like a happy train today." He kissed her until the gates lifted.

"Were you afraid I was going to spill your deepest secrets?" Caralyn asked after her toast.

"I knew you wouldn't," Nancy answered.

Caralyn grinned and said, "I will now."

"How?" Nancy asked.

"By talking about oral sex. Make him keep practicing. Make him keep doing it until he gives you an orgasm."

"Caralyn! Stop talking about that," Nancy whispered. "You're embarrassing me."

"Why? Don't you want to have an orgasm?" Caralyn asked.

"Of course, but..."

"I'll talk to him and give him some pointers."

"Don't you dare," Nancy said as the guys walked over.

"What are you ladies talking about?" Richard asked.

"We were talking about oral sex," Caralyn said loud enough for people to hear.

"Carrie, You better behave," Tucker warned.

"Nancy wants me to give you some tips about how to give her an orgasm," Caralyn said then smiled at the preacher's wife.

Derren and Natalie were standing next to Tucker and Nancy and heard everything. Derren stifled a laugh as Natalie frowned at him.

"Don't you ever talk about our sex life to anyone like that."

"I won't. I promise." Derren said, but he smiled when Natalie turned her back.

192

"He won't talk about it because you don't ever..."

Tucker grabbed her and put a hand over her mouth. "Carrie, be nice."

"I'll behave now, Tuck. But I think you..."

He tightened his grip on her.

"Caralyn, you look so pretty tonight," Dad said as they danced. "The house is so quiet without you. We miss you, but at least you will be there tonight."

"Thank you, Daddy." She didn't want to disappoint him, so she didn't mention she had another option.

Later, Richard got a glass of beer for Caralyn and Mom saw her drinking it.

"Caralyn Ann! What are you drinking?"

"Oh, Mom. It's only one glass of beer. I won't get drunk by having a little beer. I know you and Dad might not approve, but I am old enough to make my own decisions."

"Do I have to remind you the legal drinking age is twenty-one in this state?"

"Okay, Mom. I won't finish it." She handed the beer to Richard and walked away. *You just erased any doubts I had about tonight. I'm spending it at the lake with Richard.*

By eleven o'clock most of the guests had left. Tucker and Nancy were ready to depart. They said goodbye to Mr. and Mrs. Young and to Mom and Dad McKay. Tucker saw Caralyn with Richard and strode over to say goodbye.

"Good night, Carrie. We are going to head out. I will email you with our arrival time. You are going to pick us up, right? I don't want to take a taxi."

"I won't forget, Tuck. Have a good honeymoon."

"Give me a hug, Carrie. I love you, too."

She hugged him and then Nancy. She watched as they left with Derren and Natalie. Mom and Dad were ready to leave, too.

Mom put a hand on Caralyn's shoulder. "Are you coming home soon, honey?"

"I need to talk to you, Mom."

"What is it, dear? If it's about the beer, I'm sorry I made a big deal about it. Jim told me I need to let you make your own decisions about things. He said you are a smart girl, and he trusts your judgment."

"It's not about the beer, Mom." She wasn't sure now if she could go through with her plan.

"What is it? You can tell me. I love you no matter what."

"Mom, Richard and I are going to camp out by Uncle Alton's lake tonight. We were out there last night, and it was such a beautiful night. Richard has a couple of sleeping bags, and we are going to have a campfire and roast some marshmallows."

Mom froze for a moment, but asked, "Two sleeping bags?"

"Yes, Mom. Two bags. Richard and I are only friends."

"What will you do if it rains?"

"We will come home and stay at the house."

"I know you mean Grandma Florence's house. Your father will be disappointed you aren't home tonight, but I will explain it. You know where the key is if you need to come home."

"Yes, I know, Mom. Thank you for understanding and for telling Daddy. I don't think I could tell him myself." She kissed Mom and found Richard. "We can leave anytime you are ready."

"It will be fun, Cara. I promise. Did you bring a change of clothes?" Richard asked.

"I brought shorts and a t-shirt. They are in that bag I threw in the trunk. I didn't want to ruin this dress by wearing it at the lake. Did you bring extra clothes?"

"Yes."

"Where are we going to change? If we change here, people will see us and wonder what we are doing."

"We could change at the lake, Cara. You could change in the car, and I will change by the shed."

Caralyn thought about it. "That will be okay."

Chapter Twenty-Six

Caralyn and Richard said good night to Sandy and Lloyd and scurried out of the building. They reached the car without seeing anyone else and arrived at the lake twenty minutes later.

Richard opened the car door. "I will change by the shed, so you can have some privacy."

"You don't have to, Richard. I just have to take off this dress and my slip. Oh, and these pantyhose too. I forgot about them—doesn't matter. I will change in the backseat." She climbed over the seat and got in the back.

Richard got their clothes out of the trunk while Caralyn slipped off her dress and struggled with her pantyhose.

"Here's your bag, Caralyn." He handed it to her and walked behind the car to change.

"Thanks, Richard. God. I hate pantyhose." She put the shorts on under her slip. She put on her white socks and tennis shoes. She looked to see if Richard was looking but he wasn't. She pulled the slip over her head and quickly put on the t-shirt.

"Would you help carry the sleeping bags and stuff, Cara?"

"You brought two bags, right?"

"Yes, I didn't want to force you into sharing a bag."

"Thank you."

"I thought about buying one of those two-person tents, but they were too expensive."

"So, you put a monetary value on sleeping with me, huh?"

He held his hands out palms up. "I am but a poor college student, Cara."

"How much am I worth?" she asked without cracking a smile.

"The cheapest one I saw was forty bucks, but it was junk. They had some for around a hundred, but..."

"How much do hookers charge?"

He stared at her.

She rolled her eyes. "If you had to pay for sex, it would cost you."

"I get it. What will I do with a tent after tonight?"

"You could give it to me. I would cherish it as the place I surrendered my virtue to you."

"Shoot! The store's probably closed now."

She wrinkled her nose at him. "Your loss."

They carried the gear to a flat area by the picnic table. Richard spread a large piece of plastic on the ground and placed sleeping bags on top of that.

"You know, Cara, we could put the sleeping bags under the picnic table and even if it rains, we would be somewhat protected."

"Maybe, but if we sleep under the picnic table we won't have much room. Besides that, if I have to get up during the night I would probably hit my head."

Someone had stacked some firewood near the fire ring and covered it with a tarp. Richard worked on getting a fire going.

"City boy, you need kindling to start the fire."

"Fine. You do it, Daisy Mae." He handed her the lighter.

She had the fire going two minutes later.

"Can anyone see this?" Richard asked looking toward the road.

"No, the lake's far enough off the road that no one can see it because of the hill."

"Yeah, I knew that. I'm in law school, you know."

"Are you ready for something to drink, Richard?"

"Thanks, I'll take a beer."

Caralyn looked in the cooler and got a beer for Richard. "Should I have one now?"

"That's entirely up to you, Cara."

She didn't know if she should, but she decided to have one, too. She grabbed a package of cookies, but left the marshmallows. They sat on the sleeping bags which were still in their stuff sacks. Soon they were laughing and reminiscing about school and the things they did over the years.

"You are totally different than my sisters," he said.

"How long was it before you realized Tucker was not my brother?"

196

"I can't remember exactly, but it was quite a while. What was I supposed to think? Derren said Tucker was his cousin and you were his cousin, too. You called the McKay's Mom and Dad, like they were your parents. You know the way you guys acted you might as well been brother and sister. You obviously loved each other very much, and he was so protective of you."

"We will always love each other, Rickey. Do you miss Elsa?"

"Not really. She wasn't the right one for me. She was so serious all the time. It was like she was twenty-two going on fifty."

"Tell me about it. I don't think she liked me at all."

Richard finished his beer and got another one. "Do you want another one?"

"No, I will be lucky to finish this one. You aren't planning on getting me drunk, are you?"

"Nope. I've told you before. I want you stone cold sober. If anything happens I want to know it was because you wanted it and not because you were drunk."

"These are my favorite cookies. Did you know that?"

"I remembered you saying that once. There are donuts for the morning, too."

"You thought of everything, huh?"

He shrugged and said, "I try my best."

"Nancy told Tucker what we were doing here last night was foreplay. What do you think?"

"Foreplay, huh? Maybe in a way. I know I had to wait to come out of the water."

"You mean you had an erection?"

"Couldn't you tell?"

"I wasn't thinking about it. Nancy told Tucker I was letting you touch me all over, and I was touching you a lot, too."

"I don't remember exactly, Cara. We were just having fun. If I touched you where I shouldn't have, I'm sorry." He munched on a cookie and said, "Actually, I'm not sorry."

"I could tell, but it was only innocent fun," she said then was quiet for a while.

"What are you thinking about?"

"Now that Tucker is married, things will be different between us." She grabbed two cookies. "Last night was fun, but you shouldn't have thrown me in the lake. I could have drowned."

"I wouldn't have allowed it. I would have rescued you. Too bad Derren and Natalie didn't come. I don't want to say anything bad about her, but..."

"I know. She's a control freak like her mother. I feel sorry for Derren. I know he loves her, but I wonder if it will last. I know Derren wants to have kids, but I heard Natalie tell him once she never wants any."

"Do you ever want to have kids?"

"Mom used to ask me that, and I always told her no. But I've changed my mind. I want a little girl and a boy. Not necessarily in that order, but I want to have them close together so they will be friends."

"I think I will want kids, too, but not for a few years. I want to be finished with school and established in my law practice before I even think about kids."

"Are you going to get married before you have kids?"

"No way. I'm never going to get married. There are too many beautiful women out there needing my attention."

Caralyn looked at him.

"I'm kidding. I want to get married someday... before I have kids."

"I'm going to write books. Romantic books about first love... and falling in love... and making love."

"If you need help with research let me know. I will help out in the last part. I am an expert."

"Oh, believe me, I know. You have more experience than ten other guys put together."

They laughed and Caralyn jumped suddenly and grabbed his arm. "Did you hear that?"

"No, what was it?"

"Not sure, probably a critter of some sort. Maybe a deer.

"Or a mountain lion," he teased.

198

They sat quietly by the fire for a time then a flash of lightning startled them.

"Wait! Be quiet," she said touching his arm.

The thunder boomed and she said, "It's a mile away. I can smell the rain, Richard. I hate to spoil your night, but I think we need to head for the car before we get soaked."

He grabbed the sleeping bags. "We can leave the tarp and cooler here."

Seconds after they were in the car, the rain started coming down in sheets.

"I should have checked the forecast again," he said. "Sorry."

"It's all right. Even if it stops pouring soon, I think we should go home."

He looked out the window and saw another flash of lightning. He turned to Caralyn. "Should you call home? They will be worried."

"I didn't bring my phone, but they know I'm smart enough to get out of a storm."

They waited ten minutes.

"I'm calling this game on account of rain," she said. "When it slows down, we can scramble and get the cooler and tarp."

They made a dash a few minutes later, stashed the gear in the trunk and got back in the car.

"How soaked are you?"

She wrung out her hair. "I've been wetter, but usually in the shower."

"I almost slipped, but kept my balance. I'm sorry about tonight. This hasn't been an easy day for you."

"You have been very sweet to me today, and I appreciate it. I cried during the ceremony partly because Tucker married Nancy and not me."

"Someday you will find the perfect man. You will fall in love with him, and he will fall head over heels in love with you."

He started the car and drove back into town.

"We have to crash at Grandma's tonight," she said.

He pulled into the driveway, and they dashed onto the back porch. She opened the door and they scooted inside as the wind picked up and it started pouring again.

"There's a light next door, Cara. Should I run over and tell your parents we are back?"

"I could do it. I should stay in my room anyway."

"If you insist," he said as he ran a hand through her wet hair.

"We can leave everything in the car tonight. I will see you in the morning." She kissed him and stood on the porch. She waited for the rain to lessen and sprinted home. She dashed up the utility room steps and threw open the door. "We're back!"

Mom appeared in the kitchen doorway. "We were ready to drive out to the lake. Your father heard a report of a tornado touching down in Sanders Creek."

"Richard is going to crash at Grandma's."

"You should change out of those clothes before you catch a cold."

"Do you think Tuck and Nancy are okay? Will the storm bother them?" Caralyn asked.

Mom smiled and whispered, "I doubt if they even notice it."

Chapter Twenty-Seven

By the time Caralyn woke up, Richard, Mom and Dad were sitting at the kitchen table having a late breakfast.

"That was some storm, huh?" Dad said.

"Hi, honey. Are you hungry?" Mom asked. "I can make more breakfast if you want. We were lazy this morning and stayed in bed until nine o'clock."

"I'm hungry," she said looking at Richard.

Dad asked, "Did you guys have a good time at the lake? Before the storm, I mean."

"Oh, Daddy. I hope you aren't mad at me for wanting to spend the night at the lake with Richard. We had two sleeping bags and weren't going to sleep together," she told him as fast as she could.

"Mom told me about the sleeping bags last night, and I'm glad you came home when you did. Alton called earlier. The storm uprooted several trees and ripped part of the roof from his old shed. He's going to knock it down."

"Oh, that sucks. I love getting on the roof to watch the sunset or the stars."

Caralyn hugged her dad around his neck and kissed him. She sat next to him and smiled at Richard.

"Do you want to hear about our night camping out?"

"Tell me all about it, sweetie."

"You know about the sleeping bags. We had snacks and something to drink..."

"I told them about the beer," Richard admitted. "Sorry, Cara."

"I don't approve of it, but you have to face the consequences," Dad said then ate the last bit of eggs on his plate.

"Did you tell them about my plan to go swimming?" she asked Richard while running a hand through her hair.

Richard shook his head.

"Ooops! I guess I just did, huh?" She looked at her father. "I wore purple underwear, and was going to swim in it."

"I don't need to know about your underwear, Cara," Dad said. He turned his head when he noticed her chest.

"It would have been like wearing a bikini, Daddy. In fact the underwear covers more of me than my bikini."

"That's comforting to know you weren't going skinny dipping again, but you need a larger bikini," Dad said.

Caralyn ate breakfast while Dad enjoyed a second cup of coffee and listened to Richard's tales about living in New York.

"Would it be all right if I took a shower at Grandma's?" Richard asked. "I woke up and threw on some clothes earlier."

"Of course. Cara, will you make sure there are clean towels in the bathroom."

"Okay, Mom. As soon as I finish breakfast."

She finished, cleared the table and took Richard next door.

"I'll be back in a minute, Cara. I need to get my clothes out of my suitcase."

Caralyn made sure there were clean towels and wash cloths.

Mom and Dad sat at the table and talked about Caralyn and Richard.

"They are just friends, Jim. I'm sure they are not romantically involved, but you have to understand she's not a little girl anymore."

"I know, but it's still hard to think of her spending the night with a boy even if they had separate sleeping bags. Another thing, I couldn't help but notice, but I don't think she had any underwear on. It didn't faze her to sit in front of Richard without... you know."

"I'm sure she didn't wear any underwear to bed. I'm glad she planned to wear it to go swimming," Mom said then laughed.

"Why are you laughing?"

"Knowing her the way we do, I can picture her making Richard turn around and close his eyes so she could get undressed. She may not be a little girl anymore, but she is still shy in some ways."

"Thank goodness for that," Dad said with a sigh.

Back in Grandma's house Caralyn kissed Richard with her arms wrapped around his neck.

"More foreplay, huh?"

"Just a little, Richard. Don't get too excited. I feel kinda sexy without any underwear on."

"You look rather sexy without any underwear on."

She was close enough to arouse him.

"Oooh! Someone is excited."

"I think someone else is, too, and I think your parents knew you weren't wearing any underwear."

"In a way I'm glad we got rained out."

"Why?"

"I can imagine the hurt on Daddy's face if I had to explain spending the night at the lake with you."

"And going swimming?"

"There is that. We might have gotten carried away and forgot about keeping our underwear on."

He grinned, kissed her and said, "No maybe about it. I wasn't going to wear my boxers in the lake."

You are pretty naughty for a city boy." She backed away and glanced down. "I should let you shower, and I need to take one myself."

"Maybe we could conserve some water and shower together. We need to save the planet for future generations."

"Richard," she said slowly.

"Should I start the water running?"

"How would I explain to Mom and Dad I took a shower over here? And besides all my clothes are at the house."

"It was only a thought."

"Yeah. The thought of a dirty mind," she said then poked his stomach. "You should take a very cold shower, Richard. I am going home to shower and get dressed. See you in a little while."

She ran home and Mom and Dad were still in the kitchen talking.

"You came back. Did you make sure Richard had what he needed, Cara?"

She blushed because she was thinking about how they were flirting with each other. "I gave him some clean towels. I'm going to shower and get dressed."

Richard had an early Monday morning flight out of O'Hare, so he and Caralyn headed back to Chicago late Sunday afternoon.

"Drive carefully, dear, and call me when you get home."

"Okay, Mom, I will."

"It was good to see you again, Richard. Have a safe flight back to New York."

"Thank you. It was a pleasure to see you and Mr. McKay again. Thanks for everything. I will make sure Cara calls you when we get to her place."

They took turns driving to Chicago and arrived at Caralyn's apartment shortly after dark. She pulled into the alley and into her spot in the garage. They entered the building through the back door.

"I'm supposed to check Tucker's place for him while they are gone. Do you want to see it?"

"Sure. It is much different than your place?"

"It's bigger, and they have a porch and there's a roof patio. Come on. I'll show you." She led him up the stairs.

"It's big. You know how small my place is."

"I remember. Come on, let's go downstairs, and I'll show you my place. I've been fixing it up."

She showed Richard her apartment.

"Very impressive. I like all the little feminine touches. The Bulls photos on the wall and pictures of you as a cheerleader. Nice legs, by the way."

"What did you expect? I'm still a sports fan." She poked him in the ribs.

She showed him her bedroom.

"I see you have your teddy bear on your bed. Do you keep him there at night?"

"Maybe, but you will never know, Mr. Laderman."

"You can tell me, Cara. I won't tease you."

"I need to have some secrets from you."

"Maybe I will sneak in here during the night and see if you are sleeping alone."

"You better not. I might be sleeping in the nude."

"Then I am definitely sneaking into your room."

"I will have to make sure I lock my door and stick a chair under the doorknob so you can't sneak in." They teased each other back and forth. "This is the spare bedroom. Where you *will* be spending the night."

Richard smiled at her. "We'll see about that."

During the night Richard woke up and used the hall bathroom. When he came out he noticed Caralyn's door was not even closed, let alone locked. He stuck his head in the door. There was enough light for him to see her in her pajamas, and next to her on the bed was teddy. Richard smiled as he headed back to his room.

"Do you want me to make you some breakfast before you head to work, sweetheart?" she teased in the morning.

"That is a difficult offer to pass up, but strong coffee is all I need right now."

She drove to the airport and pulled into an empty space in the departure lane. "I'm not getting out. Give me a hug or something quick before that cop thinks we're making out."

"Like that's gonna happen." He hugged her and kissed her cheek. "I had a great time this weekend, Cara. We will have to get together again soon. You can come to see me anytime."

"How can I refuse such an offer. It was a great weekend."

Chapter Twenty-Eight

Two weeks after Tucker and Nancy's wedding, Caralyn sat on the couch alone in her apartment on Saturday evening. She opened a bottle of wine and thought about her best friends. They would be returning from their honeymoon the next day, and she had promised to pick them up at the airport. After a couple glasses of wine, she decided she needed some company so she called Beth.

"Hey, what are you guys doing tonight?"

"We are on our way to a party in Lancashire. Why?"

"I'm in my apartment. I'm bored, lonely, feeling sorry for myself, and I'm horny as all get out."

"And your problem is...?"

"Don't tease me, Beth."

"I'm sorry. Would you like to join us?"

"You don't mind if I tag along?" Caralyn asked.

Beth laughed as she teased, "Yeah, but I'll get over it."

"I'm sticking out my tongue at you."

"We'll be there in thirty. Be ready to party."

She put on a blue dress that allowed her bright gray-blue eyes to really stand out. It showed only enough leg to be sexy. She waited downstairs for Beth and Ray.

"Is that a new dress, Cara? It looks adorable on you." Beth said as Caralyn got in the back of Ray's car.

"Rats! I was hoping for sexy, but I guess I'll settle for adorable," Caralyn said then giggled. "Where is this party? Is it for something specific, or just a party?"

Beth explained the where, why and who of the party as Ray drove out of the city.

"Would you mind if I join you?" a stranger asked as he smiled at Caralyn.

She looked into his deep brown eyes and with a quick glance took in his ruggedly handsome features. His fifty-dollar haircut, his chiseled chin and a small scar below his right eye made him appear tremendously sexy.

She smiled. "I don't mind at all."

"I don't believe I've seen you here before. My name is John Smith." He offered his hand.

She shook his hand as she giggled. "If you don't want me to know your name, you should at least make up a better one than that."

They fall for it every time. I love proving I really am John Smith. He grinned as he reached for his wallet. He flipped it open and produced his Texas driver's license.

"Either that is a good forgery, or you really are John Smith." *Like I would know what a forged license would look like.*

"I'm used to people giving me crap about my name. You didn't tell me your name."

"My real name, or the one I'm using tonight?" she asked. *What name should I use? I really don't want him to know who I am.*

"I bet you twenty bucks I can guess your real name."

"You're on."

"Let me see... you look like a Cynthia... no wait... a Bridgetta. No that's not it... I know it's Gertrude because you are named after your great great grandmother's favorite aunt."

Caralyn giggled.

"I bet it's Caralyn Ann Dawson, and you're from Stockton Woods."

Her jaw dropped. "How did you know?"

"I cheated. I'm an old friend of Ray's, and I saw you come in with them. So I asked." He shrugged and then grinned.

"Do I still owe you the money since you cheated?" She put her hands on her hips, but she smiled.

"Maybe I can think of another way you could pay off the bet."

She gave him a dirty look.

"Crap! That didn't come out right. I'm sorry. Ray told me you are an aspiring writer, and I work for Baldacci Publishing in Fort Worth. We have an office here, and that's where I'm working this week. I thought we could talk about your writing."

"That's quite a line. I came here looking for someone to spend the night with," she boldly told him to see his reaction.

"Uh... well... hmmmm..."

"I'm feeding you a line, John Smith, and you fell for it hook, line and... kerplunk." She made a motion as if fishing and she had hooked a large one.

"You got me good." He looked around the room. *You're rather young-looking, but you look fantastic in a virginal sort of way. I doubt if I could find anyone else any prettier than you.*

"So what do you do for Baldacci Publishing...?"

For the next hour John and Caralyn talked about their common interests. He made sure she always had a full glass of wine in her hand.

"Cara, Ray and I are going home. Do you need a ride?" Beth asked.

Caralyn had to make a quick decision. She would love to talk all night to John about writing and editing and everything. She learned he lived outside of Fort Worth and had been married until two years ago. He was charming, handsome. He would make a perfect one-night stand.

"If you need a ride, I would share a cab with you. I'm staying in the Loop at the River Central Hotel." They both knew he was asking her to spend the night with him.

She chewed her lip. She gazed at him and then at Beth and Ray. "Crap! I'm sorry, John, but I have to be at O'Hare in the morning. I have to pick up my friends who've been on their honeymoon. It's been a pleasure talking to you."

"Likewise. This is my cell phone number if you ever want to call and continue our conversation. I wish you luck with your novel." He kissed her cheek, and she left with Ray and Beth.

On the drive back to Caralyn's apartment, Beth turned in the seat, saw Caralyn staring out the window, and asked, "Did you really want to go with John?"

"Yes, and if I didn't have to make an airport run, I would have. He is charming, and we have similar interests."

"And he's handsome and you're horny..."

"Crap! He's only going to be in the city for a few days. It would have been perfect. Simply a casual fling with no strings attached."

"Caralyn, I'm surprised at you." Beth's face expressed her surprise. "Since when are you into one-night stands?"

"Since tonight."

Ray mentioned, "If it will make you feel any better, his wife divorced him because he cheated. Actually, he cheated a lot."

"Are you saying that to make me feel better about not going with him?" She looked in the rear-view mirror at Ray.

"It's true. I knew him in college and he was quite the womanizer back then. He didn't change after he got married. His wife finally got fed up and took him for all his money in the divorce. He landed on his feet and has some rich, older woman supporting him now."

"Then I guess I made the right choice," Caralyn said trying to convince herself. *But I'm still horny, and I drank too much wine. I wonder how Trent is doing.*

Caralyn spotted them as they came out of the gate, waved and hollered, "Nancy! Tuck! Over here!" She ran to greet them, hugged Nancy, and then turned to Tucker. "Wow! You look great after two weeks in the Virgin Islands. Next time take me with."

He took her in his arms and held her tight. He swung her around like a little girl.

"It is so good to see you, Carrie. How have you been?"

"I'm all right. I have been busy. Nancy, you have to tell me all about your honeymoon. You can leave out some of the details, but not all of them."

She and Nancy walked arm in arm as they let Tucker take care of the luggage. Nancy told Caralyn about the place they stayed, and how they had a section of beach for their use alone. The girls giggled as they talked while Tucker struggled to keep up.

Caralyn looked at Tucker and whispered, "You naughty boy," as she smiled at him.

Tucker blushed because he didn't know for sure what Nancy told Caralyn, but he could imagine.

Caralyn said, "Now don't make too much noise tonight or else I will have to call the super and complain."

Nancy looked alarmed, but Tucker reminded her, "Don't worry, Nancy, she can't hear a thing from our place because the floors are so thick."

On the way home they talked about the honeymoon. Caralyn told them about camping at the lake with Richard.

Nancy asked, "What would you have done if it hadn't stormed?"

"Nothing that night, but I would have gone swimming in the morning."

"What were you going to wear?"

"My underwear unless he promised to behave."

Nancy told Tucker, "The next time we are home we have to go skinny dipping, okay."

"Whatever you want, Nancy. I am your obedient husband."

A couple of days later Tucker and Caralyn were sitting on his porch swing talking about where they were going to be living next year when Caralyn blurted out suddenly, "I almost got laid the night before I picked you and Nancy up at the airport."

Tucker nearly choked on his pop. "What? Carrie? I didn't know you had a new boyfriend."

"I don't have a new boyfriend."

Tucker looked puzzled. "I don't get it."

She shrugged then said, "I invited myself to a party with Beth and Ray and met a guy. We spent some time talking, and he asked me to spend the night. Not in those exact words, but that's what he meant. I actually thought about it, but I couldn't go through with it because I had to pick you guys up. I did find out his name though. It's John Smith."

Tucker was speechless. She noticed the dumbstruck look on his face.

Finally he asked, "John Smith, huh? Did you believe him?"

210

"He showed me his license, and his name really is John Smith. He works for a publishing company in Fort Worth. I was feeling horny and sorry for myself, and I thought since you and Nancy were probably making love I wanted to meet someone, too. Are you going to say anything, Tuck?"

After a moment of silence broken only by an ambulance siren, Tucker stammered. "I'm glad you didn't go through with it."

She began to cry and Tucker held her close.

"It's all right, Carrie. Don't cry. I still love you no matter what happened. We will always be best friends."

"I am going to miss you so much, Tuck. It was so hard last year at school without you there, and after this year you and Nancy might be so far away. I'll never get to see you."

"That's not true, Carrie. Nancy and I will be right here."

"Yeah, unless the Bulls decide to trade you. What if they trade you to the Warriors, or the Clippers. That would be awful."

"Maybe if I hang around long enough, I can have a no-trade clause in my contract. But you can come and visit us anytime no matter where we live. If you move to New York, Richard will be close to you while he is in law school, and he can keep you company."

"That's not the same as having you with me." She snuggled close to him as he held her tight. "John Smith cheated on his wife and she divorced him. I don't want you to ever cheat on Nancy. Promise me you won't."

"I promise, Carrie. If I ever lost her I would be devastated. Will you promise me something?"

"Yes, I will. What is it?"

"Don't ever fall for a John Smith again, okay?"

Chapter Twenty-Nine

"Nancy, since we have classes about the same time, we can walk to campus together when the weather is good, and take the bus when it isn't," Caralyn said. "Driving to campus would be my last option because of parking."

"It will be so much fun to be in school together again. High school seems like such a long time ago."

Even though they didn't have any classes together, they were able to spend time with each other. Caralyn kept Nancy company when Tucker and the Bulls traveled out of the city. A few times Nancy spent the night with Caralyn.

"Tell me about your sex life, Nancy. I want to know everything. I want to use it in my book."

"You can't put us in your book. You haven't forgotten what he was like, have you?"

"I remember all right, but how often do you do it, and do you have an orgasm every time? Just for my book."

"Not every time, but maybe about half the time. Sometimes we have quickies if we don't have a lot of time."

Caralyn pretended to write on her laptop. "How are you going to make it through a whole week without him?"

Nancy sighed and said, "I don't know. I could ask Coach to cut him."

Caralyn looked up from her laptop. "Don't say that. He's lucky to even be on the team."

"When was the last time you had sex, Cara?"

"About a hundred years ago. I barely remember what it feels like." Caralyn smiled and told Nancy, "After I returned from France I kinda dated Trent Cussler for the rest of the semester."

"I know that, and I know you slept with him. Has there been anyone else?"

"No, that's been it, and I'm feeling really horny all the time."

"I can understand. I get horny if we go more than a few hours without having sex," Nancy said then laughed.

"You are so bad now. You were so naïve and innocent when you and Tuck first dated. Remember? I had to tag along with you guys."

"I remember."

"Did I ever tell you about Mr. Green?"

Nancy tilted her head and twirled her long brown hair around a finger. "What about him?"

"I had a crush on him in high school."

"That's nothing unusual. All the girls had a crush on him. He was so handsome."

"After the second semester of my third year at Midwest, I buzzed into the school to see him. We spent some time together. Alone!"

"Caralyn, don't tell me you and Mr. Green did it."

"No, but I thought about it. I wanted him to take me in his arms and ravage my body. I wanted him to give me multiple orgasms."

"You are so silly." Nancy giggled and asked, "Did Mr. Green make a pass at you?"

"No! He was a perfect gentleman. Darn it." Caralyn remembered Trent's offer. "Trent wanted me to move to Oregon. He might have married me."

"Oh, too bad, Cara," Nancy teased. "He would have been a real catch."

"I couldn't leave my family though."

"Tell me more about Mr. Green."

"I did my best to let him know I was available, but he didn't take advantage of me. He lives in Fremont now. Maybe I should get in touch with him. He might be more willing to ravage me."

"I wonder if he's dating? He might even be married again," Nancy pointed out.

"I don't think I will ever have sex again. I can't bring myself to do it with anyone I'm not in love with anymore."

"Cara, can I ask you something really personal?"

"Of course you can. You can ask me anything."

"You know I've never been with anyone but Tuck, right?"

"Yeah, I know."

"Well, is it a lot different with other guys. I don't mean... the way they do it. I'm wondering if they feel different inside you."

"I don't think so. I don't remember much about Jeremiah, and I don't remember thinking Trent was a lot different than Tuck. Maybe they were about the same size. I don't know for sure about Mr. Green since we never... I was never... I never saw Mr. Green naked. I guess if a guy had a huge thing it would be different. Why the sudden interest?"

"I was only wondering."

"You aren't planning to find out for yourself, are you?" Caralyn was teasing because she knew Nancy would never cheat on Tuck.

Nancy blushed and hung her head.

"Nancy, what are you thinking about? Tell me."

"Is it cheating if you and I sleep together?"

"If you mean only sleeping, I don't think so, but if you mean sleep together like lesbians do, then I would say it is cheating."

"Could we sleep in the same bed and hold each other?"

"Yes, if you are lonely and need some company to help you fall asleep, then we could share a bed."

Nancy stayed with Caralyn several times when Tucker was gone for extended periods of time. Nancy didn't hide this from Tucker, and he didn't mind them staying together. He thought it was safer.

One night after they had eaten dinner together, Tucker said, "Caralyn, you and Nancy spend so much time together I can't remember if I'm married to Nancy, or if you are, or if I'm married to you. It's really confusing,"

"Well, first off, Tuck, you and I are married so you need to stay with me at night. You can't sleep with Nancy," Caralyn told him with a straight face.

"Hey, wait a minute. I thought I was married to him, Cara."

214

Caralyn waved a hand. "That was last month. This month he is mine. You can have him back in December if you want him."

"I don't know. Maybe you can keep him, Cara. I really don't have any need for him anymore."

"Are you sure?" Caralyn looked at Tucker. "I suppose I could keep him around, but sometimes he is just in the way."

Caralyn and Nancy kept pretending and teasing Tucker until he crossed his arms over his chest.

"Fine! If neither of you ladies want me around, I'm going to move. Then you'll miss me and wish I was still here."

Nancy and Cara looked at each other. "Do you care if he moves away?"

"Not really," Nancy answered. "I would have more room in the apartment, and I wouldn't have to deal with his dirty laundry."

Caralyn and Nancy agreed. "If you want to move out, we don't mind."

"You are going to get it, Caralyn Ann, and you, too, Nancy McKay. I'm going to hold you both down and tickle you to death."

He chased Nancy around the couch and grabbed her. He carried her over his shoulder while he chased Caralyn. She didn't try hard to get away and soon Tucker had both of them deposited on the couch. He began to tickle them both.

"Careful, big guy. That was my breast you were tickling."

"Sorry, Cara. I didn't mean to."

"I don't mind as long as Nancy doesn't."

Nancy answered, "I don't mind if he messes around with you, Cara. That way he leaves me alone."

Tucker and Caralyn stopped goofing around and looked at Nancy. "Do you have another headache, honey?"

"Yeah, it just started. I'm going to lie down for a while."

"Do you need anything, Nancy?" Caralyn asked.

Nancy shook her head. "I'll be okay. I need to rest until this goes away."

"I'll stay with you until you fall asleep," Caralyn said.

"Thanks, but that's my job, Carrie," Tucker said.

"What are you doing, Cara?" Tucker asked one morning.

"It's my first attempt at a romance novel."

"For real?"

"Yes, why not? I've written short stories before and even had some published."

"What's it about besides sex?" he teased.

"A few of the characters are based on our experiences growing up."

"What? Did you change the names?"

"Oh yeah, I changed all the names, and even the names of the locations."

"What are you going to call it?"

"Right now it's *Love In a Small Town*, but that will change as soon as I think of a better title."

She let Tucker and Nancy read parts of her novel as she worked on the first draft.

"Cara, I love it. I can't wait until it's all finished. I want to know what happens in the end," Nancy told her.

Tucker read her story, and she begged him for a critique.

"Okay, I'll tell you what I think. I'm impressed by your talent. It's like a real book."

"It is a real book, dweeb brain."

"I like the story and the names you use, but it's a romance novel."

"Good. You figured that out. I knew that college education wasn't completely wasted. What else?"

"Cara, it is very good, and I will read it when it's done. If the guys on the team knew I was reading a love story, they would harass me all the time."

"Well, I'm not going to tell them as long as you keep being nice to me."

"I guess that's not too steep a price to pay for your silence."

Chapter Thirty

"Hey! What's this about a birthday?" Tucker asked Monday morning. "Nancy said you're legal today. What did she mean?"

Caralyn rolled over in her bed and kicked the covers off. "Why did you call so early? I don't have any classes today. I wanted to sleep until noon."

"Is that because you were partying until two this morning?"

"No. I was home all day."

"It's nine o'clock. You need to get your butt out of bed. Am I supposed to take you to dinner tonight?" Tucker asked.

"Yes, and I can order a glass of wine legally."

"Dad will not like it if you drink in front of him."

Caralyn sat up. "Are they here already? I didn't think they were coming until this afternoon."

"They got here last night. Dad wanted to beat the weather. He said it might snow later. They were supposed to get freezing rain today."

"Where are you taking me for dinner?" she asked as she stood up and stretched her arms over her head.

"I was going to order pizza."

"No way, bucko. You have to take me to a fancy restaurant and buy me something ultra expensive."

"Now that you're of legal age and entitled to start using your trust money, I seem to remember you owe me some cash. I have the total right here." He rustled some paper then said, "According to my accounting, you owe me $23,186 for room and board from your years at MCU. That doesn't include gas money for the 873 times I chauffeured you home."

"Good luck collecting anything, Tucker McKay. I should make you pay me for being your friend for twenty-one years."

"Are you going to ask Beth and Ray to join us for dinner?"

"Yes, why?"

"Better bring your checkbook. You owe her millions for paying your rent for the last fifteen years."

"I haven't been paying rent since I was six, dweeb brain."

217

"Whatever. Get dressed and come up to see Mom and Dad. I have to leave for practice in an hour and won't be home until five. Give or take."

"I'll be there when I get there. How does Nancy feel today?"

"She is eating breakfast right now. She hasn't complained about a headache. I think it must have been too much caffeine, or not enough," he said then shrugged.

"She's not pregnant, is she?"

"Not unless her pills and my condoms aren't working right."

"You're a cretin. I'm going to order the most expensive item on the menu for dinner."

"Go ahead. How much is a deluxe cheeseburger at Burger Chef, anyway?"

"Can you see my finger?"

"No, should I ask Dad if he can see it?"

"I hate you, Tucker James."

"You can order a glass of red wine," Ray said to Caralyn, "but I'm ordering a bottle of champagne. This calls for a proper celebration."

"You don't need to, Ray," Dad said.

"Jim, this is Cara's party. Let her choose," Mom said.

Caralyn grinned at the six people sharing the table and replied, "We need wine to go with the meal. All Italians drink wine. Even the children."

She placed her order in Italian and drew a smile from the waiter.

"Your accent is off, but otherwise, I would think you were a native of Milan like me," he said.

After the waiter walked away, Nancy asked, "What did you order?"

Caralyn grinned and answered, "Spaghetti and meatballs in marinara sauce with a garden salad and Italian dressing."

An hour later, the waiter carried a small cake with the candles burning to the table.

"Are you going to sing and embarrass me?" Caralyn asked.

"Of course," Tucker said. "But we have to wait until the whole restaurant is staring at you."

"You are such a cretin," she said sticking out her tongue.

They sang and then Beth said, "Make a wish and blow out the candles."

Caralyn closed her eyes, made a wish then blew out the candles. "Can I tell you what I wished for?"

"No!" everyone shouted.

"You know the rule, Cara," Tucker said. "It won't come true if you tell anyone."

"That's a silly tale for children, but I will keep it a secret for now." She smiled at Nancy and Tucker.

"I'm ready for the champagne," Ray said. He caught the waiter's eye and beckoned him over. He placed the order, and the waiter grinned and nodded.

"Now I have to pay back all the money I've borrowed from Beth over the years," Caralyn said as Mom cut the cake.

"I've thought about it, and I decided to wipe the slate clean," Beth said. "My trust has grown quite a bit, and we really don't need the money."

"Beth, you have to let me pay you back," Caralyn said.

Beth waved a hand. "No, and that's it. No arguing, little sister."

At that moment the waiter returned with the champagne and a ten ounce plastic bottle of 7-Up. He set the champagne next to Ray, walked around the table and set the 7-Up in front of Caralyn.

She turned, stared at him then asked, "Why?"

"I know a fake ID when I see one, child. You can't be older than sixteen because you are so sweet and innocent."

Caralyn turned to her father. "Daddy! Did you set this up?"

"Yes, but you can have a sip of champagne if you want."

Chapter Thirty-One

In January, Tucker called 9-1-1 and an ambulance arrived within three minutes. Caralyn saw the flashing lights and heard the paramedics rush up the stairs. She followed a moment later and stood in Tucker's doorway.

He saw her and shook his head. "It's serious, Carrie."

"What happened?" she asked fighting tears.

"She's been suffering headaches and enduring bouts of nausea all week, but tonight she had a seizure," Tucker explained. "She saw her doctor two days ago. I should have insisted he admit her to the hospital."

"Is she conscious?"

He looked into the living room. "Not really."

They stepped aside to allow the paramedics to pass.

"We're taking her to McCormick," one said.

"I'll drive you," Caralyn said. "You better call her parents and Mom and Dad on the way."

Tucker grabbed his wallet and phone. "Let's go, Carrie."

She pulled into the McCormick University Hospital ER valet parking area and got a ticket while Tucker rushed inside. By the time Caralyn found him, he was filling out paperwork.

"Where is she?" Caralyn asked looking at the scores of people in the waiting area.

Tucker hooked a thumb over his shoulder. "Through there. Someone said he would get me in a minute."

"I'm not waiting," she said and started to walk away.

"Carrie, we have to wait and let the staff do their job."

Fifteen minutes later a nurse appeared and took Tucker and Caralyn through the double doors, down a hallway and into a smaller waiting room.

"How is she? What's happening now?" Caralyn asked.

"Dr. Moriyama is with her now. The important thing now is to stabilize her. I will come back as soon as I know more. Can I get you anything?"

They shook their heads.

"We are doing everything we can, and the doctors here are the best in the city."

An hour later Tucker and Caralyn talked to Dr. Moriyama in the small room. He explained the treatment so far. "She is going to be admitted, and I have called Dr. Guzauski. He is the hospital chief of neurology. He will check the tests, and we should have results in the morning."

"Can we see her?" Caralyn asked holding Tucker's hand.

"You can see her, but she's sedated. She can hear you but not respond." He checked the chart in his hand. "She has stabilized, but we need to find the cause. She is very young for this to occur. Mrs. Henkel will take you to your wife."

Tucker and Caralyn followed the nurse.

"I will have someone find another chair. You can stay as long as you want. She will be moved for tests soon, and then moved upstairs to the fourth floor ICU."

"Did you call everyone?" Caralyn asked after Nancy had been taken for testing.

"I think so."

"Did you call Coach Bender?"

"Yeah. He said to take all the time I need."

Two frustrating weeks later, the tests revealed a brainstem glioma. Tucker and Caralyn met with the doctors to discuss treatment.

"They should have discovered this earlier," Caralyn said.

"We can't blame the doctors, Carrie."

Dr. Guzauski walked into the room where Tucker and Caralyn waited. He was joined by another man. Caralyn stared at the slender doctor who studied a chart intently.

"This is Dr. Galuten. He's in charge of oncology," Dr. Guzauski said.

Dr. Galuten looked up from the chart and shook Tucker's hand. "There is no easy way to put this, so I will be frank."

"Thank you, Dr. Galuten. I want to know everything."

"The glioma is much farther advanced than I expected. We will need to be extremely aggressive in our treatment." He described the treatment in detail for several minutes. "I'm sure you have questions."

"Is she going to be okay?" Caralyn asked because Tucker couldn't.

Dr. Galuten took a deep breath, looked directly at Tucker, raised a finger and said, "That is up to God."

Nancy was treated with chemotherapy and radiation, but to no avail. When it became obvious the treatments were causing more harm then good, they were suspended. In May, Nancy was moved to a hospice care facility and made as comfortable as possible.

In the last month of her life when she knew she didn't have long to live, Nancy talked to Tucker and Caralyn about the future.

"I don't want you to spend a long time grieving for me. You need to carry on with your life. You and Caralyn love each other, and I want you to take care of each other. You should marry her, Tuck. I know right now you can't think about that, but don't wait too long."

Tucker couldn't think of anything to say, so he just held her hand.

She turned her eyes to Caralyn, "You will have to take care of him after I'm gone. He will be lost. He will starve to death because he can't even boil water."

"You shouldn't talk like that. You will get better. I know it in my heart."

Nancy slowly moved her head back and forth even though it resulted in extreme pain. "Caralyn, you have to face the truth. I am not going to get better," she whispered softly.

Chapter Thirty-Two

"Tucker, I realize your parents just left, but you should call them back," Dr. Galuten said. "I don't think it will be much longer."

"I will call them," Caralyn whispered.

Tucker clenched his jaw and nodded. He returned to his chair at his wife's bedside and took her hand.

Nancy's parents sat against the wall and alternated staring out the window and checking the machine monitoring their daughter.

"Mom, I'm sorry, but Dr. Galuten thinks you should come back," Caralyn said.

Sarah McKay took a deep breath, looked at her husband, Jim, and said, "We will be there as soon as possible."

Caralyn ended the call and walked over to Mr. and Mrs. Young. "You should tell her something. She might be able to hear you."

"Thank you, Cara," Mrs. Young patted her hand and moved to the empty chair on the opposite side of Nancy's bed from Tucker.

Mr. Young wiped his eyes, stood behind his wife and put his hands on her shoulders. "Go ahead, Donna," Andrew Young whispered.

Caralyn walked around the bed and put her hands on Tucker's shoulders and squeezed. She looked at the clock and noted the time. 8:01.

Mrs. Young whispered to Nancy for another minute, then she and Mr. Young moved back to their chairs against the wall. He put his arm around her shoulders and moved her head to his chest.

"Carrie, you should sit down," Tucker said.

She walked around the bed, sat down and took Nancy's other hand and allowed the tears to flow. She watched as the nurse entered, looked at the monitor and turned off the alarms. The nurse moved to the doorway, stood beside Dr. Galuten and whispered, "She's gone. Do you want to check and call it?"

He nodded and walked up to Tucker. "I have to make sure."

Tucker clenched his jaw and nodded once, ever so slightly.

Dr. Galuten checked Nancy for a pulse and turned to Tucker, put a hand on his shoulder and said, "It's over. I am sorry for your loss."

Caralyn let go of Nancy's hand, looked at the clock, noted the time, 8:07, and sobbed.

Tucker squeezed Nancy's hand and lowered his head to the edge of the bed.

Dr. Galuten and the nurse left the room. No one else moved until the McKays rushed in.

"We're too late," Jim whispered after seeing Tucker and Caralyn.

"She's gone, Mom," Caralyn rushed into her mother's arms.

Dad moved behind Tucker and patted his shoulder. "I wish I knew what to say, son."

Tucker lifted his head, looked at Nancy, then patted his father's hand. "Just because we knew it was close, doesn't make it any easier."

"I'm sorry we didn't make it back in time," Sarah said to the Youngs.

"You've been with her all night for almost a month," Mrs. Young said. "We couldn't ask for more."

"Would you like more coffee, Donna?" Sarah asked the next morning.

"I shouldn't, but half a cup, please."

Sarah poured the coffee then sat beside Mrs. Young. "I wasn't hungry, but Caralyn made me eat. I could make something for you and Andrew. Tucker hasn't eaten a thing since yesterday morning."

Mrs. Young looked over her shoulder to where Tucker, his father and father-in-law sat with blank expressions. "He needs to eat to keep up his strength."

"I'm not hungry," Tucker said.

224

"You have to eat. I will make pancakes and scramble some eggs," Sarah said. She got up, walked around the counter to the fridge. "He has bacon. I'll make that too."

"Andrew! You need to make Tucker eat something," Donna said. "All of you need to eat. We can't sit around moping. We have to make calls and arrange for the service."

"Okay. You need to shower and get dressed, Caralyn Ann," Beth said. "I know you are hurting, but you have to be strong for Tucker." Beth walked to where Caralyn lay on the couch, grabbed her hands and pulled her to a sitting position. "You need to be upstairs with Tucker and the McKays."

Caralyn looked at the ceiling. Her apartment was directly beneath Tucker and Nancy's unit.

"Ray is coming over. He will be here in thirty minutes. Do you want him to see you like this?"

Caralyn stood up. "Fine. I will get dressed. Are you guys coming to the funeral?"

"Yes, but you need to help Tucker and her parents with the details."

"We made the calls to family yesterday. The people from the funeral home were coming to pick her up today, I think."

"Is there anyplace large enough in Stockton Woods to hold the service?" Beth asked. "The church isn't by any means."

"I think the high school gym would be the biggest place in town unless we have the service outside."

"That's not happening," Beth said waving her hands.

The funeral was held on the 11th in the Stockton Woods High School gym because it was the only place in town spacious enough to accommodate the large number of expected mourners.

After the service, the long funeral procession slowly wound its way through town as it snaked to the Lincoln Ridge cemetery. The wind blew gently through the large maple trees surrounding three sides of the old cemetery as everyone exited their cars. They walked along the gravel road and made their way to the tent erected over the freshly dug gravesite. The funeral home staff worked feverishly to place as many of the floral arrangements inside the tent as possible. Mr. and Mrs. Young, Sandy and Lloyd sat with Tucker in the front row along with the McKays and Caralyn. Grandparents and other family members sat behind them. Hundreds more gathered outside. The sun shone brightly as it highlighted the fluffy clouds in the blue clear sky. The frail old preacher said a few final words in a barely audible voice.

After shaking hands with family, Tucker said, "Mom, will you excuse me? Cara and I will be back in a minute. She wants to visit the graves."

"We will cover. Take your time." Mom smiled and patted his hand.

"Do you remember the first time we came her after you realized who they were?" Tucker asked Caralyn as she put her arm around his waist.

"I remember, Tuck. I was afraid so you had to hold my hand. Even though I don't remember them at all, I still love them."

"I know you do, Carrie, and I know you love Mom and Dad, too." Tucker put his hands on her shoulders and held her for a moment as he looked up to watch two white doves riding the warm air currents above them. He looked back at the rest of the mourners. "We should get back, Carrie."

"I'll be there in a minute, Tuck. I need a minute."

Tucker squeezed her hand and rejoined everyone as Caralyn spent a moment alone with her birth parents and Grandma Florence. She knelt to remove two dandelions from the tall green grass next to the grave marker. Her heart was heavy as she remembered one of the last times she talked to Nancy. She remembered her exact words.

"I know you love him, Cara, and always have. I know it hurt when he married me instead of you. Maybe it was because God knew I wouldn't be here long, and Tucker was mine for the time I had left. You have been very patient, and now he is yours. I

226

want you to marry him and have the family we never were able to. I don't know if it works this way, but I'd like to think I will be able to look down from heaven and see you. I'll try to watch over you and Tuck. I will be the sun and rejoice with you when you are happy, and I will be the thunder when your heart aches. I will be the rain when you cry. I want to watch you grow old together. I love you both more than life itself, and I will be waiting for you when your time is through."

Tears streamed down Caralyn's face as she remembered her promise to Nancy. She looked at her parents' headstone again and stood up. She turned to face the still gathered crowd and saw Tucker talking to his mom and dad. As she walked toward him, the whistle of a slow moving freight train made an eerie mournful sound.

She laced her fingers with his, saw him watching the train and asked, "What are you thinking?"

"I hate trains."

Check out these other titles by the author. Visit the website:
kennethleemcgee.com

The Emmy's Story Series

1. We Were 'posed to Get Married
2. One Of The Guys
3. A New Friend
4. Did You Like the Ravioli Tonight?
5. Completely and Forever: A Wedding
6. It's Time To Go!
7. How Difficult Can It Be?
8. Forever... Isabella... Forever
9. The Forgettable Year
10. Turning Thirty
11. Hello, I'm James
12. Remember The Struggle
13. But God! I Write Songs
14. A Lifelong Dream
15. Gideon's Tree
16. New Priorities
17. Christmas Surprise

The Annie Mercer O'Dell Series

1. Roosevelt High
2. North Park College
3. Smoky Mountain Summer

The Stockton Woods Series

1. Sounds Like a Mournful Train Today
2. Sounds Like a Happy Train Today

<u>The Rex Ford & Clay Horn Books</u>

1. The Amazing Adventures Of Rex Ford & Clay Horn

<u>Stand Alone Books</u>

1. Growing Up In Kinmundy Junction
2. Grandpa, Lions and Kitty Cats: A Collection Of Short Stories For Children Of All Ages
3. The True Stories Of Ol' Melvin, Obadiah, Perkins MacGhee and other Characters

www.ingramcontent.com/pod-product-compliance
Lightning Source LLC
Chambersburg PA
CBHW030304200626
46816CB00002BA/760